THE
RIVAL
POTTERS

(Book Three of The Drayton Trilogy)

RONA RANDALL

HAMISH HAMILTON LONDON

HAMISH HAMILTON LTD
Published by the Penguin Group
27 Wrights Lane, London W8 5TZ, England
Viking Penguin Inc., 40 West 23rd Street, New York, New York 10010, USA
Penguin Books Australia Ltd, Ringwood, Victoria, Australia
Penguin Books Canada Ltd, 2801 John Street, Markham, Ontario, Canada L3R 1B4
Penguin Books (NZ) Ltd, 182–190 Wairau Road, Auckland 10, New Zealand

Penguin Books Ltd, Registered Offices: Harmondsworth, Middlesex, England

First published in Great Britain by Hamish Hamilton Ltd 1990
1 3 5 7 9 10 8 6 4 2

Filmset in Monophoto Baskerville

Printed in Great Britain by
Richard Clay Ltd, Bungay, Suffolk

A CIP catalogue record for this book is available from the British Library

ISBN 0-241-125200

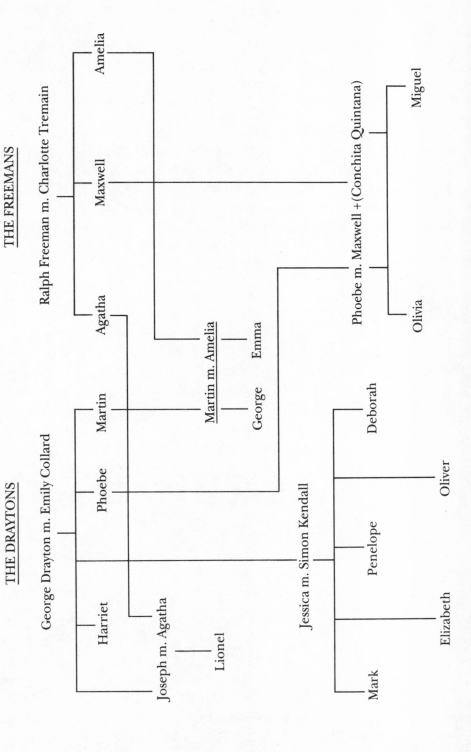

CHAPTER 1

If he rode to Merrow's Thicket at about seven o'clock in the morning, he could be sure of seeing her. There was a bridle path running along the western side of Tremain Park, so emerging onto it would appear to be quite natural since he was heir to the place. The meeting would therefore seem to be by chance rather than intention and this impression would be reinforced by the fact that, since his father's injuries now rendered him even more incapacitated, many extra duties fell upon the son.

One of these duties was a regular inspection of all boundary fences, so a weekly examination of those bordering Merrow's Thicket could be timed for when Deborah Kendall went riding by. She invariably took this route homeward from her favourite early morning ride. Country folk were not like city folk, lying abed until all hours.

But a weekly glimpse of her was not enough. When she commented, as she occasionally did, on how frequently he inspected those boundary fences, he merely smiled and said it was unwise to neglect such things. 'It's better to keep an eye on property than to let it deteriorate. But no doubt you know that, Ashburton being your home and your father a conscientious landowner.' With such remarks he concealed his true motive.

Sometimes he even avoided a meeting in an attempt to convince himself that he could do without seeing her, but love made a man impatient; hungry for the sound of her voice and the sight of her face and the warmth of her smile. The damnable part was having to hide it because, to her, he was no more than a longstanding friend, much older than herself. How could she regard him as anything else since she hadn't reached the age of seven when his father brought him from Grenada to the family home of Tremain Hall at the age of seventeen?

When, precisely, had he fallen in love with her? That was not so easy to pinpoint as the moment when he realized that he had been aware of her for a very long time. At one of the charity functions her mother frequently held at Ashburton, she had seized his hand and dragged him on to the ballroom floor, saying urgently, 'Dance with me, I beg you, Uncle Michael, or I'll be burdened with Horace Prendergast again! The man is a pest!' And shock that was almost painful had run through him, made worse by a rush of sexual desire. The touch of her hand, her smile, her radiance, her vitality, her undisguised delight when whisked away from a tiresome admirer, her slender waist beneath his hand, the lightness of her movements, the sheen of her mane of auburn hair and the dark blue of her deep-set eyes – everything about her stirred this desire, but also the pain of knowing that she regarded him only as an uncle. And elderly, at that. Uncles were always elderly.

Spinning about the floor she had smiled up at him and said, 'Is it true that some people consider the waltz to be wicked? If it is, then I enjoy being wicked! Does that shock you, Uncle dear?' And the pain and the desire had increased.

More than ten years. The gap in their ages was not really enormous although, when they first met, it appeared so to the small girl. That was why he had always been linked, in her mind, with her elders. He was turned twenty-seven now and, thank God, she no longer used the hated appellation; but if she no longer saw him as avuncular, she certainly saw him only as a family friend. A good friend, even a close one, but no more than that.

There was an ancient gazebo in Merrow's Thicket, close to the gate leading on to the bridle path. It was his habit to tether his horse and linger there until the sound of approaching hooves told him she was coming and then, very casually, he would emerge on to the path, pretending to examine the boundary fences and straightening up only when she greeted him.

On the other side of the bridle path was a right of way leading to the hill above Burslem where Deborah's mother had been born in a house called Medlar Croft. Generations of Draytons had been born there and Draytons lived there still – widowed Amelia and her two children, whom Deborah visited frequently. That gave him other opportunities for chance meetings and he seized them as often as possible, but always casually and with an air of mild if pleasurable surprise. Never must she guess that the encounters were anything but accidental. Embarrass her, and she might avoid him thereafter. He wasn't prepared to risk that.

He was early today, as always. By the time she reached the bridle path after her long ride she would have slowed down, and the deliberate tread of her horse would be heard as far away as the gazebo, giving him plenty of time to emerge. And so he waited, seated on the ancient stone seat on which, his father had once told him, many trysting couples had sat in the past. 'And done more than that, I'll warrant, lovers being lovers – though *I*'d've chosen something more comfortable for laying a woman, wouldn't you, m'boy?' His father usually made remarks like that when Aunt Agatha was present. His father always enjoyed shocking 'poor Aggie'.

He jerked his mind to other thoughts. It wasn't wise to think of trysting lovers because they would be immediately transformed into himself and Deborah Kendall, quickening his blood. He must be calm when they met. His English side must control his Latin side. Nothing must betray him. Disciplining himself, he continued to wait.

The moments dragged. He was vaguely aware of the early morning bird chorus, but didn't consciously listen to it. There was no room in his mind for anything but Deborah and nothing could distract him from the need to listen for distant hoofbeats. Outside the gazebo, his own horse cropped unhurriedly, oblivious of anything but equine contentment; from the distance came the sound of Tremain sheep, bleating as shepherds led them out to pasture; from even further away, down in the valley where Burslem crouched, came the clang of bells summoning potters to work. These late summonses were for the lucky ones employed at potteries like Drayton's, where the traditional starting hour of six had been changed to seven and the traditional knocking-off time of eight in the evening also changed to seven.

That had been Martin Drayton's doing, of course. Other potters thought him a fool to reduce the working day from fourteen to twelve hours, but Martin had been the instigator of many changes in the smoke-ridden world of the potteries; changes which other Master Potters either resented or reluctantly adopted rather than lose some of their best workers. Too many turners and throwers and glazers and firers had sought work at the

Drayton Pottery; too many had considered Martin Drayton to be not only the best potter in Staffordshire, but the best Master Potter to work for. He had established new traditions, new methods, all of which would continue under the supervision of his widow and his niece, though everyone in the potteries was now predicting failure.

'Whoever heard of females managing a pottery?' they said. 'Whoever heard of a Mistress Potter?'

That had inflamed Deborah. 'Then it's time people did. Everyone will eat their words, believe me!'

But Aunt Agatha, siding with the general prediction of failure, had merely smiled – the faintly malicious smile that he never liked but always excused because she was a disappointed and lonely woman. She had emphatically stated that a pottery needed a man at the helm. 'A man as clever as my dear Joseph was. *They*'ll find out, those two silly women . . .'

There it came at last – the first, distant hoofbeat! His ear was so attuned to the sound of it that he could estimate both pace and distance. The air was still and sounds told him now that she had reached the curve beyond the ford by Badgers' Brook. From there, once the shallow water was negotiated, she would be faced with an uphill climb and she would not press her horse at that point because she would have already galloped across Tremain's fields. Everyone in the neighbourhood was now free to use them (to Aunt Agatha's disapproval). Now Deborah would be letting the animal relax before traversing the bridle path and taking the alternative route back to the village of Cooperfield and thence to the Kendall home of Ashburton.

So he had plenty of time to listen for her approach and to anticipate the moment of meeting. What would she be wearing today – the royal blue riding habit with the black silk hat swathed with matching blue, or the dark green which so strikingly set off her rich auburn hair, or the tartan with the sweeping black velvet skirt and black velvet toque with upstanding quill feathers? And would her lovely hair be drawn back into a snood, revealing small ears and emphasizing a firm but delicately formed chin and a nose as straight as her mother's? Some said that her mother had once been the most handsome young woman in Staffordshire. She was handsome still, but of course her youngest daughter was lovelier than Jessica Kendall could ever have been.

Now! The moment had come and his pulses were throbbing and his Latin blood was stirring and, dear God, how could he go on pretending?

4

'Miguel – how nice to see you! Isn't it a beautiful morning? And isn't it good to be alive on such a day?'

She used his real name now; no longer Michael. That was pleasing, because from childhood she had used the Anglicized version which came more easily to the local inhabitants and which sounded more English coupled with the surname of Freeman. 'But Miguel suits you better,' she had said one day, and from that moment had never called him Michael, or Uncle, again. It was a step forward, but by how much did it narrow the gap?

She lifted her young face to the sky and took deep breaths of the clear air. Down below, in the valley, the pottery furnaces were belching smoke as always; clouds of it could be seen in the distance, drifting away on an obliging wind. Some of the more venturesome potters were already investing in Simon Kendall's new smoke-reducing scheme, involving complicated revolving fans based on windmill sails. But that invention still had a long way to go. 'If I fail to perfect it in my lifetime,' Kendall would say, 'someone will carry on where I leave off, *some*one will rid the potteries of air pollution . . .'

Meanwhile, he had a new project underway. Had there ever been a time when this man, born of the poorest in Staffordshire and now one of the richest, had *not* had a new project underway in his valley workshops behind and below Ashburton? Stable blocks, disused byres, barns . . . every abandoned outhouse on the estate had been put to good use once he inherited the place. The former Surveyor General of the Grand Trunk Scheme which had linked the river Trent with the Mersey and the Mersey with the Severn, who had also been responsible for building hundreds of miles of canals criss-crossing the Midlands and the North like a giant grid, was forever embarking on new projects from which the fast-growing county of Staffordshire benefited handsomely. The latest was a new type of watermill about which, with characteristic reserve, he talked little. Simon Kendall had always been a man of few words.

But it wasn't Si Kendall in whom Miguel was interested at this moment. It was the man's youngest daughter.

She was wearing the dark green and, at her throat, a white lace jabot. Hands neatly gloved in doeskin held the reins and her mane of hair was coiled into a net in the nape of her neck, for the wind was gusty today. This, no doubt, accounted for the small, head-hugging hat she wore, for many were the times when she had bemoaned the disadvantages of a high hat in the wind. When

5

younger, she had raced across the countryside with unrestricted hair streaming in a cloud behind her, but at seventeen she was acquiring decorum. And about time, too, in Aunt Agatha's opinion. 'The girl's a romp; as bad as her mother when a girl . . .'

But his father had contradicted that. 'Jessica Kendall was unlike any other young woman in Burslem, and certainly different from that twin sister of hers whom I was fool enough to wed. But a romp – no. Independent, yes.' When they spoke like that Miguel would listen, saying nothing, avid for any item which had some association with Deborah.

He said now, trying to sound casual, 'I have to visit the northern end of the park, so I'll ride with you,' and untethering his horse he mounted and rejoined her. His heart lifted when she welcomed his company.

The bridle path brought them to the highest point on the edge of the Tremain estates and here they paused to survey the panorama below. The vast acres of Tremain Park, sweeping toward the Tremain Woods, surrounded the mansion like a rich, undulating green carpet. The immensity of what would one day be his inheritance never failed to awe him. Even now he could remember the impact of the place when seeing it for the first time. All the descriptions he had absorbed throughout his boy-hood in Grenada had not prepared him for such magnificence. But awe had not extended to intimidation; it had stirred gratitude and pride and a permanent desire to be worthy of such a home.

'I do believe it means more to you than it ever did to me, my son . . .'

But his father had been born to it and had therefore taken everything for granted – the wealth, the splendour, the sheer enormity of it all. None of it had meant anything to Maxwell Freeman when young. Appreciation had only come years later, when unexpected parenthood wrought a change which no amount of hereditary influence had produced in him. The birth of a son and love for the child's mother had been a catalyst in his life so that, on her death, he had wanted to do only one thing.

'I'm going back. I'm taking you home, my son. The time has come.'

He had not added that without Conchita Quintana he could no longer endure Grenada, where everything would be a re-minder of her.

So the nutmeg plantation was sold; everything was sold. After more than twenty years, during which he had not communicated with his family, Max Freeman had abruptly returned to England, bringing with him another heir in line for Tremain Hall and all that went with it: the spreading park, the rolling acres of farm-land, the prime herds, the valuable flocks, the miles of forestry, the coal mines at Spen Green. 'And there's nothing you can do about it,' he had told his astonished relatives, who had thought him long since dead (except his mother, Charlotte, who had never given up hope). 'Contesting things will make no difference and you can't brand my son a bastard. I've legalized his birth and he bears the family name by deed poll. He is my son, and will succeed me. You may not accept him, but you cannot reject him.'

Only three people had wanted to reject Miguel – his father's wife, Phoebe, his father's nephew, Lionel, and his father's sister, Agatha; Phoebe because she coveted Tremain for her daughter Olivia (not because she was outraged as a wife, though she pre-tended to be), Lionel because he had confidently expected to inherit, and Agatha because she was Lionel's mother. But Phoebe was now dead, Lionel had chased off to America after a woman, and Agatha lived in self-pitying comfort in the West Wing, surrounded by luxury and over-indulged by her ageing French cook.

The rest of the family had not only accepted the half-breed Mexican boy, but welcomed him; his uncle Martin Drayton and pretty Amelia, his wife, who had herself belonged to Tremain before marriage; Old Ralph, his rumbustious grandfather; Char-lotte, his elegant grandmother, and Olivia, the half-sister who might have been expected to dislike him. Instead, Olivia had become his first and immediate friend. He often wished that she still lived at Tremain and sometimes he even envied her the happiness she shared in her unorthodox union with Damian Fletcher. For himself, life had become an isolated affair in this magnificent place, for a light seemed to have gone out of it with Olivia's departure, followed in time by the deaths of old Charlotte and Ralph.

Now he lived alone with a father who had never been wholly good, but whom he loved, and an aunt who had never been wholly likeable, but whom he pitied – three members of the Tremain family, far outnumbered by the retinue of indoor and outdoor servants whose welfare was the family's traditional re-sponsibility.

It had been a surprise, to a youth born and reared in totally contrasting circumstances, to learn that, contrary to the widely-held belief that indulged aristocracy owed no allegiance to servants, a lord of the manor's responsibilities toward his employees were immense.

Surveying Tremain Hall now, with Deborah beside him, Miguel thought it resembled nothing so much as a self-contained world sleeping placidly in its endless acres, with its farms, its workers' cottages, and its stables which were amongst the best-stocked in the country; its workshops for carpenter and glazier and blacksmith; its slaughter-houses where home-cured carcasses were hung, along with game killed on Tremain's own lands – killed not merely for the exhilaration of the chase but, more importantly, to feed and provide for the large number of inhabitants within the estates.

The immediate grounds demanded a whole team of gardeners, with more working in hothouses and kitchen gardens and orchards. Even the spreading woods required a permanent forestry staff. Additional outdoor workers were gamekeepers and wardens, park-keepers and handymen, coachmen and grooms, stable boys and blacksmiths.

This regiment of employees, together with their dependants, had to be housed and fed and eventually supported in retirement. A mansion like this, with its spreading wings, its countless bedrooms and innumerable reception rooms; its sprawling kitchens and sculleries and servants' quarters; its still-room, laundry, dairy, brewery; its stone-floored larders which had to be perpetually chilled and perpetually filled, and its wine cellars and store-rooms which housed supplies big enough for a siege – all demanded an army of attendants compared with whom, Miguel sometimes felt, the three remaining members of the reigning family were insignificant.

He loved Tremain. Heart and soul, he belonged to the place and would devote his life to it, as his late grandmother had done. Charlotte Freeman, who had been Charlotte Tremain before her marriage, had had no difficulty in imbuing into her unusual grandson her own sense of dedication. 'But who would have expected it?' Miguel had once accidentally overheard her say to Old Ralph. 'Who would have imagined that such pride in an English home could be inborn in an offspring only half English and whose formative years were spent in a foreign environment?'

'Aye, he's a good lad,' his grandfather had said. 'You'll be leaving your precious heritage in safe hands when you go.'

'*We* will be leaving it,' Charlotte had corrected gently. 'You have served and loved the place as diligently as I. It is ours equally.'

8

Concealed by a half-open door, Miguel had been unable to see their faces. But he knew that a smile accompanied the old lady's words, and he knew the quality of it. Warmth and affection had always been there when talking to her husband, and it had always been there for himself.

Deborah brought him back to the moment by saying, 'Aren't you ever lonely in that huge place? I mean . . . the three of you living in your separate wings . . . so isolated from each other . . .'

Startled, because such a thought had never occurred to him and he had certainly not expected it to come from her, he said, 'I've never thought about it. I never have time! The days are too busy. And we're not isolated. At least, my father and I are not. We take all our meals together, even breakfast because he insists on getting up for it. On his good days he gets out and about with me. There's nothing he enjoys so much as driving all over the estate and seeing how everything is getting along. He used to ride, when he was able to, and during my grandparents' last days he brought them regular reports about every development. That pleased them because in his youth he had taken no interest in Tremain. Only on bad days now, when his injuries plague him, does he shut himself off with a decanter for company. I have learned to leave him alone then, but not for too long.'

'And Aunt Agatha?'

He smiled. 'She never changes.'

'Still being indulged by Pierre?' Deborah's tone was kindly, not critical.

'How do you know about that?'

'Doesn't everyone? Don't forget that she is my aunt as well as yours because she married my mother's elder brother, the legendary Joseph.'

'It sounds as though you disliked your uncle.'

'How could I? I never knew him. He died long before I was born. But of course I haven't grown up in these parts without hearing things –'

'Such as?'

'Such as the way he died. People still whisper about it, and about Carrion House which they declare to be haunted, or worse. "'Tis cursed!" they say. "Violent deaths be natural to that there place. In times begone the bodies of a woman an' 'er lover were walled up there, an' 'tis said as 'ow folk've disappeared, nivver t'be seen agin!"'

She gave a passable imitation of the local dialect, making him laugh.

'Good – you're laughing. You don't do it enough, Miguel.'

'Perhaps because I don't see *you* enough, to make me.'

Her lovely eyes saddened. She reached out and touched his hand. 'Dear Miguel, are you unhappy? Or don't you smile so much these days because you are lonely? My mother wishes you would come to see us more often. Why don't you?'

Because I don't want to thrust my company on to you, he wanted to say. Because I wouldn't be able to hide how I feel, but meeting casually like this, spending a brief time riding alongside you, I can keep things light and impersonal. Because seeing you too often would make me want you more and more and then I would certainly give myself away and you would begin to avoid me. Because of several things but one in particular – I don't trust myself.

He evaded the disturbing touch of her hand by moving on and saying lightly, 'So people still declare that Carrion House is haunted, do they? I heard that tale when I first came here, but didn't believe it. Nor do I believe it now. I can't see Aunt Agatha going to such pains to care for the place on her son's behalf if *she* believed it either. She spends endless time preparing for Lionel's coming, poor soul.'

'*Is* he coming?'

'Not that I've heard, but she lives in hope.' As Grandmother Charlotte had once done, he reflected. There was a tragic similarity in the two situations.

Deborah said thoughtfully, 'Had he wanted to, surely he would have returned when he heard of the bequest all those years ago, but he didn't bother.' She finished lightly, 'Perhaps he was alarmed by Carrion's history!'

If he were, thought Miguel, it could be understandable. Lionel must surely have heard the details of his father's violent death. Although it had occurred some months prior to his own birth, the facts were public knowledge and could not have been withheld from him for ever. Joseph Drayton's body had lain in Carrion's summer house for a week, stabbed through the nape of the neck just below the skull. The exotic interior of the place had lent a macabre touch . . . Oriental furniture, rich carpeting, silken cushions piled on a luxurious divan . . . and Joseph Drayton's figure, clad only in a Chinese robe, sprawled on it, as if awaiting a lover.

Or left there by one.

How it happened and who was responsible, had never been discovered. His widow had returned to her former home, Tremain Hall, there to give birth to his son and there to remain. Twenty-one years later, she had sold Carrion House to her brother Maxwell, who settled his estranged wife in it: spoilt Phoebe, tiresome Phoebe, who for all her faults surely didn't deserve to die by strangulation in the midst of the tawdry, gaudy setting she had created for herself?

But these things belonged to the past and Miguel had no intention of reviving them now. If Deborah's knowledge of events was scanty, let it remain so. Let her attribute the unhappy reputation of Carrion House merely to local legend.

He said, 'Remembering Lionel, I doubt if he would pay much heed to superstition.'

'I have only the vaguest recollection of him.'

'He was very much like his father, I'm told.'

'Then he must have been handsome, because everyone recalls my late uncle as a very good-looking man. But Martin was always nicer, always kinder, my mother says. Dear Uncle Martin. I remember how he welcomed me on a visit to the pottery when Olivia took me there as a child, and how his workers were at ease with him, and what a happy place it was – and still will be, with Olivia and Amelia at the helm, not to mention Meg Tinsley to help them, still the best turner in all the potteries.'

They were reaching the point where she would take the road to Cooperfield and he, having no excuse to accompany her, would ride downhill and re-enter Tremain Park, returning to the vast house in which he occupied the Heir's Wing, with his father in the Master Wing and his aunt in the West. Lonely? He had never thought about it, but now he realized that what the place lacked was the echo of voices and the sound of life. Once it must have been filled with both, but there was only one way in which they could be revived – with a wife and a family of his own; with young people growing up there and marrying and rearing *their* children, as generations of Tremains had done before.

When Ralph Freeman, a man lacking equal estates but successful in his own field, married Charlotte, who was to inherit the Tremain fortune, he too had made the place his home. 'Didn't much want to,' he had confessed to Miguel one day, in his bluff way, 'but I wanted dear Charlotte a great deal more, so it was worth it. And I've never regretted it; never felt like an intruder or a guest or anything like that. I was her husband and as such I established myself here, and in time the place came to mean as much to me as it does to her.'

In a short time, Deborah halted again. 'I often pause here to look down on Tremain Chapel. How pretty it is! My mother

11

once told me that her sister married your father there and what a pretty bride she must have made. That struck me as an odd way of putting it – not that she *was* a pretty bride, but that she must have been, as if she, her twin, hadn't seen her. So of course I asked what she meant. "Weren't you there?" I said, and she said no. That was all.'

'I never liked Phoebe, my father's wife. She made me far from welcome when my father brought me to Tremain. She couldn't be blamed for that, of course, since she had neither seen nor heard of her husband for more than twenty years and had long since concluded she was a widow. Turning up with a son of seventeen must have been an unpalatable shock.'

'And so she went to live in Carrion House?'

He nodded. 'It was the only house she wanted, so my father persuaded Agatha to sell it to him, which she did willingly enough. It had fallen into a terrible state of neglect, but Phoebe insisted on it being restored to her liking, whatever the cost.'

'And then didn't live to enjoy it very long. Perhaps the superstitions aren't superstitions after all and the place does have a curse on it, as some villagers declare.'

'That's nonsense. Pay no heed.'

'I don't really, but all the same, don't you think it odd that she bequeathed Carrion House to her nephew and not to her daughter?'

'Olivia didn't like it.'

'I know. She told me. But not *why* she didn't like it.'

'Olivia is too realistic to be troubled by superstition.'

'Don't try to dampen my imagination, sir! It can't be done.'

'Then find another outlet for it.'

'I try. I scribble poetry. I paint. I'm no good at either. I am now trying my hand at designs for decorative pottery. I mean to show them to Olivia when I'm satisfied with them, but at the moment they lack originality. I have studied the pots in the Drayton Museum – all lovely, but I want to do something *different*. Something in complete contrast.'

'Then I must show you some of my mother's Mexican pots.'

'You have them still? Aunt Amelia once told me about them.'

'Of course I have them still. They are amongst the few things I possess of my mother's. She would never be parted from her cooking pots, and when she and my father left Mexico for Grenada, she insisted on taking them with her. You've probably heard that she was a servant in a Mexican household before she met my father and became what people here call his "mistress". To me,

12

she was a wonderful mother. To him, she was a wonderful wife. Before she became either she had saved his life after an earthquake . . . he was dug out of the rubble badly injured and she nursed him back to health. She was beautiful in every way.'

A warm smile wreathed Deborah's face. 'And she had a splendid son,' she said, 'and I would love to see her Mexican pots. When may I?'

'Today, if you wish. I shall finish all essential work by early afternoon.'

'Then early afternoon I shall present myself at your door, after which I shall call on Olivia and Amelia at the pottery.'

She waved and blew a kiss to him as she rode away. The kiss meant nothing and he knew it, but a glow of happiness and anticipation accompanied him until he reached the family chapel and memory suddenly gripped him. He could see all of them again, walking up toward the great house – Old Ralph and Charlotte, Olivia and Agatha and Phoebe, then the household staff following at a respectful distance . . . butler and housekeeper, footmen and underfootmen, housemaids and scullery maids, all in their Sunday-best. From within the coach, sitting beside his father, he had taken a good look at everyone, suddenly apprehensive and remembering his father's words as they drove along the road from Burslem. 'We will arrive just when they are coming out of chapel. I have planned it so because my parents will then be in mellow mood and Christian charity will compel them to welcome us.'

'But why shouldn't they?'

'You will find out, my son.'

He recalled again his father's unease, covered with much bravado. Throughout the long voyage from Grenada and the long coach journey via Stoke-on-Trent, even during the two days spent in Liverpool on business which had demanded immediate attention, his father's spirits had ebbed and flowed, but since Conchita's death these variable moods had been understandable and therefore to be forgiven. But shortly before reaching the immense wrought-iron gates opening on to Tremain's three mile drive, he had cleared his throat and said, 'There's something you ought to know, Miguel. Should've told you before. Cowardly of me to shirk it. So here it is – before I met your mother I had a wife. Still have. If she's still living at Tremain our reception may be – well, unpredictable. Got to face it though. Come so far; can't turn back. Nor do I want to. This is your rightful home and I've come to claim it for you. And there's something else. When I left

13

my wife she was with child and making a great to-do about it. Anyone would've thought no woman had ever given birth before and the tortures of hell awaited her. She didn't want to be a mother, and as things were I didn't want to be a father. All the same, I shouldn't have turned my back on them and I'm not going to do so now. Well, here we are – and that's the family chapel where we were married, an ill-matched pair if ever there was one. Some day you'll be married in it, too, and you'll make a better Master of Tremain than I am likely to, but please God you will choose a better partner for the marriage bed than I did . . .'

After a long moment, Miguel had said, 'If she – your wife – was with child, then you have another. One who was born before me. It is he who should inherit, not I.'

'But I choose otherwise. That was my reason for staying in Liverpool. I visited the family lawyers there and legalized every-thing – your identity *and* naming you my heir.'

'But if another son was born before me, I won't want to usurp him. Surely I can refuse to?'

His father was a genial man, but hated being thwarted.

'I forbid you to. Understand? And let's hope it wasn't a son.'

It wasn't. It was Olivia, a half-sister whom he liked on sight.

As for choosing the right wife in marriage, there had been no doubt in his mind on that point for a very long time.

On an impulse, he dismounted and entered the chapel and walked to the altar rails and let his imagination take over. It was a foolish thing to do and he knew it, but he could visualize only Deborah's lovely face turning to smile at him as they knelt together.

Abruptly, he left, and continued on his way to the great house where life seemed to be standing still. But this afternoon, for a brief while, it would come alive again because Deborah Kendall would walk through its doors.

CHAPTER 2

The pump had stood in the middle of the potters' yard for as long as Meg Tinsley could remember, and that was going back a long way. She was in her mid-forties now and still working at Drayton's as head turner, with a team of twenty workers under her, boss of the whole shed. She had come a long way from being Meg Gibson, the village whore. She was respectable now, a widow earning good wages with a bonus at Christmas and an extra shilling for every hundred pots she turned; likewise each of her workers received an additional threepence or sixpence for the same number, depending on their skill and the quality of their work. No other Master Potter in Burslem paid so well, but Martin Drayton had always been a generous employer and now he had gone his widow, Amelia, was carrying on the tradition.

On top of this affluence, Meg occupied a cottage down Larch Lane. What matter if it had once housed that old witch, Ma Tinsley? The woman had been laid to rest nine years ago, her troublesome spirit along with her.

Meg took a swill of cold water, then dropped the iron drinking cup. It swung clanking on its chain as she wiped her hands on her potter's slop and turned back to her workshed, but some impulse made her glance over her shoulder as she went. There had been no particular sound to attract her attention and all she saw was the gatekeeper's lodge beside the entrance gates and beyond them a stationary coach. It must have been there for some time, she decided, since she had heard no rumble of wheels. No doubt it had deposited a customer and was awaiting his return.

Then why not drive into the yard, as everyone did? There was a sign directing visitors to the main doors, ample space to accommodate carriages of all kinds, and tethering posts for horses. There was no need for anybody to wait in the lane outside.

The coachman sat patiently on his box. She was on the point of beckoning to him when a movement from within the coach halted her. A man leaned from the window, his glance wandering comprehensively over the sprawling sheds and the cobble-stoned yard, finally settling on herself.

She shivered. At this distance his features were indistinct, which made her reaction illogical. Nevertheless, it was there; chilling, oddly frightening. She turned sharply on her heel and closed the door of the turners' shed firmly behind her.

Once inside, she forced her mind to think of other things – Abby Walker, for one. The girl worried her. At fourteen she was as tempting as a piece of ripe fruit. She plainly enjoyed masculine attention; was even persuaded to court it by her slut of a mother who brazenly plied a profitable trade and looked upon a pretty daughter as a possible asset to business, meanwhile making sure the girl earned useful pence at the pottery.

15

That was where Abby's girlhood differed from her own. Meg's mother had never suspected what her daughter had been forced to do to ease their circumstances. The extra coins she had brought home were reputedly earned by putting in extra hours at the turning wheel. Once established, the lie had never been questioned and the supply of old Ma Tinsley's herbal brews to lull her mother's ceaseless pain had been worth every penny. But Abby had no such incentive. She had only her mother's loose morals for guidance.

Sometimes Meg had been tempted to talk to the Master Potter about Abby. Martin Drayton had been an understanding man, always compassionate, never condemning. If she had gone to him and said, 'Master Potter, there be a girl in my shed wot needs protecting; a girl with talent who'll rise in t'pottery unless 'er ma makes 'er earn money other ways,' he would have removed the girl from Kate Walker's influence somehow. By discreetly suggesting to the woman that she could earn more on the streets of some rising Midland town without the encumbrance of a daughter?

That would have been as good a way as any. Kate Walker would have jumped at the chance to expand her trade in Leicester or Nottingham, leaving Abby here in Burslem where she, Meg Tinsley, could befriend her without let or hindrance. But it was too late now. The Master Potter had gone and despite his widow's valiant efforts, supported by her talented niece, Olivia, an air of uncertainty hovered over the Drayton Pottery. Could two lone women really keep it going? The scepticism of rival potters seemed to be spreading insidiously. Some regular clients were hesitating before renewing orders, or were reducing the size of them for fear of delayed production and ordering the balance from elsewhere as a precautionary measure.

Damn them, thought Meg. Damn the lot of them. M's Amelia and M's Olivia were as good as any men and a great deal better than some. And when Master Kendall's new grinding wheel was ready, what a surprise everyone would get and how jealous other potters would be when they saw Drayton's new white stoneware – finer and whiter than any stoneware yet produced throughout the potteries!

But that must remain a well-kept secret as yet, the Master Potter's widow had warned her. Proud to be so trusted, Meg's lips were sealed. If there was one thing life had taught her, it was to keep silent when silence was needed.

She was surprised when, despite her efforts to think of other things, the recollection of the stranger at the gates thrust itself back into her mind. What *was* it about him that made her feel uneasy? Why should he seem like a disturbing echo from the past? She wished she had been close enough to see his face because faces revealed so much.

Thrusting the thought aside she set her wheel spinning and, turning tool poised above an upturned pot, began to create a foot by placing the point of her tool dead centre and peeling away thin ribbons of moist clay until the width and depth of the rim were defined, then she repeated the process by working from the outside until the ring stood up clearly. She did it speedily and expertly, assessing the thickness and the strength required for a pot of this particular size and weight.

She had spent the major part of her life as a turner and her work was faultless. Some said she could do it in her sleep. Certainly she could let her mind wander while her hands automatically continued their delicate work, and it wandered now to the unknown gentleman whose face she had not seen but who filled her, illogically, with apprehension.

Above the quiet hum of kick-wheels and the rhythmic throb of the treadles, she heard, through the open window, the grind of retreating carriage wheels. So the vehicle was moving on, for which she was obscurely thankful. But still the man's identity troubled her and the chill remained.

Ten years. In all that time he hadn't seen Burslem, nor thought about it much. Nor had he been in any hurry to return. It had taken more than the bequest of Carrion House to bring him back. Though the legacy had been unexpected and property was always worth owning, it was neither so grand nor so vast as the inheritance he had always hankered after and which, after Olivia's extraordinary but gratifying rejection of it, he had confidently assumed would be his.

Of course, it was reassuring to know that his doting mother had kept her eye on Carrion House during his prolonged absence. That meant it would be in good shape – as good as when his pretty aunt had restored it at enormous expense. Her estranged husband's expense, of course. That was the way Phoebe did things. She had always known how to make the most of other people's money without squandering her own; how to extract every possible penny out of the Freemans. And other things. Like the rubies.

But he rarely thought about the rubies, useful though they had been to him. Just occasionally he would take the last remaining

17

one from a well-concealed inner pocket, admire its rich colour and fine gold setting, and ponder on whether to have it mounted in a ring or made into a fob to hang from a quizzing glass. No matter. There was no hurry.

He had always intended to come home, of course, but not until his pursuit of Damian Fletcher's wife had ceased to be a juicy scandal in Burslem and local tongues stopped wagging. And everything had gone so well for him from the moment he stepped on American shores that he had settled there contentedly. As expected, he had impressed her wealthy family with his air of good breeding, though their underlying hostility because he was English proved an unexpected obstacle, and one he never fully overcame. Of English origin themselves, after five generations of colonial life the Hopkeys no longer identified with what had once been their mother country. The War of Independence had alienated them further, expanding the barrier which, to his surprise, Caroline herself seemed unwilling to surmount, for the divorce he had expected her to seek had never been sought, though she was willing, when the mood took her, to continue their liaison.

It had not taken him long to realize that Caroline's sexual appetite was whetted more by illicit love than by a marital union blessed by God, a fact he should have recognized in those long-ago days in Burslem when she had given her body to him any time, anywhere. Hay-rick, meadow, the back room of an inn, any secret place had sufficed – with the exception of the Carrion garden house, from which she had fled after they once made love there. 'If you had *told* me your father's dead body had been found on that couch,' she had reproached him much later, emphasizing her words with a shudder, 'I would never have gone near the place!'

Prior to that, deceiving her husband had added as much zest to her passion as it had to his.

'And I suppose it would be the same were you married to me,' he had accused before their affair finally ended in Savannah. 'You would deceive any husband you had, and enjoy it.'

'Why not? It adds spice to life.'

'So that's why you're in no hurry to be free? You like having the status of a married woman so long as a husband isn't around to restrict you.'

'Again, why not? It's *good* this way, Lionel! Let's not change things.'

To this tune their see-saw affair had proceeded while her family now held themselves aloof, plainly suspicious, plainly disapproving, but unable to control their wayward daughter.

'I'm not a young miss!' she would declare in the face of their protests. 'I don't *have* to live with my parents any more, but I thought you'd be happy to have me back. You did your best to make me give up Damian, but now I have left him and returned to the fold, you are still displeased!'

That had amused him. No family fold could ever have penned the wayward Caroline, so adept at flaunting her independence. She was equally adept at displaying indifference if a lover became too possessive. She was like quicksilver; volatile, emotional, petulant – and eventually a bore.

But she didn't become a bore until he began to realize that the Hopkeys' business was on the decline, that the War of Independence was hitting them financially because fewer and fewer clients could afford their costly legal representation. Once her eminent grandfather died the practice began to ebb away. William Hopkey had been not only Savannah's Chief Magistrate, but its most famous lawyer. His sons, however, failed to match his success. Signs of deteriorating wealth gradually became inescapable, and it was then that the affair with Caroline began to lose its attraction. He had moved on quickly, taking what he wanted from life as he had always done, retreating from entanglements and avoiding responsibilities, constantly seeking safety as the tide of political upheaval in the Colonies swept him on.

And now – here he was, home again in the year 1781, with no obligations, no family, no children, no ties, no worries, and no angry women following in his wake. Oh yes, he had been wise to turn his back on the lovely Caroline, and it amused him to think that Damian Fletcher was still not rid of her, which meant that after all these years Cousin Olivia was still living with the man without the Church's blessing.

What DO you think the wretched girl has done now? his mother had written at the time. *Packed a bag and moved in with the village blacksmith! Imagine leaving Tremain Hall for a farrier's humble cottage, but that is what she has done without a pang of conscience. You had scarce left Burslem and her poor murdered mother was scarce cold in her grave before she upped and went. Brazen, as always. But her grandparents – M Y father and mother! – will not hear a word against her. I have always wondered why they like the girl so much. Society will have more sense, of course. She will be shunned by everyone who matters. Only rough women labourers at the pottery, those women whose level she has now sunk to, will accept her. Her poor mother would turn in her grave if she knew!*

He doubted it. Phoebe, whom he had called 'his pretty aunt'

19

because he knew she loved flattery, had surely become immune to the outrageous things Olivia did.

Now, thank God, he would move in and take control, appoint an experienced potter to run the place and reign supreme as his distinguished father had done before him. He would even be occupying his father's house, in which he had entertained all the best people. He himself intended to do likewise. History was repeating itself, and very much to his liking. He was thirty-one, handsome, possessed of a fine figure and a fine wardrobe; independent of means and with more waiting to drop into his hand; self-assured and without a care in the world.

This was the way to arrive. He could not have timed it better.

No one could have been more surprised than Lionel when the news that he had inherited Carrion House eventually caught up with him. It had never entered his head that anyone but his aunt Phoebe's only daughter would benefit.

He remembered that Olivia had never liked Carrion House. Even after her mother had done it up with great show and extravagance, she had still disliked it.

Restored to Phoebe's exacting standards, the place had increased in value and, by now, would be even more acceptable. Even so, it bore no comparison to Tremain Hall and everything that went with it. All the Tremain wealth would have come to him but for that misbegotten son of his Uncle Max. The thought was as galling now as it had ever been. For this reason he had stayed away, even after his affair with Caroline Fletcher had sunk in a sea of boredom. He had had no desire to come face to face with that half-breed youth and no desire to look on while others accepted him. Nor would he acknowledge any wife he might have taken. The thought of swarthy, olive-skinned brats swarming all over Tremain Hall appalled him.

This time his mother's summons had been imperative, not because she had grown tired of keeping an eye on Carrion House (*It will be as immaculate when you return as it was when Phoebe died, I promise you, dear boy* ...) but because the Drayton legacy could now be fulfilled.

You have come into your own at last, my son – the Drayton Pottery is yours! Poor Martin Drayton has been thrown from the saddle – the stubborn man WOULD insist on riding there daily, despite that crippled leg of his – so when his horse tripped in a pot-hole he was unable to hold on and shot clean over the beast's head. He died within the hour, but he had had a good life and much success so we mustn't mourn for him. Amelia, of course, is distraught, though she will never weep in public; unlike myself, too sensitive to do otherwise . . .

More family oddities, he had reflected. More contrasts in character; more variations in nature and in looks. People had always been surprised to learn that Agatha and Amelia were sisters.

Martin's will is not yet read, his mother had continued, *but I am hastening this missive to you without waiting for that because whatever the will might contain can make no difference to the fact that the rule of primogeniture establishes you, by seniority, as head of the Drayton family and therefore Master of the pottery. Amelia and her children will obviously be well provided for and, no doubt, continue to live at Medlar Croft; that should appease her, and I hope cure her of the ridiculous idea that she can carry on where her husband left off. Olivia seems to have some similar notion and silly Deborah (the Kendalls' youngest daughter, only seventeen and therefore empty-headed) actually champions them. Everyone else has more sense. There can be no such thing as a Mistress Potter. The very idea is ridiculous. Amelia will have to be content with an allowance from the family industry (it need only be modest, dear boy, depriving you of little) and Olivia must be content with her clay-working – I am confident you will make sure of that.*

The crown is yours at last, my son, and will do much to compensate for your loss of Tremain. The Drayton Pottery is more prosperous than ever, exporting extensively as well as outstripping all rivals. It also supplies some of the most noble families of the realm, and what tone a man like you will add to the place! My only regret is that my news will take long to reach you and that your voyage home will be equally long. Pray book an early passage the moment you receive this. Your return is now imperative. Hurry, dear boy, hurry!

So here he was, obeying his mother's behest at last. Throughout the years she had written her pleading letters; cajoling, begging, appealing to his good nature, reminding him that she was now ageing and utterly alone.

He had intended to go straight to Carrion House where he would no doubt find his mother. Her letters revealed that she spent endless hours there, seeing that everything was in impeccable order and chastising servants if it were not. Knowing her well, he had not let her know the exact date of his arrival, thus delaying a reunion which would consist of cloying embraces and tears and endless questions while he struggled to hide his displeasure over her appearance, which had no doubt become gross with the years. Apart from himself, food had been her main joy in life, and in his absence self-indulgence had doubtless become dominant.

He had half-expected to see her on the dockside, for he wouldn't have put it past her to take lodgings in Liverpool and to drive to the quay daily, watching for every ship that berthed and hoping against hope that he might have availed himself of any suddenly cancelled booking rather than wait for the costly reservation he had made – though she should have known him better than that. No substitute accommodation for him! Not even for something so important as claiming the Drayton Pottery would he discomfort himself to that extent. The place would still be there and would still be his, no matter when he arrived.

His relief had been great when he saw no sign of his mother, as a result of which he had been able to spend an enjoyable night at the best inn Liverpool had to offer and to hire this elegant cabriolet for the rest of the journey next day. (There had been an obliging chambermaid to warm his loins in the night.) Tomorrow he would see about purchasing some smart vehicles of his own – a curricle for local travel and a britzka or dormeuse for longer journeys. In England the Continental influence, particularly the French, had crept into carriage design, or so he had heard. As soon as possible he would journey to Stoke in search of a good coach-builder. Money, thank God, would be no object now.

In the midst of these pleasant thoughts *en route* for Burslem, he had realized that he was driving through the outskirts of the village and was astonished to see how vastly it had grown. Scattered country cottages were now surrounded by industrial buildings as well as potteries, though the huge bottle ovens were still predominant. One imposing entrance was spanned by a magnificent arch of wrought iron, with the name FLET-CHER'S FORGE emblazoned on it. Good God, surely this wasn't Damian Fletcher's place? Surely the man couldn't have progressed from being a humble farrier to anything so prosperous as this? But apparently he had, for a sign displayed the proprietor's name and the location of an additional establishment at Tunstall.

The entrance before him opened on to an immense yard, flanked on three sides by a range of stone buildings from where the clang of metal and the roar of furnaces confirmed that the place was a hive of industry. He resisted the temptation to halt his driver because the last thing he wanted was to attract attention from the team of workers in the yard. Instead, he ordered the man to drive faster unless he wanted to forfeit a portion of his fee. Threats to withhold money always worked. He had leaned back complacently as the man obeyed, then rapped out a command to stop when the gates of the Drayton Pottery loomed ahead.

They were handsome gates and he remembered them well. They were the first commissioned wrought ironwork Caroline's husband had produced, marking his advance from farrier to blacksmith, but his humble trade had shamed the rich Savannah belle. To her, it marked his descent from scholar to labourer, so small wonder she had been ready to tumble into bed with another man. Lionel had sensed this very quickly and, as quickly, taken advantage of it.

He now wondered how she would feel were she to learn how prosperous her husband had become. It would be amusing to let her know, amusing to be instrumental in bringing her back. Hot on the scent of money as she always was, she would pursue it without hesitation. He could visualize her arriving unexpectedly on her rich husband's doorstep, to the humiliation of dear cousin Olivia. How he would enjoy that! It would pay her back, after all these years, for the humiliation she had administered to himself on the night of his coming-of-age celebrations, causing him to return to the ballroom bearing the mark of Cain on his face. It was never too late for revenge; one had only to await the opportunity.

Idly, he noticed a woman drinking from a pump in the middle of the potters' yard. A striking woman; not young, but erect and shapely. He was too far away to see her features clearly, so leaned from the window to take a closer look, though it was insufficient to gain more than an impression of handsome features and black hair streaked prematurely with silver.

The woman wore the traditional potter's slop, typifying her worker's rank. She paused, holding the chained iron cup while levelling a searching glance at him, then dropping the cup before crossing to a nearby shed. The turners' shed, wasn't it? It was so long since he had visited the Drayton Pottery that he scarcely remembered the layout of the place; indeed, he had paid little attention to it in the past, never having been interested in such a grubby trade. Dirt and mud and dust and chaff had never been to his taste, and his Uncle Martin's stipulation that if he ever hoped to earn a share in the family industry he would have to soil his hands with it, had been resolutely dismissed.

Now he felt differently. If there was money for him in dirt and mud and dust and chaff, he was more than ready to pick it up.

But let others soil their hands. He would be like his father before him, the gentlemanly overlord, ruling the roost.

He was vaguely aware that the woman in the clay-soiled potter's slop glanced back at him before disappearing into the shed and closing the door behind her. Absently, he ordered his driver to continue, but had travelled barely a few yards before changing his mind. His mother could wait, and so could Carrion House. This moment, the moment when he claimed his major inheritance, could not.

The driver wheeled the carriage round at his command, and drove into the potter's yard.

CHAPTER 3

It had changed, but subtly. The layout of the place seemed the same, flanked by workers' sheds on one side and administrative ones on the other. Off cobbled alleyways were glaze stores and stock-rooms and packing areas and, beyond, the huge firing section with its massive bottle-shaped ovens. Finally there were the long open-fronted canalside sheds where clay from the barges was hacked into workable lumps before going to the cleansing sheds for riddling and sifting and raking, thence to the wedgers' benches to be transformed into perfect clay, free of air bubbles or pinpricks. 'Satin smooth,' was how his cousin Olivia had once described it. 'Beautiful to touch. Perfect for modelling and ideal for throwing.'

Only an odd creature like Livvy, who turned it into figurines, or throwers, who spun it on their wheels to form bowls of all imaginable sizes, could have regarded the unpleasant, dun-coloured stuff as 'beautiful to touch'. Not he, though he was now ready to participate in its financial rewards.

Judging by the increased number of workers' sheds and what was plainly a vastly expanded area overall, these rewards would now be substantial. His mother had apparently been right when saying that the pottery was more prosperous than ever. And, bless her (which he rarely did), her oft-quoted prophecy that he had only to wait and his day would come, had also been right. **His day had certainly come.**

Bolstered by the thought, he began to stroll about the main yard but, with so much development around him, getting his bearings was like trying to study a map from which essential signs had disappeared. Where, for a start, was the office his father had occupied? It had been built at his wife's insistence, because she considered a workroom on a par with all the others to be unworthy of a Master Potter, especially one who had married into such an elevated family as the Freemans of Tremain Hall.

'And I furnished it more handsomely, too,' Agatha had once boasted, 'with a splendid desk to replace the old-fashioned one that previous Draytons always considered good enough. *That* had been no more than a table with a couple of drawers, shabby to a degree. But Martin will be content with it . . .' Whereupon she had presented the handsome new desk to her father, Old Ralph, who had been quite touched by the thought, though sitting at a desk wasn't his idea of how a country gentleman should spend his time. 'What'll I do with it, m'dear?' he had said to Grandmother Charlotte, well out of Agatha's hearing. 'Put your feet up on it while you read your daily news-sheet,' the old lady had laughed. At least, that was how the story went, although he couldn't vouch for it, not having been born at the time.

He could now imagine unlikeable Uncle Max putting it to the same use. No matter. When established as the Master of the Drayton Pottery he would buy an even finer desk for himself.

As he strolled through the potters' yard, viewing everything possessively, he became aware of an old man hobbling after him. He had apparently emerged from a small gatehouse at the entrance. Such a thing had never been there in the old days and Lionel Drayton could see no necessity for it now – nor for a gatekeeper, if such he was. Superfluous employees like that would have to go, he decided, and when the old man's quavering voice asked for his identity and the nature of his business, he brushed him aside, silenced him with a glance, and then continued his tour, counting the rows of sheds which seemed to have increased in size as well as in number.

Finally, he halted before a door which he seemed to recall as that of the Master Potter's office. It looked less impressive now, flanked by neighbouring ones which had surely not been there in his youth. He remembered how he had once sauntered into that office when his uncle had been touring the sheds and how he had found his Aunt Amelia, in an adjoining room, scribbling in what he had assumed to be a ledger, and how startled he had been to discover, when left briefly alone, that it did not contain the financial figures he expected but a sort of diary; recorded episodes in Drayton family history that had proved highly intriguing. With amusement he recalled how, on her return, he had teased her about romancing and how she had accused him of spying, angrily telling him that these Drayton archives would one day be of value.

A vivacious, nonsensical creature, his Aunt Amelia. In one of her rambling letters his mother had likened the youngest Kendall daughter to her. *Deborah is as silly and flighty as Amelia when young, but men don't seem to see it, alas. I even suspect that Max's boy is in love with her* . . . Agatha rarely referred to Miguel, knowing of Lionel's own bitterness toward him. *But I suppose I should not call him a boy, for he is now more than seven-and-twenty* . . .'

As if that half-breed was of any interest! Nor Amelia Drayton, who must be approaching fifty now, a widow sitting at home with a lace cap on her head and her feet on a footstool and a crochet hook in her hand, no longer busying herself in Drayton affairs, no trouble to anyone. He could safely anticipate the future without her meddlesome interference.

As for Olivia, when she threw in her lot with Damian Fletcher she must have abandoned her whimsical idea of working as a ceramic modeller. From the size and prosperity of the man's forge (not to mention another at Tunstall) it was plain that he could easily support her, and because she had been inordinately fond of Martin and Amelia she would surely have spared them the embarrassment of her continued presence at the pottery. An unmarried woman living with a married man was always a target for disapproval, some of which would extend to anyone willing to employ her. Even Olivia, unconventional as she was (brazen, said his mother) would not have exposed her uncle and aunt to that.

It was good to know that there would now be no tiresome females underfoot, other than women labourers in the sheds. For as long as he could remember, female clay workers had almost equalled the men in number, driving carts to and from the canal barges, unloading clay at the canalside sheds, hacking it into lumps for riddling and cleansing, wedging it until it was free of air bubbles, turning the bases of pots, making handles and fixing them on with clay slip – there were manifold jobs for women in potteries, but not for refined ones. Rough ones fitted into such a background, but wellborn women like his aunt and his cousin were totally out of place. No doubt Martin Drayton had yielded to their desire to participate because he was too weak to do otherwise. (Indulgent, said Lionel's mother.)

26

Well, there would certainly be no indulgence from the new Master Potter, a title he would bear once the reins were in his hands, even though he had neither knowledge nor experience of the craft.

Confidently, he headed for the Master Potter's office, only to pull up abruptly when faced with a sign that had never been there before. *The Drayton Showroom and Museum.*

A showroom? What in hell's teeth was a showroom? And a *museum*? What sort of a museum, what did it contain? Relics, shards, ancient pots? What ridiculous nonsense was this and whose fanciful mind had conjured it up? The idea was so absurd that he was almost laughing as he flung open the door, only to halt yet again.

The room which had once been the Master Potter's splendid sanctum was lined with tables on which seemingly endless rows of pottery were displayed. They even adorned the walls, the choicest pieces encased in glass. And surely those were additional windows in the roof, admitting greater light? What wanton extravagance! What an absurd waste of money! The place must be a joke amongst Staffordshire's rival potteries.

Cynical amusement gave way to critical assessment as he walked from table to table, from display cabinet to display cabinet, from shelf to shelf, finally halting at a section labelled 'New Productions', where samples of present-day ware were prominently featured and, to his surprise, individually marked with workers' names. What further nonsense was this? And who imagined that prospective customers would be interested in a craftsman's identity? The only important thing was the quality of goods and how quickly they could be delivered. The name of the thrower, decorator, or modeller meant nothing to a buyer, but even a turner was included here, not only in the modern section but in the so-called 'museum'. A whole table exhibited samples of her work, past and present.

Studying them, he saw that they dated from the time when she had been lowly Meg Gibson, once a child labourer working alongside her mother, to the time when she became known as the best turner in the potteries whom many a rival potter wanted to lure away from Drayton's.

Despite his lack of interest in the muddy process of pot-making, Lionel Drayton found himself studying Meg's samples with interest. After her girlhood there was a halt, but the samples were renewed after her return to Burslem as Meg Tinsley, related by marriage to that evil-smelling old witch from Larch Lane – the poor people's substitute for fee-demanding doctors. And suddenly recollection sharpened – the woman at the well, the woman who had cast a fleeting glance over her shoulder, that woman *was* Meg Tinsley. He should have recognized those gypsy features and that swaggering walk, but time had obliterated many memories and many people – and, after all, she had left Burslem before he was born so she had been unknown to him until she returned when widowed, years later.

Even then, he had never really met her, though her reputation had intrigued him. She was known to have been Burslem's most successful whore from the age of thirteen or fourteen, disappearing at the age of sixteen or seventeen and not being heard of again until her unexpected return after many years. She must have been into her thirties then, but he had been too besotted by Caroline Fletcher to spare a glance for the good-looking turner, of whom most people thought the worst.

Memories were long in these parts, so people had predicted that Meg would start plying her old trade on the side again, but as far as he knew all she did was to pick up a turning tool at Drayton's and start putting rims on the bases of pots, as good as any she had done in the old days. 'Everyone should see Meg at work,' his uncle had said. 'No one can create a foot as dexterously as she. She is an artist.'

So once, in an idle moment, Lionel had visited the pottery, sauntering confidently into the place because he bore the name of Drayton and knew no one would dare challenge his right to be there. He had gone straight to the turning shed and stood beside her. When she failed to glance up he remained there, watching as she peeled away leather-hard clay from the bases of revolving pots, each curling strand equal in thickness until a firm, neat foot stood up, always of the right dimension and strength to support the article. Even he was impressed by her skill, but when he complimented her she ignored him – something he was so unaccustomed to, especially from women, that he never went near that shed again, nor glanced at her, except covertly when catching sight of her in the village.

Although she was older than he, her indifference had challenged him.

A woman's voice cut into his recollections.

'I'm sorry there was no one here to receive you, sir . . .'

At his abrupt turn, the voice cut off.

Its owner was silhouetted against sunlight streaming through the open door, her face in shadow while light shone full on his

28

own. Although unable to see her features, something about the outline of that slim figure was vaguely familiar.

'Great heavens!' she gasped. 'I do believe it's Lionel!'

At that she stepped forward, her quick light tread, as well as her voice, identifying her at once. Both attributes had typified his cousin Olivia.

He was too astonished to speak, but she demanded with characteristic frankness, 'What brings *you* here?'

Besides incredulity there was amusement in her voice, though he failed to see the cause. Sharp as ever, she hastened to enlighten him.

'Lionel Drayton visiting a *pottery*? My fastidious, idle cousin who would soil his hands with nothing except an overful glass of wine and would immediately change his fine linen if so much as a drop sullied it? Your clothes must have collected a deal of dust even when stepping down into the yard – I presume that carriage outside is yours? I thought it must have brought customers from Stoke, so I came to attend them until Amelia returns. Naturally, I am amused! And so will Amelia be, I swear. I'll linger until she comes. She is with the potters' children at the moment. You remember how we started classes for them while their parents work? Of course, you don't. You were probably not even aware of it. You took no interest in the pottery or anything to do with it, so your presence now astonishes me. We knew you were coming home because Agatha has talked about nothing else for many weeks, but we were unaware of your arrival. You are already installed in Carrion House, I take it. Is this the first time you've honoured the village with a visit? If so, Drayton's is honoured too.'

The old, teasing note was there; the note that had so often made him feel ridiculed.

When she reached his side he saw that the past ten years had altered her looks only by improving them. He had always, unwillingly, thought her attractive in her fashion, and even found her seductive on occasion – such as his coming-of-age celebrations at Tremain Hall when she had had the audacity to attack him because he did what any man had a right to do if he fancied a woman. He remembered the marks of her teeth on his hands and the weal she had left on his face. He had had the devil of a task trying to conceal the blemishes for the rest of the night's festivities.

He could remember insults vividly and the old, familiar resentment came flooding back. Olivia's mockery had always inflamed him – but, by God, he could turn the tables now.

'It is I who should ask what brings *you* here, Cousin. Surely you should be gracing hearth and home? But no – how foolish of me! That is a wife's place. Aren't the same duties expected of a woman who merely occupies a man's house?'

At her angry flush, he laughed. 'Have I touched you on the raw, Cousin? Do you expect me to apologize? You should know me better than to hope for that.'

She said contemptuously, 'Any apology you made would be worthless. Nor would it make any difference as far as I am concerned. I am Damian Fletcher's common-law wife and content to be.'

'But Caroline is still his legal one. I know she has never divorced him.'

'That is of little consequence to either of us, nor to anyone who knows us. Not only are we accepted by most people (the rest don't matter) but Damian is highly respected and a valued member of the parish.'

'But not in the eyes of the Church.'

'As far as the local church is concerned, you are wrong. We worship there together and although we avoid embarrassing the clergy by seeking Holy Communion since the Church forbids them to administer it to "sinners" like us, we are not treated as outcasts either by the clergy or congregation – not merely because Damian is Burslem-born and bred, nor because he made the beautiful new reredos and altar rails, but because we live honestly. And though no doubt this will amuse your cynical mind, we even feel that we have received God's blessing because we pledged ourselves before the altar, privately, with no one present but ourselves, and have kept our vows to each other ever since.'

'How very touching . . .'

Olivia said calmly, 'State why you are here, and then leave. Even a customer can outstay his welcome.'

She had lost none of her ability to snub him. He turned the tables by reverting to his earlier question.

'And why are *you* here, dear Livvy? As a customer yourself?'

'I work here, as you must well remember.'

He noticed then that she wore that unbecoming garment, a potter's slop, her long skirts finishing at her ankles, her feet in dusty boots. So absorbed had he been in parrying her thrusts that he had spared no glance for her clothes.

He said, hiding a smile, 'And you imagine your employment will continue?'

'Of course. And so will Amelia's. You seem to be unaware that

30

we are running the pottery jointly. It was Uncle Martin's wish.'
A sound from the door cut into the moment. 'And here she is.'
Dropping her voice, Olivia added, 'Be gentle with her. It will be
long before she recovers from her loss. Don't upset her, I beg.'

'I will be the soul of discretion. What else would you expect of
me?'

Olivia cast him an eloquent glance, as if nothing he did or said
would surprise her, then she was crossing the room to meet her
aunt and asking how the children had behaved. 'Well, I hope?'

'If by well you mean quietly, the answer is no, but if you mean
naturally and boisterously, then yes – they did behave well,
thanks to your suggestion that they should each model something
of their choice, which yielded some surprises. Young Timmy
Collard chose to make an elephant, memorizing a picture from a
book and producing something not in the least like it, but he was
ecstatic and begged to be allowed to take it home instead of
putting it on display with the others.'

Her voice was unchanged, soft and musical as it had ever been,
but her nephew detected a forced note. He was glad to be
unnoticed by her, as yet, and took the opportunity to study her.
Strong light from the windows above beamed down on her,
revealing lines of strain. Her smile was bright, but forced, and
there was sadness in eyes which he remembered as sparkling. Her
figure, to his surprise, had retained its youthfulness, but her face
had not. It was the face of a woman struck down by sorrow, and
fighting it. That aroused in him not pity, but hope. She might
not be an ageing woman, ready for rocking chair and crochet
hook, but grief made her vulnerable, which meant she would be
easy to dispose of.

All he had to do was to display compassion. 'You must rest,
dear Amelia,' he would say. 'You must give up all responsibilities
but domestic ones. You must live quietly and peacefully at home,
away from the noise and dust of the earthenware industry. That
is what Martin would wish for you.'

By dropping the titles of 'Aunt' and 'Uncle' he placed himself
on an equal footing, no longer a mere nephew but a contemporary
who had the right to deal with a situation as he thought fit. And
his position as Master Potter would strengthen his hand.

Complacently, he waited. His aunt was carrying a tray bearing
crude clay models and Olivia was examining them with interest,
but when Amelia finally deposited them on a nearby table Olivia
said, 'We have a visitor –' at the precise moment that Amelia saw
him and stood stock still.

31

'Yes, it is Lionel,' Olivia added, as lightly as if it were no surprise at all. 'He has changed little, don't you agree? He was waiting here when I came across from the modelling shed.'

At that, Amelia came toward him, her graceful step as unchanged as her voice. Both attributes had typified her in her youth, and still did. Here was no heavy, ageing woman; no lace cap, no mittens, no thickening figure. Surprise placed him at a disadvantage and that piqued him, but before he could speak she forestalled him.

'Why didn't Agatha let us know you had arrived? We knew you were coming, of course, but not that you were already here. I'm so glad you made yourself at home in my treasured museum.' A gesture of her slender hand indicated pride in the place. 'It has taken me years to assemble. I expect your mother told you all about it in her letters.'

His mother had done no such thing. Nor had she told him in what way Amelia had been involved at the pottery; only that she still 'meddled in the place' and that her indulgent husband permitted it. But Agatha never referred much to her younger sister, her letters being too full of inquiries about Lionel's welfare and when he was likely to come home, then on to her own trivial affairs coupled, as always, with laments about her 'delicate constitution'.

Bowing gallantly over his aunt's hand, he then looked up and said admiringly. 'You mean *you* planned all this? My dear Amelia, how clever of you, particularly at your time of life.'

'I started it long before I reached "my time of life",' she answered with some amusement. 'I began the collection even before you decamped – I mean before you went away,' she added with apparent negligence.

He ignored the correction, remarking that even so it must have been a fatiguing task and one she must be glad to see behind her.

'On the contrary, it was an enjoyable one and continues to be. It meant much to Martin and it still does to me. It is a permanent tie with him. I shall develop and increase it as we both planned. There is an adjoining room which can be linked with this and the place can be enlarged in other ways as well.'

Reference to the adjoining room reminded him of the moment when he had discovered her scribbling there and, in her absence, taken a good look at what she had written, becoming so absorbed that he had not heard her return until her voice demanded to know whether it was his custom to read private documents. Her anger had amused him, but vexed him too because reading those ancient diary entries had entertained him as vastly as reading someone's private letters, a practice he had always indulged, given the opportunity. Her rebuke had rankled, becoming a score which he would be happy to settle when the time came. Opportunity came for everything, if one waited. So he continued to smile, hiding his thoughts.

'I take it you are comfortably settled in Carrion House,' Amelia continued, 'so we must drink a toast to your happiness there.'

She moved to the communicating door and though her erect back seemed to be maintained with an effort, her step was brisk. With time and the fading of her grief, she would be as energetic as she had ever been, a picture which ill fitted his imagined one.

The opened door revealed the Master Potter's desk – the ancient table that former Draytons had been content to use. So Martin Drayton had vacated the fine office used by his elder brother, and moved into this smaller and less impressive room – how typical of the man! He had always been unprepossessing, though his wife had been known to call him modest and unassuming, seeming to admire such qualities.

Lolling in the open doorway, Lionel watched as she took decanter and goblets from a corner cupboard. 'Martin always kept wine at hand for important customers,' she said. 'You may not be a customer, Lionel, but you will certainly be regarded as important now you are the owner of Carrion House. I have no doubt your health will be drunk by the villagers and others, but ours will be the first toast. Be so good as to carry this decanter for me, dear nephew.'

The affectionate term surprised him, because Amelia had never spared many endearments for him in the past. To use one now perhaps indicated the mellowing of advancing years. The thought pleased him, as did any sign of age taking its toll of her, emphasizing her vulnerability.

'Why did my uncle use that smaller room?' he asked as his aunt poured wine. 'Surely this one was more suitable for the owner of a pottery such as this?'

'He thought it unnecessarily large, and I confess to agreeing because I very much wanted it for my museum. Even then, he insisted on enlarging it – the better to display things, he said. He designed the vaulted roof with its sloping windows for greater light and had the south and west walls pushed farther out. He predicted that eventually it would be necessary to build a special place to house it all, and he was right. I shall carry out our plans for it, exactly as he would wish.'

33

'Always providing the new Master Potter agrees,' he said, raising his wineglass to the pair of them.

There was an imperceptible silence in which he saw Olivia's hazel eyes flicker toward the older woman, but Amelia did not see the glance. She was looking at him speculatively and then saying, 'But there isn't going to *be* a Master Potter for a long time yet. In the meantime, Olivia and I are running the pottery exactly as Martin planned. It was his intention to leave it in our joint care.'

Lionel's glass halted half-way to his mouth.

'Impossible. He could bequeath it to no one. The inheritance descends by right of birth to the next Drayton in the male line and that, my dear aunt, happens to me. *I* am the new Master of Drayton's.'

'You are mistaken. Our son, George, is his father's heir, so you see why there will not be a Master Potter at Drayton's for a long time to come, for he is not yet ten years old. Surely your mother told you about the birth of our two children, George and Emma? Until the boy comes of age, Olivia and I will continue to manage the pottery together.'

'You are forgetting that *I* have rights.'

'But you were Martin's nephew, not his son. And George will not qualify as a potter until he has grown up and served the customary five-year apprenticeship.'

'By which time he will be accustomed to my authority – as will you, my dear aunt, long before that. I am the son of the eldest Drayton –'

'Who was succeeded by Martin,' Olivia interrupted.

'– whom *I* now succeed, being the eldest male in my turn. That means head of the Drayton family and all that concerns it, for the rule of primogeniture still prevails.'

He heard Olivia's indignant protest, and whipped round to her. 'This is no concern of yours, Cousin. You were born a Freemen, not a Drayton. So was Amelia, exchanging her name only through marriage. Apart from Martin's son, who is a minor, I and I alone am in the direct male line, and my seniority means that I now take the helm.'

In the midst of an appalled silence, the door opened and Deborah Kendall's young voice cried, '*Look* what we have brought to show you! I made Miguel bring them at once. Did you ever see such exciting designs? They are Mexican, and all belonged to his mother.'

Amelia rallied and went to meet her. Olivia, too, welcomed

her. She was always glad to see Deborah, whose parents she loved and respected. The girl resembled both, having inherited her mother's high cheekbones and finely bridged nose, her graceful carriage, her wide mouth – a mouth considered too big for beauty – but she had also inherited a strong strain of her father. Simon Kendall's red hair, 'the Armstrong red', was quietly reflected in the deep auburn of Deborah's, and the proud angle of his head and cool challenge of his eye were also very evident. Both depicted characteristics which he had needed in his legendary struggle to rise above circumstance and to achieve the recognition he so richly deserved. Simon Kendall's rise from deprivation to success was part of Burslem's story; his genius the spur that had brought vital canals to the potteries.

It had also brought him the support of Sir Neville Armstrong, whose family features and colouring so plainly ran in him though not through Sir Neville himself, as Phoebe had always maliciously declared. Even now, Olivia remembered her mother's fury when the sister who had 'married beneath her' had eventually become mistress of Ashburton, ancestral home of the Armstrongs, with 'that upstart of a canal-builder' at her side.

Still chattering, Deborah was unwrapping a pot decorated with primitive and colourful patterns, while Miguel quietly unwrapped others. Amelia's attention was immediately caught, but Olivia remained aware of Lionel Drayton standing aside, quietly watching.

'Don't you think it would be a good idea for Drayton's to produce something similar –', Deborah was saying, but broke off, becoming aware of the unknown man whose glance was fixed on her with an interest plainly spiced with admiration.

Their glances held and Lionel was pleased to see colour flood her face. So this was Deborah Kendall, the young woman whom his mother called flighty. He studied her with interest, liking what he saw.

Not so pleasing was the fact that the upstart Miguel accompanied her. *I suspect Max's boy is in love with her* . . . From the way Miguel looked at the girl, Lionel's mother again appeared to be right.

The situation became immediately entertaining, with boundless, challenging, and very satisfying possibilities.

CHAPTER 4

Olivia put an end to the encounter by saying lightly, 'This is your cousin Lionel, who left Burslem so long ago that I don't suppose you even remember him. He is just leaving.'

'When we have exchanged greetings,' he corrected, extending his hand to Deborah. 'You must be dear Aunt Jessica's youngest. I recall that she had a leggy little girl much younger than the rest of her brood, but I can see no resemblance to that child in your lovely self . . .' He kissed her hand, then held it. 'Alas, as dear Livvy says, I am just taking my leave, but I look forward to entertaining your parents and their family at Carrion House.'

Faintly embarrassed by his lingering grasp, Deborah withdrew her hand. She was rarely self-conscious, but this man made her so. She forced herself to say brightly, 'We shall look forward to that, Cousin Lionel, though you are no doubt unaware that the family is now somewhat depleted. Elizabeth, my eldest sister, is now married and living in York, and Penelope is also wed and gone to Lincoln. As for my brothers, Mark, the elder, is a lawyer practising in Exeter – his wife's home city – and Oliver, who comes next, is away at university so we see him only during vacations.'

'Then I shall look forward to entertaining your parents and yourself, since you appear to be the only chick still in the nest.'

He smiled and moved away. As he did so, his glance rested briefly on the collection of Mexican pots. 'Somewhat crude, are they not?' he murmured before bowing in a general farewell which somehow excluded Miguel.

Then he was gone and Olivia was exclaiming indignantly, 'Who is *he* to judge? He knows nothing about pottery or anything pertaining to it! Amelia dear, just look at these! Deborah is right – they are beautiful.'

The four gathered in an enthusiastic group and the atmosphere lightened. So too did Amelia's tension, but Deborah was glancing from one to the other, sensing something amiss.

'Is anything wrong?' she asked in concern, but was reassured when Olivia declared that there was absolutely nothing which she and Amelia did not know how to deal with.

Even so, the undercurrent was there. Deborah could always tell when her spirited cousin was inwardly fuming.

From the West Wing of Tremain Hall, Agatha Drayton could see everyone who approached along the winding drive that cut through the surrounding park to the main doors of the mansion. These formed the apex of a three-sided courtyard, the East and West Wings being projections commanding unrestricted views. Only the Heir's Wing did not overlook the house and had its own private entrance. Not that Max's son used it very frequently; he would come riding up to the main doors, more often than not in that Mexican jacket of fringed leather which he had worn as a youth and which never seemed to wear out, and she would think how handsome he looked, and how nice his smile was when he glanced at her window and waved in greeting. Such a warm and friendly smile. The sort a mother would delight in from a son.

She always felt disloyal when responding to Miguel, because dear Lionel had ample cause for resenting him and therefore so had she, but he had only to greet her in that friendly way and to inquire after her health with his disarming air of concern, for her to find herself liking him as greatly as everyone else did – Jessica and Simon Kendall especially, which was not surprising since Miguel was obviously attracted by their youngest child and they would no doubt consider him eminently suitable for the girl's hand.

Whether Deborah felt a reciprocal attraction was difficult to tell, for the girl was an obvious coquette. She flirted outrageously at local balls and accepted male homage with indifference although encouraging it, but if Miguel succeeded in winning her hand, what a match it would be, uniting two great Staffordshire houses, Tremain and Ashburton – but how very undesirable from Lionel's point of view, and therefore her own, because any marriage Miguel made could ensure further heirs to take precedence over any issue of her son's.

Such things didn't bear thinking about, and it was comforting to reflect that since Deborah was only seventeen any interest she felt in any man was likely to be transient, whereas Miguel seemed so enamoured of her that he had eyes for no one else. Agatha was surprised that he was unaware of the girl's fickleness, for he was old enough to sum her up. Her own son, she was convinced, would have had more sense.

She was also convinced that Lionel would never have gone away had Miguel not usurped him. The dear boy had been driven by a sense of rejection, and when unkind friends declared that he had gone in pursuit of Damian Fletcher's wife, she stopped their wagging tongues with a whiplash from her own. She knew that Lionel would never have left home if her brother Max had not brought Miguel to Tremain and established him as his legal heir. And if Lionel had wanted to pursue a woman, there were plenty in Staffordshire for him to choose from, every one of whom would have been more than willing to be wooed and won by him.

Memories of the past were Agatha's constant companions and she had plenty of time in which to brood on them, sitting at the windows during her many idle hours. Her only relief from boredom was to drive over to Carrion House and chivvy the servants whom she had installed to care for the place until its master came to take up residence. As he must. Particularly now. His unwillingness – not indifference, as Max said so unkindly – had of course been due to his extreme sensitivity. No doubt the dear boy shunned the idea of living in a house wherein two people had died, especially people so closely related. Such a sensitive spirit would naturally shrink from unhappy reminders.

Although Lionel had been born after his father's death, she had kept Joseph's memory alive by stressing how fine he was, how dignified, how handsome, how greatly admired. She had done her duty in that respect with great diligence, believing that a boy should have an ideal to look up to and to emulate.

She had been equally diligent in extolling the beauties of Carrion House, which Lionel had visited only once when Phoebe held her first reception there.

Seeing Deborah Kendall arrive unheralded, and Miguel's subsequent departure with her, aroused Agatha's curiosity. Where had they gone, and for how long? She remained by her window even when Pierre sent up one of his delectable snacks.

The taste of Lent Potatoes, flavoured with almonds and raisin wine, still lingered in her mouth from the small repast he had served an hour or two after the midday meal. 'A little fortification, dear Milady . . . a little sustenance to keep fatigue at bay . . .' There had also been a small mound of *Puits d'Amour* and a glass of the particular brand of Madeira that Joseph had taught her to appreciate. Now, a full two hours later (no wonder she was beginning to feel a little faint!) came a tray bearing a portion of flummery and a wedge of Chantilly cake. Not a great deal, but fortunately she was not a greedy person and this would suffice for the time being.

The evening meal would be something to look forward to after that. Pierre's menus were submitted to her daily (apart from these tasty snippets) so she knew that tonight she would be enjoying grey plovers stewed with herbs and spices, accompanied by an array of well-seasoned vegetables, with green plovers on toast as a side dish – or plovers' eggs served on a napkin? She couldn't quite remember, but she did recall that spit-roasted ortolans were to be a second choice (she would eat well of all, to avoid hurting Pierre's feelings) followed by a delicious Tansey and a goodly serving of Sack Cream. And, of course, the choicest wines. Age could not wither her cook's genius, nor custom stale the infinite variety of his menus.

Now she signalled for the tray to be placed beside her at the window, instead of by the fireside where she usually partook of these lesser refreshments. She was determined not to miss Miguel's return. He would surely be accompanied by Deborah because she had left her small gig in the courtyard and driven away in his curricle, into which Agatha had watched him load a box of some kind – quite a large one, too – but from this upstairs window she had been unable to see it at close quarters so had no idea of what it contained. It was all very tantalizing.

As she so often did following a meal (though one could scarcely apply that name to light refreshments such as these) she fell into a doze, from which she aroused only when her maid, Rose, came to remove the tray. Had she missed the return of those two young people? Had she been caught napping? Seeing no sign of Miguel's curricle in the courtyard, she felt reassured – although, of course, he might have driven straight round to the coach-house. However, Deborah Kendall's gig was still there so it seemed that, after all, she had missed nothing.

Agatha yawned, stretched her buxom arms, rubbed her fleshy neck, and said, 'Tell Pierre that the flummery was very good today, Rose.'

The woman nodded. Rose had grown somewhat surly with the years, but even when young she had not been very attractive. She had plainly been in love with Pierre, though never succeeding in catching him as a husband. For that reason alone Agatha had never believed that he had been regularly bedding her, as Lionel had once declared. Her son had been joking, and very naughtily, an endearing habit of his.

39

If there was any woman to whom Pierre was devoted, it was his mistress. He was her trusted servant and even, occasionally, her confidant, so when she became fretful over her son's absence and needed a sympathetic ear, it was Pierre who offered it. He would do more than that. He would bring up a bottle of vintage Burgundy, not sending it by an underling but serving it personally, so naturally he deserved to partake of it with her, replenishing her glass every time she paused to wipe away a tear but only refilling his own when she indicated that he might. He would stand there deferentially, waiting to be dismissed, so if she occasionally rewarded him by gesturing to a chair – which he accepted with just the right amount of humble gratitude – he fully deserved such consideration.

He also deserved her other occasional rewards, such as financial help when his distant French family were in need. 'Which is more frequent than ever in these troublous times, Milady, and all the blessings of the saints be on your head for your kind and generous heart . . .' The reverential way in which he called her 'Milady', although the title was not due to her, was always sweet to the ear.

What the troublous times were in France, she had no idea, but she believed every word he said. He had served her since her marriage and in so long a time an employer grew to know an employee very well indeed, so her maid's disgruntled hints about Pierre's dishonesty merely indicated the woman's basic jealousy. No doubt she was still smarting beneath the man's rejection; many ageing women nursed lifelong grievances, and Rose was certainly ageing – as indeed everyone seemed to be. The few friends she now had were all sadly aged, but she was glad of their infrequent visits because there was little enough company in this sprawling mansion.

Perhaps one dwelt too much in the past when one was lonely, but until dear Lionel returned she would continue to be lonely. Despite her sister's regular visits, and those of her unconventional niece Olivia, nothing and no one could fill the gap Lionel had left in her life. Olivia's visits could be embarrassing if respectable folk were present, because introducing her as Mistress Fletcher, when she was nothing of the kind despite all this talk about common-law wives, really did go against the grain.

Agatha knew she was always welcome at Medlar Croft when she felt inclined to call – which she sometimes did following one of her visits of inspection to Carrion House – and she was often included in Sabbath suppers there, but here in Tremain Hall her brother Maxwell paid her little attention beyond cursory visits when he felt more physically active than usual, and these only occurred when she sent urgent messages demanding attention to this or that – draughty windows, smoking chimneys, ill-fitting doors which rattled in the wind and kept her awake at nights – but beyond that she rarely saw him. Plainly, he preferred one of his stewards to deal with her complaints. Even when she invited him to share one of Pierre's excellent meals, he would send excuses. *Then some other time,* she would write in pleading. *Remember we are brother and sister . . .*

Sounds from below cut into her rambling thoughts; sounds of wheels on gravel, driven at a spanking pace. They were back – Miguel and Deborah. She had not missed their return after all.

She was wrong. It was her niece, Olivia, come to visit her father, no doubt. She was conscientious in that respect. She even seemed fond of him, which was surprising since she had not met him until she was half-way through her twenty-first year. In her way, Olivia wasn't a bad person, despite her regrettable lack of morals.

Agatha was not surprised to see that she was still clad in those dreadful pottery garments. She often arrived like that to call on her father, travelling straight from work before continuing to her own home, but today she seemed in more than her usual hurry. Olivia did everything zestfully, as if life was so full that each moment had to be chased, but as her sporting little gig whirled to a standstill and Agatha leaned from her window to obtain a better view, it was plain that something more than zest prompted her niece's haste this time. There was anger in the way she hitched the reins, anger in the way she jumped down, anger in the clutching of her skirts as she raced up the imposing front steps.

Agatha was curious. If Olivia had come to have words with her father, it would be interesting to know why, and what provoked her. It would be unusual, too, for slowly throughout the years Olivia and Max had grown to know and like each other. Friction between them was rare. Olivia accepted her father without criticism and without resentment; she had never shared her mother's bitterness toward him.

Agatha decided to go downstairs and greet Olivia. She was curious to know just why her niece seemed so agitated. Feeling self-righteous, she approached the splendid staircase leading down into the Great Hall. She had scarcely begun the descent when her niece, her hurrying footsteps echoing on the stone-flagged floor, looked up at the sound of her aunt's heavy tread and burst

41

out, 'Aunt Agatha, you are the very person I've come to see! Why didn't you *tell* us Lionel had returned? At least poor Amelia would have been prepared!'

The vaulted roof, the echoing walls, the lines of family portraits, the footman closing the double front doors, the sweeping stairs, the treacherous steps yawning at Agatha's feet – all seemed to sway so that she reached out blindly for the banister rail, and then Olivia was racing up to her and flinging a supportive arm about her and exclaiming, 'Dear heaven, I thought you *knew*! Forgive me – forgive me –'

In the stunned recesses of her mind Agatha recognized compassion in the young face; no more anger, no more urgency, nothing but concern which was then cut through by a male voice demanding to know what was amiss.

'Is Aggie ill, or something? We'd best get a doctor. Jarvis, ride into Burslem and fetch Smithers and tell him it's urgent! Now then, sister, lean on me . . . there, there, gently does it. You've eaten too much as usual, shouldn't wonder . . .'

How ridiculous! And how could she possibly lean on a man who was himself leaning on sticks? Her brother's heartiness made her want to push him away. She wanted to push them all away – her brother, his daughter, the gawping footman. She wanted no one near her at this appalling moment. How could anyone be jovial at a time like this? How could *any*one try to make light of a situation which struck right to the heart?

Remotely, she heard Olivia saying, 'I am to blame. I shocked her. I'll fetch hartshorn and stay with her until the doctor comes.'

With a supreme effort, Agatha rallied. Thrusting her niece away with a pudgy, beringed hand she gasped, 'Leave me alone! I want no one . . .'

No one but her son. No one but Lionel, who had sent no word of his coming, and certainly no one who suspected how deeply that hurt. Turning away from the compassion in Olivia's eyes she stumbled back upstairs, and when her brother called after her, 'Nonsense, Aggie! Olivia'll take care of you . . .', she stumbled even more in her haste to get away.

Now her isolated wing seemed a most desirable refuge; she couldn't get there quickly enough and was grateful to her niece for not following. In the back of her mind whispered the thought that Olivia was kinder than her mother had ever been. Had Phoebe witnessed her shock and guessed the cause, she would have prattled and probed, taunted her with questions, hurt her

42

with innuendo, and mocked her for having so inconsiderate a son.

But Lionel was not inconsiderate. Just a little thoughtless, perhaps, in the way of the young. Perhaps he had even wanted to give her a pleasant surprise, or to spare her the long journey by highways and byways to Liverpool. How stupid not to have thought of that! And how could he have been expected to know that she would have preferred not to hear of his arrival from someone else – or, indeed, that she was likely to?

She had reacted foolishly and now regretted it, particularly since Olivia had witnessed her shock and put an obvious inter-pretation on it. That was regrettable, but could be rectified. Lionel was definitely not to blame and it had been wrong of her to do him such an injustice even in thought.

But then came another. How had Olivia been the first to learn of his coming? And why had it angered her? And what was all that about poor Amelia being prepared? Prepared for what? And why 'poor' Amelia? It should be poor me, Agatha thought self-pityingly as she at last reached the privacy of the West Wing and immediately summoned Rose, whom she then sent hurrying to the coachman's quarters.

'And on your way, send Pierre to me. Tell him I am unwell and need reviving . . .'

A glass of that vintage Burgundy was essential to calm her. On no account must she betray agitation when she arrived at Carrion House. It would distress her son to see his mother so upset.

Half an hour later, fortified by hastily gulped wine and her cook's unspoken sympathy (had the kindly man guessed that something momentous, and somehow dreadful, had happened?) she was arriving at the door of Carrion House and her coachman, after tugging the ancient bell rope and then returning to the carriage, was unfolding the steps and helping her down. When he tried to lead her to the entrance she shook his arm away, determined that no one should see how difficult she found the steps. By the time she reached the top, the door had opened and a footman was loftily asking for her name and the nature of her business.

That enraged her.

'My good man, you must know full well who I am since it was *I* who engaged you!'

With that, she swept past him, mentally resolving that he should be sent packing without delay, but forgetting both indigna-tion and disappointment when her son appeared. At the sight of

43

him, she stumbled to a halt, holding out both arms and crying his name, but to her consternation he remained where he was, staring. But only briefly. In seconds he had recovered and was hurrying toward her.

Kissing her on both cheeks, he exclaimed, 'My dear Mama, you are quite unchanged! How well the years have treated you!'

Sobbing, she cried, 'And what of you! You look wonderful, more handsome than ever!'

That, he certainly was. With his tall figure, and features resembling Joseph's more strongly than ever, and the costly brocades and lace of his elegant garments, he made a more impressive figure than had been seen in this country district for a long time.

Inwardly preening with gratification, she relished the triumph ahead. When presenting this splendid man to local society she would no longer be regarded as 'poor Agatha Drayton', living out her lonely life in a forgotten wing of Tremain Hall (oh, she knew how malicious tongues wagged!). Instead, she would be envied by many a mother of unprepossessing sons and sought after by many a mother of unmarried daughters, but she would naturally hide her satisfaction. Once re-established as hostess at Carrion House, she would smile on such people with condescending grace and bask in the sunshine of their envy.

With a sudden swoop, she gathered her son in a voluptuous embrace, enveloping him in draperies and tears, pouring out endearments and reproaches, totally unaware of his struggles to be free.

'Why didn't you let me know when you were coming, dear boy? Why didn't you let your mother *know*? It was all such a shock, hearing it the way I did . . . Oh, my son, how *could* you be so cruel? After all this waiting . . . these endless months and years . . . to arrive without warning, without giving your poor mother a chance to meet you at the dock . . . oh, cruel, *cruel*!'

Plump, beringed hands pawed his face, tangled his hair, clutched his shoulders, clung possessively. Writhing and protesting, he struggled for freedom, concerned for the state of his clothes and his carefully pommaded hair.

'For God's sake, Mama, *stop*! Until a *perruquier* has serviced my wigs – all sadly messed in the packing – I must survive without. It takes hours to dress my hair and almost as long to tie this neckcloth, and until I get a really competent valet I will have to struggle with both myself. The fellow you engaged doesn't impress me, for he is still unpacking my clothes, although I have been here these two hours. And do be careful of this brocade – those rings of yours could do untold damage and it cost no mean a price, let me tell you. And why such a fuss? I detest women who fuss.'

Detaching himself at last, he stroked the long flares of his coat, smoothed his hair, and straightened the immaculate bow in the nape of his neck, scowling as he did so. She was penitent at once, begging forgiveness. 'It is only because I am your mother and love you, my son . . . you have been away so long and written so rarely . . .'

When tears overflowed he turned away impatiently, protesting that she should realize how little time for letter-writing was available to a man of affairs. At that she sniffed disconsolately, adding that she had no notion of his affairs.

'I thought you were simply travelling in the New World, dear boy. I had no idea you were engaged in anything more serious. Forgive your loving Mama. So silly of me . . . so silly . . .'

'More than silly. Stupid. And I detest stupid women as greatly as I detest fussers.'

The reprimand silenced her briefly, but did nothing to halt her tears. 'It wouldn't have been so bad,' she said reproachfully, 'if I had not heard of your arrival through Olivia, who must have sensed my surprise. You could have spared me that by coming straight to Tremain.'

'But Carrion House is now my home. You must have known I would come here. Besides, you have been pestering me to return and take up residence here. And what is all this about Olivia? Don't tell me she is spreading the news all over Burslem.'

'Olivia doesn't gossip, I will say that for her, but if the news is all over Burslem by now, are you surprised? No doubt others, as well as she, saw you drive past the pottery.'

'Not past it. Into it. I made it my first port of call.'

'Even before seeing *me*? Oh, Lionel, that was cruel.'

'No – natural. Claiming the Drayton Pottery is not to be delayed, and the sooner those two women and everyone else accept the situation, the better. I made sure they did.'

'You mean you have seen them, *told* them? So that was what Olivia meant by 'poor Amelia'. Dear boy, was it wise, was it tactful, wouldn't it have been better to wait and let the lawyers handle everything?'

'Why? It should come as no surprise to anyone, so why the need for "tact"? As you yourself pointed out, in letter after letter, I am now the Drayton heir and the fact that my uncle left a son makes no difference.'

45

'As yet,' Agatha said uncertainly, 'but everyone knows that Martin planned to make a will, changing the old order. I had no knowledge of this when I sent you news of his death. I wanted to waste no time because it was absolutely vital to bring your home as quickly as possible. Or so I thought.'

'And you thought rightly, my dear mother. You have nothing with which to reproach yourself – if that doubt in your voice does indicate self-reproach?'

'Well . . . I confess I do feel rather badly about my sister's position, but of course when I wrote to you I had no idea that Martin planned to leave the pottery in the joint care of Amelia and Olivia until George grows up.'

'What nonsense! How could he break the old order? The Drayton tradition –'

'– was never really more than a tradition.'

'But it was observed, and strictly. By generation after generation. Besides, Martin didn't own the pottery exclusively.'

'He was Master Potter exclusively, which amounts to the same thing.'

'And that now applies to me. Don't argue that I know nothing about the trade, my dear mother. I shall master it quickly enough and appoint an experienced potter to run the place in the meantime. There must be plenty available in these parts, so you have nothing to fear on that score.'

'Dear boy, I know you will be splendid in every way . . . and once Amelia and everyone else accepts the situation, everything will turn out well, I am sure.'

Agatha's concern faded in the light of her son's self-assurance, and since Martin had died before his will could be finalized, there could be no possible trouble. She was thankful for that. At her age, troubles were to be avoided, and now her son was home all she wanted was a pleasant life, fulfilling her hopes and dreams.

Lionel continued, 'As for Martin's son – about whom, let me remind you, you never warned me – I shall make a place for him when he is old enough, upholding the precious family tradition as always. But don't forget that I too may have sons, who will take precedence. As head of the family now, my rights cannot be disputed. You yourself pointed out that the rule of primogeniture still prevails. You should be glad of that.'

His reference to eventually having sons of his own was wonderfully reassuring, for it confirmed his decision to remain. Meanwhile, there was no hurry and therefore no need to worry about

46

whom he would marry and what sort of a daughter-in-law she would make, and whether she, his mother, would be expected to take a back seat. She could look forward to a life about which she had been dreaming while waiting for his return. Nothing could threaten it now.

She was tearful no more. Beaming, she said, 'Have you had time to inspect the house yet? I hope not, for I look forward to showing it to you. I have been diligent in my care.'

'I know. Your letters told me. Truth to tell, it became somewhat monotonous. Now don't look so crestfallen. I appreciate all you have done, but you'll be troubled no more.'

'It's no *trouble*! How could you imagine such a thing? I shall continue to supervise it as conscientiously as ever. We will be so happy here – as happy as your dear father and I once were. When he died I couldn't face living alone in this house, but now I shall be proud to be its mistress again, receiving guests at your side. Dear Joseph took justifiable pride in it. He restored it to its original splendour and I never shared Jessica Drayton's – I mean Jessica Kendall's – dislike of it. But Jessica was always odd, always unpredictable . . .' Agatha took a few clumsy but excited steps and glanced around happily, quite unaware of her son's silence. 'Did you know that Max and Phoebe's wedding breakfast was held in this very hall? Such a lavish affair! As head of the Draytons, Joseph spared no expense. And now *you* occupy his shoes! I know you will do so admirably –'

She broke off, suddenly aware that her son was staring at her in what appeared to be disbelief.

'It is true, Lionel – you *are* master of Carrion House.'

'I am well aware of that, but you are not its mistress. Nor will be. Surely you didn't imagine so? My dear mother, did my revered father have *his* mother living with him in his bachelor days? I'm quite sure he did not. Nor shall I.'

There was amusement in his voice, and in the stunned recesses of her mind she realized that he found the whole idea comical, and herself as well.

When he led her out to her carriage she knew she was dismissed. She had served her purpose. She had done her duty. She had been useful, as a mother should be, but he needed her no longer. She was to go back to her own life, in which he had no interest, and leave him to his own, in which she was to have no part.

CHAPTER 5

The twenty workers in the turners' shed flanked two walls, ten along one side and ten along another, with Meg at her wheel overlooking them. From floor to ceiling the room was lined with slatted wooden shelves on which pots waited to be turned, with completed ones waiting to be collected for drying. In fine weather there would also be lines in the yard outside. Not until thoroughly dried out would they be ready for bisque-firing – the first firing of raw clay – and not until the kilns cooled could they be decorated, glazed and, after standing for a further drying period, fired yet again.

Days of patient waiting lay between each vital operation. The only speedy steps were the actual throwing and turning, and between these it was necessary to wait for the pot to become leather-hard. Only then was it ready for the turner's tool. Too wet, and a foot would be impossible to carve; too dry, and the tool would merely scratch the surface. There was an art in knowing when clay had reached the right consistency and to Meg's delight Abby Walker had grasped it quickly. Sharp as a needle, she was, with an unerring eye.

Meg had been much younger than Abby when she began to master the skill. How proud her mother had been when the small daughter, whom she took with her to the pottery daily, had picked up a turning tool and jabbed at a mound of clay, drawing a perfect circle with unerring instinct! 'Ye'll mak' a better turner than me, our Meg . . . you be me own clever lass, that ye be!' And how proud she had also been when George Drayton offered employment to her daughter on her tenth birthday, the earliest age at which he would employ children. More caring than many potters, who employed them as soon as they were sturdy on their feet, setting them to rake out ash from beneath the massive ovens because they were small enough to crawl through the apertures. Then their mothers would wipe their ash-covered faces with their sacking aprons, comforting them when they cried and giving them water from the pump to clear sediment from their throats.

Mercifully, Meg had escaped all that, for George Drayton had been one of the first Master Potters to provide long-handled iron shovels to remove debris which was then riddled and sifted, the resultant ash being carted to the glazing sheds where it was a valuable ingredient. For such work the strongest lads were used. Even George Drayton's eldest son, Joseph, had continued to provide these shovels, not because he was a considerate employer but because the practice was economical – though he was less concerned about the age and strength of the boys who did this and other arduous tasks.

Meg could well remember the lines of spindly-shanked, under-sized lads leaning over troughs, backs bent and shoulders straining as their thin arms wielded heavy sieves . . . round and round, shaking and tossing, pausing only to pick out larger pieces of grit and stone until their hands were raw from the icy water and their finger nails broken to the quick.

It had been a merciful day when Joseph Drayton died, though the way of it was something she never cared to think about. The mercy was that his younger brother had stepped into his shoes and from that day the Drayton Pottery had never looked back. She now resolved not to look back herself, though the sight of Lionel Drayton at the gates of the pottery still troubled her. Not that she had realized who he was until later, when old Peterson had come shuffling into the turners' shed in a state of agitation, babbling about the gentleman who had brushed him aside.

'Could've knocked me down with a feather when I see'd un, that ye could. Reckernized 'im soon as I got up close – spittin' image o' Master Joseph. I swear t'God 't'were 'is son, Master Lionel.'

It was true that when Martin Drayton became Master Potter conditions had promptly improved, but the back-breaking work still had to be done. It was all part of a potter's training. Even Olivia Freeman had gone through it, daring anyone to doubt her stamina. A person had to be dedicated to stay the course.

Would Abby Walker? Watching her now, eyes intent, tool poised, oblivious of everything but perfecting a foot to support a particularly delicate bowl, Meg's hopes soared. At moments like this she saw the real Abby, the one for whom she had ambitions, the one who could rise above her background given half a chance. The problem was, would the girl recognize a chance if faced with it?

The answer was the same as ever – not so long as her mother was around.

Both question and answer were presenting themselves more frequently these days, increasing with Abby's increasing maturity. Those thrusting young breasts had developed early and now her body was no longer that of a child; she was a young woman, and as patently aware of it as she was of male attention.

In anxious moments, Meg would ponder at length on the problem of Abby. She longed to protect and guide the girl, but she had no jurisdiction over her beyond the turning shed. What Abby did or where she went outside the gates of the Drayton Pottery was not the concern of the chief turner.

Nor was it the concern of Dave Jefferson, though Meg wished it were. Dave was the well-set-up young man currently in charge of the glazing sheds. His grandfather had been chief glazer once upon a time and had played an important part in the young Martin Drayton's life, taking an interest in him throughout his apprenticeship and helping him to solve many a glazing problem when he branched out on his own after being sacked by his brother. Eventually old Jefferson had died, as so many glazers did, through respiratory troubles which, Martin Drayton suspected but which medical science had not yet proved, were due to the chemicals used in glaze recipes, particularly lead.

George Drayton's youngest son had been the first Master Potter in England to ban the use of lead glazes, working for years to produce a leadless substitute which would produce an equally high gloss. The quest was still only partially fulfilled, but in it he had been supported by young Dave, who was now battling with it alone.

'I owe it to Master Martin,' he had once said. 'I'd like to solve it for his sake.'

Dave was passionately loyal. He was equally passionate in his devotion to Abby.

It had been no surprise to Meg when Dave became chief glazer at twenty, nor that he should then support the Master Potter's ruling that all glaze workers should wear masks, a practice scoffed at by many but finally accepted when benefits became apparent. Dave also insisted on the daily cleaning of benches and worktops and floors because the Master Potter was convinced that dust was equally injurious to health; but when it came to forcing clay workers to wear masks the battle proved to be a losing one. How could dust possibly be harmful? they argued. Why should they coddle themselves when their forefathers hadn't done so? To imagine that dust caused troublesome breathing was a pack o'nonsense, so wearing fancy facewear was not for them!

Dave Jefferson could be of no help there. 'There's none as'll listen to *me*, Master – not outside the glazing shed. Ye knows what potters be like. Nobbody knows ow't about *their* business so well as they does themselves!'

In that, he was right. Divisions were wide and strictly partisan. Wedgers, throwers, fettlers, turners, decorators, modellers, glazers and fire men, all had their rightful places in the scheme of things. Each department was a self-enclosed kingdom. Only when a man became General Overseer had he the right to interfere overall, and young Dave Jefferson had not yet reached those heights.

But some day he would. Meg was confident of that. Having been trained from the ground up and mastered every aspect of the craft, he even deserved to become his own boss, but in Martin Drayton's lifetime the young man refused to desert him. Nor would there have been any need, for the master had begun to depend on him more and more; without a doubt Dave would have become his right hand. As General Overseer, he would then have lived in a tied cottage close to the pottery. That would have meant security and a roof over the heads of himself and his family for life. Dave's grandfather had been pensioned off in such a way, as had others too old or too ill to work.

But if Martin Drayton's widow was stripped of authority, what would happen? Please God it wasn't true that Lionel Drayton had come home to step into the late Master Potter's shoes, but throughout the past week the rumour had gathered momentum and when he entered the turning shed this Monday morning, with Mistress Amelia at his side, Meg knew it was indeed true.

By every turner's wheel the man paused, watching them at work and occasionally asking a question or making a comment. In the old days he had been nothing but a rich and spoiled young man who squandered his time in idleness. For such people Meg had no respect and she had never hesitated to show it. It might be fortunate now if his memory was too short to remember the occasions when she had deliberately ignored him, and particularly the time when he had gone out of his way to speak to her and she had snubbed him. She had seen through the youth too well, knowing he would think it amusing to bed an older woman, particularly one with a past. She had read his mind unerringly and dealt with him accordingly. How would he now deal with her, were he to remember that?

She was not surprised when he paused beside Abby, ostensibly watching her small hands at work and possibly marvelling, as many people did, that a diminutive fourteen-year-old could

51

handle so skilful a job, but when his eyes lingered on the girl's face Meg knew precisely what he was studying: the soft, full mouth; the delicate nose and chin; the large brown eyes with their long eyelashes which lay like small fans against her cheeks as she looked down at her work; her unruly mane of blonde hair which Meg had encouraged her to wash beneath the pump at the end of a day's work, to remove its pall of clay dust. Abby hated wearing the protective cloth cap which many female potters wore, for she shared Meg's dislike of its restriction.

In the old days, Meg had washed not only her hair at the village pump on her way home from work, but her face and arms and legs as well, avoiding the one in the potters' yard because Joseph Drayton, like this son of his, had been too observant. But that had never stopped him from watching from his carriage as he journeyed home to Carrion House.

Like father, like son? It seemed so, for she saw Lionel Drayton's glance linger on Abby's young throat, move down to the immature young breasts, then still further to the curve of slender hip and thigh, and it recalled sickening moments with Joseph Drayton that she had never been able to forget.

The cheap, thin fabric of Abby's skirt clung betrayingly; better material would have hung well, concealing rather than revealing, but Kate's suggestive cast-offs always came her daughter's way. 'They'll show ye off, luv, an' ye've got plenty t' show, so mak' t'most of't!' Instil that teaching into a growing daughter's receptive mind, and it would take root.

Meg saw Mistress Amelia watching her nephew and knew that she, too, had noticed his interest in Abby. But Meg also saw the sad air of the woman. When young, Amelia Drayton had been vivacious, even what staid folk called flighty; rich and spoilt, but warm and outgiving; generous and friendly to everyone, regardless of their station in life. Come to think of it, the youngest Kendall daughter was very much the same. Everyone liked Miss Deborah. So did Meg, who well remembered kindnesses extended by the girl's parents to herself and her dying mother, all those years ago . . .

But had Deborah Kendall the ability to love as loyally as Amelia Freeman had loved? That remained to be seen. Folk said that the heir of Tremain was attracted to the girl, but so were many other young men in Staffordshire. The situation was not so very different from the young Amelia's all those years ago, but it was the struggling potter with the crippled leg whom the younger Freeman daughter had wanted and the happiness of their marriage had been self-evident and lasting.

Lionel Drayton's drawling voice recalled Meg's wandering thoughts.

'My dear aunt, we seem to have a talented person here.' (The use of that 'aunt' seemed to relegate Amelia Drayton to a very dusty shelf.) 'And so young, too. So delicately formed. Do you really think she has sufficient stamina to stand at a wheel all day, labouring over lumps of clay? Should we not find less arduous work for her?'

Amelia answered, 'Abby enjoys it, and Meg has taught her well. She is one of our most promising young turners.'

At that the girl looked up, smiling. 'An' I be strong, sir. Ye'd be surprised 'ow strong I be. Me ma sez I wear 'er out!'

'In what way?' Lionel Drayton asked indulgently.

'I be allus on the go, sir. Enjoying life.'

'And your mother does not?'

'Oh aye, she enjoys it in 'er own way!' Abby's laughter filled the shed, bringing smiles from her fellow workers.

'And what is her way, Abby?'

'Well now, that be 'er own business, sir. I asks no questions.' Mischief danced in the big brown eyes. Abby was well aware that her mother's mode of life was frowned on, but having been reared to it she accepted it uncritically. So long as Kate had money in her pocket for gin and gaudy clothes, life proceeded tolerably enough.

Meg picked up the next pot to be turned, centred it on the wheel, secured it with knobs of clay to prevent movement whilst revolving, sent the wheel spinning and set to work again.

'And you,' said Lionel Drayton, 'are Meg Tinsley, I believe? I recall your name, and vaguely your face. You were a turner here when a girl, were you not?'

'I were, sir,' said Meg, not pausing to look up. 'I've worked at the Drayton Pottery from childhood, and me mother afore me.'

Her turning tool remained steady, thin strips of clay curling like apple peel from its point.

Drayton was momentarily silent, then said, 'In that case, I think I shall not dispense with your services after all, old as you are. You must be well experienced by now, and my aunt speaks highly of your work. She even displays samples of it in that "museum" across the yard. You must not be too disappointed when I put an end to that.'

Instantly, Meg's tool was withdrawn. Her wheel slowed down. For the first time she looked directly at the man.

'What d'ye mean, sir?' She had heard Amelia Drayton's

indrawn breath and now saw distress in her eyes. No one should be allowed to hurt the woman who had been a lifelong friend to her; certainly not this man who knew little or nothing about the potter's craft.

Meg rushed on, 'Mistress Drayton's museum is important – sir. Folks travel far to see it an' customers place bigger orders because of it. Master Martin useter say it was a big asset. So what d'ye mean about putting an end to it? If ye mean taking out me own pieces, that I won't mind at all. But what right have ye?'

She was being foolhardy, and knew it. Challenging a man who was to be her new boss could mean the end of her employment. She might be considered the best turner in the industry, but he could replace her with others. Abby, for instance, even though the girl had still a long way to go. But a man such as he would only promote Abby for reasons of his own.

Meg could see from his expression that she had overstepped the mark. His eyes went cold, and despite the smile his mouth tightened. Turning to his aunt he asked if it were customary for workers to be so insolent, at which Amelia replied that Meg was never insolent; that she and her work were valued highly and that her long employment placed her in a privileged position.

'My husband always encouraged his workers to speak up and this they were never afraid to do, knowing they would get a fair hearing because he liked to know what they thought and felt. And Meg is right about the showroom. Customers value it.'

'I was speaking about the "museum", the section cluttered with relics from the past. Displaying current wares is another matter, but who wants to see samples of Meg Tinsley's work from long ago, or any other obsolete items? Only present-day work is of any importance, so the so-called "museum" is superfluous and will go. It is for me to make the decisions now, *and* to enforce them.'

The whole shed was silent as he moved to the door, but the silence was shattered when Abby spoke up.

'Ye don't mean it, do ye, sir? You ain't the kinda gent to hurt summun like Mistress Drayton, nor our Meg neether.' Her eyes were challenging. The girl had been taught to fear no man and she certainly didn't fear one whose glance had been openly admiring. 'If ye do, sir, ye'll 'ave a battle on your 'ands. With me.'

There was a momentary hush, then Lionel Drayton burst out laughing. He was still laughing when he left the shed.

From the door, Amelia looked back at Meg and smiled. The smile expressed gratitude and affection, but also concern, and Meg knew that her thoughts were the same as her own – that despite Abby's apparent victory the girl had unwittingly made matters worse. And in doing so she had whetted the man's interest in herself.

After delivering a tray of finished pots to the drying shed, Meg came face to face with Dave Jefferson.

'I want to talk to ye,' she said, and when he asked what about she answered, 'Abby. And the new boss. I'll never call 'im "Master Potter", though that's what he's to be. "Master Potter", indeed! An' all because he's a Drayton and next in line.'

'I knows all that, Meg, but what's this about Abby?'

'He likes her. Too much.'

Dave's blue eyes darkened. Not that he was surprised. Too many men liked Abby, and little did she see the danger of it. If only she would listen to himself a bit more, he'd be less worried, but she skimmed through life like a butterfly he could never pin down. Not that he wanted to curb her or hurt her in any way; he loved her too much for that, so much that he wanted to wed her and keep her safe. He had told her so more than once, but when he did she would laugh, fling her arms about him, smack an affectionate kiss on his cheek and tell him not to be daft.

'*Me* – wed? Only if I 'ave to, an' ye wouldn't do that t'me, would ye, Dave? Get me in t'family way, I mean. There's many a wench as'd be glad to get an 'usband that way, but not me. Me mam's taught me 'ow to take care o'meself when the time comes.' She added provocatively, 'An' *I'll* be the one to choose when that'll be.'

All this was cold comfort to Dave and of the gravest concern to Meg, who knew of the primitive precautions used by women like Abby's mother. That old witch, Martha Tinsley, used to dole them out to the village women, no questions asked, together with herbal brews guaranteed to force miscarriages but which often failed, thereby leading to her profitable trade in abortions. No one had replaced that so-called midwife, so heaven protect Abby Walker.

'I wish I could get 'er away from Kate,' Meg now confided to Dave. 'I've never 'ad a daughter, never 'ad a child. If I could persuade 'er to move into my cottage, I'd make room for her somehow. Better still would be a home with you, Dave.'

'Aye.' Dave was a man of few words, but that single one came from his heart.

Meg could say no more. Besides, there wasn't time. Old Peterson was ringing the ancient bell which had been used to summon pottery workers to the eating sheds ever since the place had been established. Half a pint of small ale and a hunk of bread and cheese with a raw onion was the routine meal at midday.

Rinsing her clay-covered hands at the pump, Meg looked around for Abby. The fact that both male and female workers now ate in one huge shed, unlike the old days when they were segregated, was a mixed blessing in her eyes, for the men's attention would be focused on Kate Walker's daughter, with many a suggestive glance and ribald remark thrown in her direction even though the men sat at one end of the shed and women at the other.

Meg knew what it was like to be the target for male innuendo; she had experienced it herself when young, though mercifully spared it at meal breaks, when the women ate alone. At such times she had had to parry malicious female jibes instead, but now she had achieved a position which commanded respect and when she sat beside Abby the men as well as the women showed restraint.

Perhaps she was being over-protective, but Meg didn't think so. Especially after this morning. But if the new Master Potter's interest in the girl increased, what could she do about it?

She was glad when she saw M's Olivia on her way to join her aunt for the midday meal. This they took in the room housing archives compiled by M's Amelia years ago. The volumes occupied a whole shelf, their contents immaculately written in her fine copperplate hand. Meg knew this because she had once been shown them by Mistress Amelia, who promised that when she learned to read she would be allowed to practise with certain selected parts. Jessica Kendall had promptly offered to teach her, since when Meg had hired a nag for fivepence from the landlord of the Red Lion and ridden the few miles to and from Ashburton every weekend.

She was less adept at deciphering letters than she was at wielding a turning tool, but she persevered because she knew how proud Frank would have been had he known. She was a slow reader, but writing presented less difficulty because copying letters was like drawing a design. Loops and lines had come easily to her as a child, hence her ability to draw that perfect circle with the point of a turning tool. She could now write her address as well as her name – Tinsley's Cottage, Larch Lane, Burslem. It was an achievement unknown to many another pottery worker.

56

She also signed some of her work with her initials, no longer impressing her thumbprint in the clay for identification.

When the day came that Mistress Amelia opened one of those volumes and asked her to read, Meg would reach an important milestone in her life.

Other books the Master Potter's wife had shown her contained lessons she and M's 'Livia had used for the pottery workers' children until they were old enough to become apprentices. The classes were an innovation unheard of elsewhere. Abby had been one of the fortunate children to receive basic instruction in the three Rs before her mother found a more financially profitable occupation and turned her back on a clay-worker's life.

Kate's desertion had caused Amelia and Olivia much concern, not for the woman's sake but for her small daughter's, for officially Abby had no longer qualified for inclusion in the children's classes. This had first brought the little girl to Meg's notice. Finding her in floods of tears outside the pottery gates one day, she had discovered the cause of her grief, taken her by the hand, and led her to the Master Potter's wife.

'She's crying because 'er mam don't work 'ere no more, Mistress, so Abby can't share the children's lessons an' she wants to real bad.'

'Then indeed she shall.' Wiping the child's tear-stained face Amelia Drayton had said, 'Dear Abby, there's a place for you in the class for as long as you wish.'

'An' can I work 'ere, ma'am, when I be growed?'

'You certainly may.'

'At summat good, summat important like our Meg's?'

'Yes indeed, if you work hard enough.'

'That I will, ma'am! I'll be real important 'ere, one day.' Her radiant grin had focused then on Meg. 'I betcha I'll beat yer, Meg Tinsley!'

That was the first indication that Kate Walker's daughter not only wanted to better herself, but had the will to do it.

But at that time she had not matured into a ripe young peach, ready for the plucking.

Seeing Olivia, Meg seized her chance.

'M's 'Livia, ma'am –?'

'Yes, Meg?'

Olivia spoke absently and Meg wondered if she too had something on her mind. Recalling the underlying strain in Amelia Drayton's manner, Meg decided that the advent of Joseph Drayton's son was sufficient explanation for both.

'It's about Abby Walker, M's 'Livia. She worrits me.'

One glance at Meg's face told Olivia a lot. 'Is it men?' she asked.

'Just one, ma'am. And mebbe I'm wrong. I 'opes so, but this morning the new Master Potter came to the turners' shed. An' noticed Abby.'

'Everyone notices Abby. She is extremely pretty.'

'And – and sus –' Meg groped for the word.

'Susceptible?'

'Aye. That.'

'Unfortunately, we are all susceptible when young, but what you are really saying is that the new Master Potter singled her out this morning and you don't like it. Neither do I. Let us hope he singles out someone else, someone outside the pottery, someone in his own sphere. I expect he will but, knowing my cousin, that won't stop him from amusing himself elsewhere if he so pleases. Meanwhile, what can we do about it? We must think of something . . .'

'I've already thought, ma'am. First chance I get I'll go to work on that ma of 'ers. I think I know how to get rid of Kate Walker. Then I'd like Abby to live along o'me.'

'Can you persuade her?'

'I can try.'

'And if you fail?'

'M's 'Livia, I daresn't fail. If she'd only wed Dave Jefferson, I'd not be worrit. Nor would he.'

'But she's little more than a child!'

'Fourteen, ma'am. I wed Frank Tinsley when I were sixteen, an' t'were the best thing I ever did. But till then, I'd like Abby under me own roof –'

Meg broke off. She had just seen the girl walking across the yard to the eating shed, with Dave at her side. Murmuring with relief, 'Mebbe I worrit too much, M's 'Livia. Forgive me for bothering you,' Meg turned to follow them.

'Bother me whenever you wish. Abby's a nice child and a promising worker. And Meg – if you have any further cause for concern, come to me, won't you?'

Meg hesitated. 'Well, there do be summat I'd like to ask. It be about the new Master an' Mistress Drayton's museum.'

'The *museum*? I don't understand.'

'Nor do I, ma'am, but this morning 'e hinted that it's to be done away with. It'll 'ave t'go, he said, because the only things to interest folk are what's being made right now. Fair scoffed, 'e did, an' Mistress Drayton were hurt, I could see.'

58

'And *I* am angry!'

'He can't do away with the museum, can 'e, M's 'Livia?'

'I don't know, Meg . . . I just don't know. For the time being my aunt and I can only hope that lawyers will help us. In the meantime, we both have to wait – and that is something which doesn't come easily to me.' Her hand touched Meg's briefly. 'Thank you for telling me this. And now *I* will tell *you* something – we have exciting plans for a new type of decorative ware, Mexican and very colourful. And guess who had the idea? My young cousin Deborah. My half-brother had been showing her some of his mother's possessions – her treasures, he called them. Pottery and hand-made jewellery unlike anything produced in this country. And to think he has had them all these years and never shown them to me or to anyone because he didn't think we would be interested! He had kept them for sentimental reasons – and bless him for that because Deborah Kendall wants to try her hand at producing designs in the same colourful and exciting form. We may discover that the girl has latent talent – who knows?'

Although Meg had no idea what Mexican designs were like, she did know that new ceramic lines were always important. What with Master Kendall's new grinding-mill to produce stone-ware of a whiteness never seen before, there could be exciting days ahead for the Drayton Pottery.

'The new Master's lucky to be taking over right now,' she commented, thinking that he ill deserved such good fortune.

'He is not to know yet,' Olivia said, remembering Lionel's derisory comment. 'The whole idea needs developing. By then we will know what is to happen here. In the meantime –'

'– in the meantime, ma'am, me mouth's tight shut, but I can't 'elp thinking Master Lionel don't deserve such luck and it'd please me mighty if it fell through – meaning taking over the pottery, M's 'Livia, not the new line o' goods.'

'Amen to that,' Olivia said devoutly.

Meg smiled gratefully and went on her way. Entering the huge shed she heard Abby's voice calling.

'I've save a place right 'ere beside me, our Meg!' And sure enough the girl had – at a table far removed from the men's. When Meg sat down, Abby smiled broadly and said, 'I 'opes as 'ow this pleases ye, Meg luv? I chose this table 'cos those loose-tongued women from canalside allus takes the one nearest the men, so stop worriting, will ye?'

'It isn't the women I worrit about,' Meg wanted to say. Instead, she took a welcome swig of small ale.

*

59

Olivia was glad to find Amelia waiting for her. Nowadays her aunt seemed to eat very little, frequently missing the midday meal and occupying herself with work instead. In this way she felt she was still serving her husband.

Amelia fulfilled manifold duties at the pottery. Apart from concerning herself with the welfare of workers' children, and running both the museum and showroom, she compiled the museum's catalogue, updating it regularly, and producing stock lists for dispatch to both regular and prospective customers.

'I'm not hungry,' she began when Olivia put food before her. Then, seeing her niece's face, she yielded. 'Very well, I'll eat if it pleases you.'

'You'll eat because it's necessary,' Olivia replied with mock severity, 'not only for your own sake, but for your children's. I can't have you going home feeling tired.'

'I recover the moment I see them. And if my work here is to come to an end, perhaps it will be for the best.'

'Who says it is to end?'

'My nephew – if he has his way. He hasn't actually *said* as much, but I can read his thoughts.'

Then thank heaven Damian has ridden into Stoke to get a legal opinion, Olivia reflected. She said: 'I talked to my father, whose reaction was the same as yours and mine. He immediately thought of the Tremain lawyer in Stoke, though he also considered that since he himself was not a Drayton he couldn't interfere in that family's affairs. He then said it might not be a bad idea to give Lionel his head, because he would be sure to dislike the earthenware trade as much as he himself had done. He added wryly that you would be sure to remember that . . .'

'I do indeed. Joseph made an opening for him because he was marrying Phoebe. It ended as disastrously as the marriage. What else did Max say?'

'Only that the sooner we consult Whittaker, the better. That made me impatient to see Damian, but I had to wait until he returned from Tunstall.'

'And when he did return, what did he say?'

Regretfully, Olivia admitted that Damian feared nothing could be done because Lionel was undeniably the eldest male in the Drayton line, but since Whittaker knew what Martin had in mind he would press that point home.

'Damian was always more decisive than Max,' Amelia said gratefully.

'He went to Stoke first thing yesterday and will return tonight if he has been able to see Whittaker. If not, he will remain until he does. Meanwhile, take heart. If we have to work under my unlikeable cousin, we must thwart him whenever he tries to spike our guns.'

'He is firing the first volley already. The museum is to be closed. Haven't you heard?'

'Meg has just told me, but I hoped it was nothing but idle talk – Lionel's, not Meg's.'

'Not this time. He intends to restore that splendid room into an office for himself. He told me so after we toured the works this morning. The smaller room can display samples of our latest wares, he said, and that should be quite enough. If not, the large shed given over to the children can be utilized instead. When I asked where the children's classes would then be held, he said that 'of course' they would be abolished and reminded me that no other potter in Staffordshire wastes time or money on workers' offspring.'

Olivia's fury choked her.

'As for my catalogues and stock lists,' Amelia continued, 'he considers them an unnecessary expense. Put an end to the museum, and the catalogues will end too. And stock lists, he maintains, can be done by any employee who can read and write. They can also be issued half-yearly instead of quarterly. What he is really saying is that I am superfluous here and will have to go.'

'Never! The workers would be up in arms.'

'They might want to be, but dare any of them risk their jobs?' Amelia sighed. 'Where will he attack next, I wonder. Dear Olivia, what are we to do?'

'Fight him,' Olivia declared hotly. 'Fight him every inch of the way! But let's look on the bright side – his claim may fail.'

'I fear not because he is right. I have looked at it from every angle, over and over again, and it is inescapable. Martin died before he could change the old order, so it remains. You and I, dear Olivia, have no choice but to yield to it.'

CHAPTER 6

The contrast between her own home and Miguel's struck Deborah forcibly as, with one hand lifting her skirts, she raced up the front steps of Ashburton. Both were country houses of distinction, but in atmosphere they were vastly different.

Glancing up, she saw the Armstrong coat of arms carved into the portico. At Tremain Hall the Tremain crest was featured similarly. Here at Ashburton proud griffins stood at the foot of the steps, with unicorns midway and haughty lions at the top. Corinthian columns framed a pair of fine double doors. At Tremain the statuary was classical, the columns were doric, and the entrance doors even more imposing. Both houses were approached by magnificent tree-lined drives terminating, at Ashburton, in a circular sweep and at the Hall in a fine courtyard.

As far as lands went, however, Ashburton's were considerably less because the elder Armstrong sons – the wastrel brothers – had sacrificed the Home Farm and other large sections of the estate to satisfy voracious debt collectors, leaving it to Neville, the youngest, to salvage what he could. With determination and diligence he had done so, dedicating himself to the restoration of the family's fortune and the resurgence of its pride. While Tremain had prospered, Ashburton had been painstakingly reborn – first under childless Neville, then under Deborah's clever father, Simon Kendall, whom Neville had chosen as his heir.

From behind the house of Ashburton, grounds swept toward a deep valley where every spare outhouse and barn had been turned into a workshop of some kind. None could be seen from the house, nor could the perpetual hum of activity be heard, a hum currently dominated by her father's latest experiments in harnessing wind and water to charge his latest project – a windmill to drive stampers for pounding burnt flints to powder. When perfected, such a mill would replace the laborious process of hammering and handgrinding, and the result would be the finest ground flint to mix with Drayton's white clay, thus producing the purest and whitest stoneware ever marketed. It would be the most exciting advance in ceramic manufacture for many years.

'There won't be a firm in all the potteries that won't be after it,' Martin Drayton had predicted. 'For that reason the product and the mixing proportions must be as closely guarded as the workings of Simon's mill.'

It was all very exciting, but also frustrating, thought Deborah as she flung herself into the house. Now that she was to be involved – and she was determined that her Mexican-inspired designs should actively involve her – her interest in her father's scheme was heightened. The clay of Miguel's pots had been strong enough to use for outdoor cooking, which meant that it was strong enough to withstand the elements which, in turn, meant that similar clay, such as stoneware, could be used for external work – garden ornaments, statuary, and picturesque sundials to be mounted on walls. The possibilities were endless.

Already she had committed to paper a panel design for a wall sundial, featuring pheasant and partridge instead of tropical birds; a design which would blend into an English background but, at the same time, have the life and vigour of Miguel's. Not until she had finished the drawing had she realized that, subconsciously, she had been designing it with Tremain in mind because he was the heir; consequently she was now impatient for her father's experiments to reach fruition.

The sundial plaque would need to be produced in stoneware clay, otherwise a mason would have to be employed to carve it in solid stone and Deborah found such an idea unacceptable. She wanted to execute the work herself, and to do so she would first have to understand the working properties of clay.

Unbeknown to her family, she had been sketching in a disused summer house in a forgotten corner far west of the entrance lodge, keeping the activity secret in case of failure. She had pursued so many creative hobbies, without success, that her brothers and sisters had become indulgent but sceptical. Only her cousin Olivia seemed to understand her frustrated need to express herself.

'Wait until you're married like me, Debby dear,' her sister Penelope had said, laughing. 'You'll be producing a new addition to the family every year and *that* will satisfy your creative urge, believe me!' And back she had gone to Lincoln, happy and content, amused by the little sister who wanted to do more than mark time until conventional marriage with a conventional man led her into conventional married life.

But now Deborah was eager to show her pheasant-and-partridge design to the world, so here she was, racing up the long drive and into the house, waving a roll of thick drawing paper and calling her mother's name.

In the middle of the wide hall, she stood still and raised her voice. It was a habit in this family to shout to each other through the sprawling rooms; it saved time and trouble and spared servants the necessity of plodding up from the kitchen quarters to answer unnecessary bells. Even so, they would frequently appear, as one did now.

'If it be your dear mother you want, Miss Deb'ra, last time I seed her she were on her way to the flower room. Would ye like me to tell her you be looking for her?'

'No, don't trouble – but thank you, Sarah.'

The woman was Clara's sister, younger by twelve years. Their mother had once been a lowly kitchenmaid at Ashburton, finally achieving the position of cook. By the time Clara was established as the late Emily Drayton's only servant at Medlar Croft, Sarah had been taught to read and write and to 'speak proper', thanks to the late master of Ashburton. She had reached the rank of senior housemaid by the time she was 'inherited' by the Kendalls and, like the rest of the staff, had willingly remained. Now she happily occupied the position of under housekeeper beneath her older sister, whom the mistress had brought from Medlar Croft on the death of her mother, Emily Drayton. Clara was ageing rapidly so it was Sarah's more nimble legs that brought her to answer Miss Deborah's lusty call.

But the flower room was empty. So was the sewing room, where her mother sometimes helped Clara with household needlework. The woman's hands were now so gnarled that holding a needle was difficult, but never would she admit it. 'Clara lets me help only because she thinks I enjoy it,' Jessica Kendall admitted, 'but frankly I would rather lose myself in a book!' All the family was in the conspiracy, fostering dear Clara's belief.

When neither the sewing room nor the flower room yielded Jessica Kendall, the next possibility was the writing room, where she penned those articles on social reforms which aroused ire in many people but brought applause from others. Failing that, she might be in Ashburton's extensive library, where Jessica had tutored her children until the boys were old enough to go away to school and the girls ready for individual tuition (plus home management, which she herself had learned at her mother's knee). And if she were in neither of these places, then she could well be outdoors, listening attentively to the head gardener but

64

subtly winning him over to her own ideas, or she would be down at the valley workshops, unobtrusively watching her husband at work.

They could never be apart from each other for long, those two. If Jessica Kendall were seated beneath the shade of a tree, soon her husband would be beside her. If he were working on some complicated plans in the silence of his study, after a while he would discover his wife's quiet presence, and be glad of it.

Failing to find her mother, Deborah hurried through the house, finally emerging on to a wide terrace flanking the southern side. From here she could faintly hear not only the spasmodic throbbing of the pump which was to drive her father's water-wheel, but the muted hum of activity involved in other schemes and the sound of distant voices shouting above their work. Although far removed and out of sight of the house itself, they were the very pulse of Ashburton, ceasing only for sleep.

This was the contrast between Miguel's home and her own. At Tremain, quietness reigned. Only from belowstairs and in the far-flung regions of smithy, granary, stables, carpenter's shop and other domestic and estate services came any real sounds of life. No family voices echoed in the vast house. All was peace, serenity – and loneliness.

Never had this struck Deborah so much as during the hours she had spent with Miguel on that memorable day (was it really no more than ten days ago?). 'We will not be interrupted here,' he had said, leading her into Tremain's long library, though who was likely to intrude she could not imagine. Neither Aunt Agatha nor Uncle Max were booklovers, so Miguel had exclusive use of the place, but the picture of him closeted alone for hours at a stretch struck her as sad.

He had set out his mother's treasures on the library's big drum table. They had looked incongruous in the sombre room for they included primitive cooking pots of all kinds, but their patterns were so vivid and colourful that they seemed to contain a vitality of their own. There was also hand-made jewellery created from leather and bronze, brightly ornamented with ceramic stones. The display had forced a delightful exclamation from her, and the warmth of her enthusiasm had brought happiness to Miguel's quiet face.

'Amelia and Olivia must see these at once!' she had declared. 'How *could* you have hidden them all these years?'

'They were all I had of her. Very personal, very private. Of interest to no one but myself, I thought.'

65

'*And* your father.'

'To him, yes, but he finds such reminders painful. 'Do with them what you wish,' he once said, so I told him I intended to keep them for my bride – when I have one. To that he said he only hoped the young lady would appreciate them, but that he doubted whether any English miss would. So I put them away and there they have remained until now.'

Why was Miguel so touching? Was it his simplicity, his modesty, his shyness? And why was he shy, after all these years in a country to which he had adapted so naturally? At one time he had been in the habit of visiting Ashburton regularly, becoming a close friend of her brother's and fitting easily into the family background, but recently he seemed to have withdrawn, and that concerned her. She hoped he wasn't growing away from them all. She would hate to lose such a good friend. 'Perhaps we could find him a nice wife,' she had blithely suggested one day when her mother commented on how rarely Miguel now visited them.

'And how could a wife improve the situation, my dear?'

'Why, Mama, she would come to call and he would come with her and then exchange visits would start and we would all be one happy family again.'

'You think so?' Her mother's glance had been as quizzical as her voice, but she had changed the subject by discussing the week's batch of home produce to be packed and sent to Liverpool's dockland settlements. The Kendalls had given over whole areas at Ashburton for the cultivation of foodstuffs, from which a variety of charitable organizations, as well as villagers, benefited.

'We must do *something* with our land, other than feed ourselves,' Jessica had once said when Agatha, paying an unexpected call, asked how they could possibly need so much fruit and vegetables. 'Unlike Tremain, we haven't a veritable army of dependants, so it's good to feel that someone, somewhere, enjoys our produce too. And remembering all the charities you were involved with when young, Agatha, you must surely approve?'

'Ah, but *I* supervised and organized. I didn't soil my hands with all this messy cleaning and packing of foodstuffs. Just look at yours, Jessica! Not the hands of a lady at all.'

That had sparked her mother's laughter. To Deborah's ears, there was no one who laughed so musically. 'I loved your mother's laughter from the moment I first heard it,' Papa had once said, which didn't surprise Deborah, though all she had said in reply was, 'It seems to me that you loved everything about her from the moment you first met,' to which he had nodded agreement, smiling his quiet smile.

Impatiently now, she went in search of her parents, resolving that, wherever they were, she would make them pay attention right away.

She found them in the long barn which served as her father's main experimentation centre. The water-driven pump had hummed to a standstill and Jessica Kendall stood quietly aside, watching her husband as he stooped to adjust part of the mechanism. Plainly, things were not going to his satisfaction so perhaps this was not a good moment to interrupt, but surely, just for *five* minutes. . .? Quietly, Deborah slipped her arm through her mother's and whispered, 'I have something to show to both of you, urgently . . .'

'Hush, my love. There seems to be a problem here. We must not interrupt.'

Deborah suppressed a sigh. When one was agog with excitement, it was difficult to be patient. 'Why water-driven?' she whispered more loudly. 'I thought steam was Papa's obsession now.'

Simon Kendall looked up. 'Stage whispers should be quieter than that, my child.' The words mixed admonishment with indulgence. 'As for steam, that is something to advance to when we have perfected this stage – which we will.' Wiping his hands on a roll of cheese-cloth, he called a halt. 'A short one. Just long enough for me to get rid of this boisterous girl of mine.' The men laughed and the foreman shouted for the ale-boy as Simon drew his wife and daughter outside. Workers at Ashburton were more fortunate than elsewhere, the customary small ale being home-brewed.

Si Kendall placed one arm about Deborah's shoulders, the other about his wife's, and led them to the shade of an overhanging tree.

'*Now* let us hear what you are so agog about –'

'This!' Deborah unrolled her drawing and held it up. 'And don't either of you dare to tell me that you can't recognize pheasant and partridge!'

'My dear – is this *your* work?'

'Of course, Mama. And I plan to do more. Papa, why are you looking at it like that, head on one side as if it puzzles you?'

'Because it *is* puzzling me. It's so unusual. Oh, the birds are instantly recognizable but the way they are drawn . . . so boldly, so differently . . .'

67

'They look almost tropical,' said her mother, plainly interested but also surprised.

'Good. I meant them to.'

'Is this your latest whim?' Simon asked. 'If so, I approve, though I share your mother's surprise. What sparked this dashing approach?'

'The patterns on Miguel's Mexican pots. His mother's. He has treasured them all these years, showing them to no one except, at last, to me – which is lucky for Drayton's because the moment I saw them I found them exciting and challenging and felt convinced that the Drayton Pottery should produce something similar – not copying slavishly, of course, but seeking inspiration from them.'

'They have certainly inspired you,' said her mother. 'The more I study that design, the better it seems. I would very much like to see it in colour.'

'So you shall. Vivid and bold. But it will need the right clay body, so the sooner you get your mill working, Papa, the better. Can't you just *see* how dramatic these birds would look on really white stoneware? And why couldn't the powdered flints be mixed with terracotta to produce a lovely shade of coral? What a splendid foil that would be! My dear, *dear* father, do go back to work quickly, and do abandon water-power for steam, to speed things up. You've been extolling the virtues of steam ever since you went to Wolverhampton to study Newcomen's atmospheric steam engines. There – you see how carefully I listen to all you say, and doesn't that surprise you?' Her eyes sparkled. 'I'm not the feather-brained miss you believe me to be!'

'I have never believed you to be any such thing,' her father answered mildly, 'and I acknowledge that steam will advance things enormously, but only when my watermill has reached a certain stage and can be adapted to it. One step at a time, young lady – that is the way to success. As for your sudden interest in pottery, I am gratified by it. I take it that Drayton's know?'

'Yes, indeed. And when Amelia and Olivia saw the Mexican pots, they were as fascinated as I. Not Cousin Lionel, though. He thought them crude. I know he didn't mean to be overheard – he's too charming to be impolite – and of course he will admire the new product eventually, as will everyone. Meanwhile, so long as the two Drayton partners approve, that's all that matters – and they will, they *will*! Amelia said what Uncle Martin used to say – that sometimes new lines are slow to be accepted. Even so, new lines are the lifeblood of a pottery – he used to say that too.

Well, *my* idea has sparked a whole new line and *I* intend to produce the designs for it. I'm sure Amelia will be happy for me to do so. I could dance for joy!' She hugged each of her parents in turn.

'So you've met Lionel,' Jessica commented, extricating herself from her effervescent young daughter. 'We haven't yet had that pleasure, but I suppose we must accept his invitation to sup at Carrion House.'

'So it has come?' Deborah was delighted. 'He did say he would invite us, but so often people say that sort of thing and then forget . . . I thought he might do the same . . . But why do you "suppose" we must accept? Surely the invitation was for all of us, not just for yourselves?'

'For the family, or those of us who are currently at home. And I say "suppose" because I am not wholly sure that I want to go, despite the fact that he is my brother's son . . . or perhaps because of it. I have never made any secret of the fact that I was not overfond of my elder brother.'

'But why, Mama?'

'Ancient history, my love.' Jessica added briskly, 'We will hinder you no more, Simon. I want to see where this secretive daughter of ours has been developing this newly-discovered talent. Not in her room or, knowing how untidy she can be, there would have been some evidence. I have seen none of it anywhere in the house, so where have you been hiding yourself, my child?'

'In a dilapidated summer house far beyond the Lodge.'

'That won't do. An attic with a northern light – isn't that what artists need? There are plenty here at Ashburton so let's go and choose one.' Giving her husband the smile which she reserved especially for him, and receiving the warmth of his in return, Jessica linked her arm with her daughter's and moved away.

'I imagine you will need art tuition,' she continued. 'I believe that in Stoke there are several fashionable tutors for young ladies –'

Deborah interrupted swiftly, 'If Amelia and Olivia think me sufficiently talented, I'm sure I shall be given workspace at the pottery. There I shall be taught ceramic painting, both underglaze and overglaze, because only that way can I learn the technique. *Then* I shall be able to create designs suitable for reproduction on clay. I fully expect that when Amelia and Olivia see this one, they may want it to be modified or embellished. Where better to learn all this than at a pottery? And how splendid it will be to be part of a place like Drayton's!' When her mother made no answer, Deborah finished, 'Don't you think so, Mama? And won't you be proud of me?'

'I am always proud of you. So is your father. But –'

'But what? You don't doubt my ability, do you? I know I have a tremendous lot to learn, but Olivia mastered a specialized field and I mean to do the same.'

'It isn't your ability that I doubt. It's the future of Drayton's.'

'Not you, too! Surely *you* don't side with all those gloomy folk who declare that women can't run a pottery successfully?'

'I am confident they can, if allowed to.'

'Why shouldn't they be? And who can stop them?' Deborah gave her mother's arm a little shake and was satisfied when she smiled. 'Now tell me when my handsome cousin has invited us to his house – and what shall I wear? My blue velvet? You like me in that, I know. Or may I have something new, if there's time?'

'The invitation is for three days hence.'

So soon! Deborah felt a tremor of excitement. So *soon* she would see him again, her sophisticated cousin who had looked at her in such a way that she had felt colour surge to her face and knew that he had noticed it.

'I suppose everyone will be there.' She forced a casual note into her voice, though she felt far from casual. 'Aunt Agatha and Uncle Max and Miguel, too. And Amelia and Olivia and Damian, of course. And I shall happily wear my blue velvet, Mama, for though it may not be new to the family, it will be new to Lionel . . .'

'And is that so important?' A searching glance accompanied her mother's question. Receiving no reply, and detecting a faint colour in the girl's cheeks, Jessica Kendall said no more.

It was not a family supper party, after all. Scarcely a local dignitary had been overlooked, scarcely a title or a prominent name; not an overcrowded guest list, but an impressive one.

A long table spanned the full length of the hall, with another across its head. Silver and crystal sparkled beneath hundreds of candles set in glittering chandeliers, with more in silver candelabra at intervals along the tables. Flowers, plainly ordered from one of Staffordshire's leading horticulturists since the Carrion hothouses were not yet restocked, provided great masses of colour on a background of spotless napery.

Jessica Kendall wondered whether the place had looked like this for her twin sister's wedding breakfast, and thought it very likely since Joseph had been determined to draw attention to his own success. She recalled how proud he had been of this spacious hall, which forever after he had referred to as 'the banqueting hall', but no amount of refurbishing and decoration had changed Jessica's personal reaction to it. Nor to the house itself. Carrion House was a place she disliked.

Entering now at her husband's side, she slipped an arm through his and felt a welcome pressure as he drew it closer. Fleetingly, she glanced up and saw his gentle, understanding smile. He was reading her mind, as always. There was no need for words; no need to whisper *'Do you remember?'* How could either of them forget a past that had shaped their life together?

'You look very beautiful tonight,' he said, 'but then, you always do. That's one of my favourite gowns.'

'And that's why I chose it, my love.'

Her open mantua, revealing pearl-embroidered petticoats, was trimmed with lace-edged gauze ruffles on the sleeves, and a matching neck frill formed an upstanding Medici collar to frame a still lovely neck and bosom. She wore the gown well because she carried herself well. Across her high brow she wore a *ferronière* set with pearls and moonstones, an adornment few women could do justice to but which Jessica's classical features displayed to perfection.

Behind them came Deborah, bare shoulders rising from the deep neckline of her blue velvet gown, with its top skirt looped up in polonaise style to reveal the second embroidered layer beneath, and her hair shining like polished copper under the glittering chandeliers. Unlike most young women of her age, she wore no adornment. 'I feel cluttered!' she had exclaimed when dressed for her first ball, and had promptly discarded the tiered necklace of peridots which her sister Elizabeth had insisted she should wear. Even a jewelled Glauvina pin for her hair, with its knot of upstanding feathers, had been cast aside with the protest that it not only made her look like a turkey-cock, but would surely be lost in the first Roger de Coverley.

'How can I romp in the dance with that thing on my head?'

At that, both sisters had been aghast. 'You must *not* romp!' Elizabeth had admonished. 'You must dance delicately and sedately! You cannot remain a hoyden for ever, little sister. As for wearing no adornments, have you ever seen Penelope or myself go unbejewelled to a formal social event?'

'But both of you wear jewellery well. On me, it looks fussy and overdone.' Decisive as ever, Deborah had had her way – and very lovely had she looked as a result, both then and now. Her

71

mother was gratified because her youngest child showed so much common sense and hoped this same faculty would stand her in good stead always.

Jessica hoped for this even more when she saw her nephew's seating arrangements. She herself was on his right at the top table, with Deborah on his left – a gesture so marked that not an ambitious mama in the place could fail to notice it.

Simon was placed a few feet away from Jessica, a natural arrangement since to seat husband and wife together was not customary. But where was Lionel's mother? Jessica was about to remark on her sister-in-law's absence when Deborah forestalled her.

'Where is Aunt Agatha?' she asked as Lionel seated her. 'Surely she should be seated beside you, Cousin?'

'Alas, my poor mother is indisposed.' The regret in his eyes conveyed genuine disappointment.

'Then what of Uncle Max and Miguel? I can see no sign of either.'

'For the simple reason that they too are absent. You are no doubt aware that our uncle's physical condition keeps him very much at home. I doubt if he could get through a long social evening without fatigue.'

'And Miguel?'

Shrugging, Lionel said, 'He declined.'

'I'm disappointed.'

'Why?'

'Because I think he has little social life, up there at the Hall.'

'Then he should have accepted my invitation.'

'He's shy.'

'You seem to know him well.'

'We all know him well. But what of Aunt Amelia – and Olivia and Damian? They seem to be absent, too.'

'I gather that dear Amelia has turned her back on a social life since her husband's death, and far be it from me to try to dissuade her until the requisite period of mourning has passed. Indeed, I was surprised to find her still working at the pottery.'

'The pottery is her salvation and we are glad for her to have it.' Glancing round the glittering room Deborah added, 'I see no sign of Olivia and Damian.'

'I understand he is in Tunstall.'

'Not now. I saw him in Burslem only today.'

'I was unaware of that, otherwise I would have had a joint invitation sent to them. Naturally, one could not be sent to

Olivia alone. I imagine she would avoid attending any function without him.' Lionel smiled his amiable, attractive smile. 'Their union, I gather, is as strong as if they were married.'

'In everyone's eyes they *are* married.'

'What a forthright young woman you are!'

Deborah laughed. 'So people tell me. I suppose I should try to remedy such a fault.'

'Pray don't. I would have nothing about you changed in any way.'

Jessica listened, quelling uneasiness. It was the first time she had met her nephew for many years and she was startled not only by the physical resemblance to her elder brother, but by the personality resemblance also. Lionel lacked Joseph's authoritative air, but equalled him in self-confidence. And in plausibility, too? His reasons for failing to invite the others seemed sound enough, but were they true? And did her daughter's observations indicate that she, too, was troubled? If so, then there was no need to fear for her susceptibility.

But as the evening advanced and course followed course and an atmosphere of enjoyment testified to the success of the evening, Deborah seemed to be slowly captivated by Lionel's personality – and no one knew better than her mother how easily a young and trusting girl could be trapped by a man's charm.

At length, Jessica caught her husband's eye. He was in conversation with his neighbour, but read her message. How soon would they be able to leave? The lavish meal was over, people were now lingering over their wine and, in the absence of a hostess, waiting for their host to rise and bow to the lady on his right who happened, tonight, to be his nearest female relative – his father's sister and his eldest aunt. In that respect his seating had been correct, but the placing of her daughter on his left had not been a matter of etiquette, but of choice – a significant choice, everyone must be thinking, especially now that he was making no effort to indicate that it was time for the ladies to withdraw.

His whole attention was focused on Deborah, from whom he plainly had no wish to part. He was enjoying her conversation, teasing her with his smile, sending unspoken messages with his eyes, obviously resolved not to part from her until it was absolutely necessary. And Deborah seemed to be enjoying every moment.

I never did like this house, Jessica thought unhappily, but her calm, serene face betrayed nothing, though, even while she talked to the neighbour on her right, snatches of conversation came to

73

her from the left. Suddenly her attention was sharpened by a remark of her nephew's.

'You have no need to be concerned about Amelia. She will recover from distress, in time. The best thing she can do is to retire and I intend to advise it. At her age, she deserves to take life easily and the pottery will provide for her amply.'

'Retire!' Deborah gasped. 'Aunt *Amelia*? She would hate that!'

'On the contrary, I suspect she might find the idea attractive. She voiced no objection when I hinted at it.'

'And why did you do that?'

'Because it distresses me to see a woman of her age working too hard, but far be it from me to coerce her – she will leave only when she is ready.'

'But they are to run the pottery together, she and Olivia. They need each other's support.'

'The only support any woman needs is a man's. Dear Deborah, the potteries are not a woman's world.'

'They are going to be mine! Mama –' Deborah leaned across, attracting her mother's attention – 'Lionel is telling me unbeliev-able things –'

'– but true ones, Cousin. The only unbelievable thing is that a young lady like you can even think of becoming involved in so masculine a place as a pottery. And in what possible way, I wonder?'

Deborah's cheeks were now pink – from annoyance, or response to his interest?'

'I will reveal that only to Amelia and Olivia,' she stated.

'No. To me. I am head of the Drayton Pottery now.'

Glancing from one surprised face to the other he continued, 'Surely you know that? Surely the whole of Burslem knows it? Amelia and Olivia have held the fort admirably, or as admirably as any women could, but they are now to be freed from all responsibility. You must come to me with any whim you may have, dear Deborah, and I will listen with pleasure.'

'It is no whim.'

She sounded downcast. He took hold of her hand and said comfortingly, 'Then I shall listen with the fullest attention.'

But his eyes promised a great deal more.

CHAPTER 7

Olivia was in bed when Damian returned from Stoke. One glance at his face confirmed her fears.

'We can do nothing,' he told her. 'Martin's will was unsigned. It was prepared and waiting for his signature the next day. Whittaker is willing to confirm what Martin had in mind, to any near relative entitled to know, though should anyone try to carry out his wishes, others could successfully prevent it.'

'Meaning Lionel.'

'Who else? The facts are exactly as he claims and cannot be ignored.'

'But the heritrix clause which applied to Grandmother Charlotte was broken, and was then to be restored in favour of myself, had I agreed. So why can't Lionel's claim be over-turned?'

'Because in the case of Tremain the circumstances were differ-ent. If Amelia wants to fight, she can do little. She can only console herself with the thought that her son will eventually in-herit.'

'And that will happen only if Lionel Drayton dies without leaving sons of his own, or is somehow dethroned. The first is unlikely and the second seems impossible. In any case, all the fight has gone out of Amelia.'

'But she's courageous. She will rally. Meanwhile, I shall be behind both of you, whatever you choose to do. I have never liked that cousin of yours, not because of his affair with Caroline – I had reason to be grateful for that! – but because of his attitude to you. Do you remember the days when I used to shoe the Tremain horses? You would linger in the stables to watch me. It was then that I noticed how often he followed you and the way he looked at you and I knew full well what he wanted and, being the kind of man he was (and no doubt still is), believed he had every right to take.'

'Lionel believed that of any woman, and was rarely dis-couraged.'

'Except by you. Long ago as it was, I remember the night of his coming-of-age celebrations and how you arrived on my doorstep, your hair streaming in the rain. I guessed you had ridden off in a rage to escape from someone, *and* whom.'

'And what a sight I looked! While you re-shod Corporal I tried to clean myself up –'

'– and failed. I think I fell in love with you that night. Certainly I became really aware of you for the first time.'

'I wish I'd known. I'd been in love with you for so long!' As he stooped over the bed and gathered her up, she returned his embrace with a love that had not diminished throughout the years. Then, firmly detaching herself, she said, 'Enough of ourselves! We must concentrate on Amelia. If I were to find it intolerable to work for Lionel, I would still remain at the pottery because she needs my support. She's convinced that he's bent on getting rid of her.'

'And it seems she's right. I called at Ashburton on my way back and learned that the Kendalls had already got wind of what was afoot. They supped at Carrion House last night and Lionel admitted that he thinks Amelia should retire. Si and Jessica are both indignant about it, but Deborah is trying not to be. She even struggled to defend him, saying he was surely prompted by kindly concern.'

'How gullible one can be at seventeen!'

'At least her parents are alert to the situation, and, because of the water-driven mill Simon is building for the benefit of Drayton's, he will be keeping a watching brief. I can't see a man like Si Kendall being willing to trade with an inefficient potter, and I can't see one who lacks expertise being anything else. I expect Lionel's aim will be to put an experienced man in charge, and with so many potters struggling to make a living singly, he will easily find one eager to work for a well-established pot bank. That should prevent him from making too many mistakes.'

'He has made one already. He's closing the museum.'

'And when was that announced?' Damian asked, preparing for bed.

'After you'd gone to Stoke. Everything is to be immediately packed away or disposed of because that impressive room is again to be the Master Potter's office. Where the exhibits are to be stored, I can't think. Every shed at the pottery is in use. Martin was planning to instal a cellar similar to a pump room Simon built for one of the Tremain mines at Spen Green. They had discussed it at length and Simon had produced plans, together with detailed precautions against seepage from the canal. We all know how coal pits near inland waters can be subject to flooding; those at Spen were often so until the Kendall pump was installed. But a pottery, being above ground, would be at less risk. Even so, a cellar near a canal would need good fortification. In the end, Martin abandoned the scheme, so there isn't even a good dry cellar in which to store Amelia's collection. If only Lionel would give her more time, but no, the room must be cleared immediately!'

Olivia sighed, yawned, and nestled close to Damian when he joined her. Her restless stirrings brought his arms close about her. 'Be still, my love . . . and don't worry . . . we will find somewhere to house Amelia's treasures.'

Olivia sighed. 'But *where*?'

'At the forge, but not as part of it. There is a roomy building near the entrance, at present used for storing scrap, but it could be utilized for something better.'

'I thought you planned to use that for displaying finished ironwork?'

'So I did, but as fast as things are made, they are sold, so I have never been able to accumulate enough for a display. In any case, there is enough space on the site to erect further outbuildings, as and when needed. I bought the adjoining land with expansion in mind. Housing Amelia's museum won't be an encroachment. It will be entirely separate. I'll have a sign put up, the name emblazoned, and an arrow pointing the way.'

'*Wonderful!* Damian, I love you!'

His lips silenced her. Their senses stirred, gathered momentum and finally merged. It was the never-ending miracle of their lives, eternally renewable. It was the rhythmic, recurrent pulse of their union, unthreatened by staleness, and the peace and tranquillity it brought lingered with her even as she set out for the pottery next morning – until she walked into the modelling shed and knew at once that something was wrong. The faces of her work team and the way in which they looked at her – silently, uneasily – told her so.

'What has happened?' she asked, and when no one answered she added, 'Don't be afraid to confess if something is smashed. Accidents happen.'

One of the senior modellers then spoke up.

''T'were in the firing, M's 'Livia. Your statue of Minerva for that London gallery – blown up, along with others. More than a dozen statuettes so far and an even bigger number of wildlife models for the same gallery – all gone. What caused it, nobody knows, but everything near it was smashed.'

And even beyond, Olivia knew. Hurtling fragments of exploding pottery could reach even distant parts of a kiln, ruining a whole consignment no matter how carefully stacked. Most firings had a percentage of rejections caused by such hazards as uneven glaze reactions, but such pieces could sometimes be reglazed and refired, whereas flaws such as crawling or blistering, due to bad positioning or too heavy an application of glaze, could never be overcome. Even so, these items could still be disposed of to market dealers who were glad of them to sell cheaply.

A ten per cent 'discard' per load was average in most potteries, but Drayton's prided itself on never exceeding five per cent. Faultless production in the remaining pieces more than made up for any imbalance and often merited considerably higher pricing than expected, so that in the end the load still proved profitable. Exports to Europe and America, as well as supplies to important dealers in London and leading provincial cities, had been built to a standard of perfection unequalled elsewhere. Firing cycles were carefully planned in regular sequence, but a heavy loss from only one could upset the whole programme and, this time, it was particularly serious because the order from the London gallery had been a big one.

Olivia had made all the major pieces herself, carefully supervising and inspecting the rest because responsibility for the whole department was hers. She therefore knew that no faulty item had emerged from the modelling sheds, but after such a disaster it could be difficult to prove. Piecing together masses of fragments in search of evidence could be well nigh impossible.

She was grieved over her wildlife reproductions, a line which had won for her an increasingly high reputation. Every piece had been individually commissioned from preliminary sketches, every price individually quoted and accepted – with an additional percentage for signed editions because her initials on the bases increased their value. Now each one would have to be remodelled, put aside to dry out, then bisque-fired, glazed, and glaze-fired yet again. That meant not only weeks of work and weeks of delay, but the loss of costly materials. Rutile and manganese, whiting and feldspar, not to mention chemical oxides for fusing in glazes, meant nothing to laymen who imagined that the only thing needed to produce a ceramic article was a lump of clay. To a buyer, an order was an order and failure to deliver by an agreed date was a black mark against a potter's name.

Olivia took a deep breath and told her workers not to worry. 'These things happen,' she reiterated, trying to sound more philosophical than she felt, for although there could be several causes for such a disaster, the most frequent was the omission of a vent hole in a 'closed' item. Only open pots and bowls and domestic crocks had no need for this. Blame would therefore focus on the modelling department, where everything had to be hollow and with pierced bases. Without an air hole, a piece would explode.

'Has the kiln been drawn yet?'

'They're still at it, M's 'Livia, the damage was that bad.'

She decided to visit the firing area to find out what she could. Any action was better than staying here, knowing her workers were trying to concentrate while anxiety gnawed at them, each fearful that one of their own pieces might be to blame. Tiredness, fatigued eyes at the end of the day, or sheer forgetfulness could so easily cause a simple oversight. The late Master Potter had been stern about carelessness, but compassionate when compassion was called for. In the new regime, what would happen?

Olivia was shocked by the extent of the damage. Broken pots littered the ground, intermingled with shattered figurines and fragmented models. Never before had she seen such extensive wastage from a single firing.

News of the disaster had spread on that silent wave which seeped through any pottery when something had gone wrong. No doubt it was known throughout Burslem by now, and soon it would spread throughout the length and breadth of the potteries. In the firing area, groups of workers huddled silently: glazers, throwers, wedgers, turners, riddlers, decorators, sagger-makers, packers, mould-makers and slip-casters, and even canalside women who drove carts to and from the clay-carrying barges – anyone who could steal a moment was doing so, slipping away again to describe the scene to workers back in the sheds, and all the time the firers worked on, unloading the wreckage and dumping it on the ground for people to examine if they wished. *Some*one might spot doubtful pieces and recognize their source.

Olivia saw Dave Jefferson with Meg Tinsley. Both were un-aware of Abby Walker slipping quietly into view. The turning tool in her hand testified that she had halted in the middle of a task, unable to contain her curiosity. It was possibly the first such disaster the child had ever seen and her eyes were round with dismay. 'Thanks be t'God *we* can't be blamed,' she was saying to another worker as Olivia passed. 'Turners've only to put rims on bases an' now't else.'

In that case, Olivia was tempted to say, the sooner she continued with the job in hand the better because the pottery was going to need plenty of completed stock, and speedily. But who could speak harshly to Abby?

Olivia walked on until she reached the rogue kiln and heard Lionel angrily demanding an explanation which the chief firer stonily refused to give.

'Ye cain't point blame until the whole load be out, sir. Ye'd best be patient-like an' leave us t'the job.' Such blunt speech displeased the new Master, who turned away and, seeing Olivia, held up some broken pieces. 'These are plainly from figurines,' he said. 'We will talk in my office.'

'Certainly,' she answered, and turned away. Lingering in the firing area was a waste of time and she was suddenly impatient to be working again. She and her team would now have weeks of overtime ahead, but before she made a start it might be wise to get the talk with Lionel over and done with.

Glancing at the ancient clock in the yard she saw that it was now ten-thirty, which meant that classes for the potters' children were in progress. This explained Amelia's absence. Olivia was glad of that. Such a scene could only distress her.

Studying the broken pieces on his desk Lionel thought, with satisfaction, that at least Olivia would not be able to fool him over the cause of such a disaster. Spending the major part of his life in the potteries, and overhearing 'potters' talk', had taught him more than he had realized until now. So when he accused her of responsibility for the tragedy, she would scarcely be able to argue.

She walked into the room with her customary self-assurance. Far from annoying him, it amused him. He would enjoy deflating it.

He met her with a smile.

'I thought I would give you the opportunity to apologize in private rather than in front of the workers,' he said. 'The last thing I want to do is to humiliate you.'

Ignoring his last words, she asked, 'Apologize for what?'

'No hedging, please. You know perfectly well that you and you alone are to blame for today's disaster.'

'I know nothing of the sort. Nor does anyone – as yet. The whole firing will have to be examined if any sound conclusion can be come to. That means days of searching and sorting and piecing together, and from the look of things it could take weeks. Time is too valuable for that. Every potter in the place will have to put in double time to replace such a huge loss. The best thing to do is to clear up the mess and put the tragedy behind us.'

'*I* will decide on the best thing to do. There will be a thorough investigation. Every item that can be salvaged and matched, *will* be salvaged and matched until guilt is established. That excludes bowls, jugs, bottles, and all thrown ware. So what is left? Hand-modelled pieces. Yours. Do you think I don't know how such items have to be made? Do you think I don't know the importance of air-vents and what will result if they are forgotten?'

'There can be other causes for blow-ups. Insufficiently wedged clay. Lingering grit. Air bubbles that have somehow not been eliminated in the processing. Items not thoroughly dried out. All these things can ruin any object, whether thrown or hand-built. Even too coarse a flint in clays such as stoneware, which this pottery is dedicated to overcoming, can be the root of the trouble. That is one reason why Simon Kendall has designed a new grinding mill – to provide us with powdered flints of such a fine texture that we will be able to produce better stoneware than anyone else.'

'All that is beside the point. And we were firing earthenware today, not stoneware. You are trying to shift the blame.'

'No one must be blamed. It is too serious to focus on any one person or on any one shed. Every potter in the place will know the seriousness of it and wonder if he or she is to blame. Anxiety of that kind is punishment enough. Now let us all get on with our work.'

'That would suit you admirably, no doubt.'

'I am thinking of what would be best for Drayton's, and I doubt if a single worker would disagree with me.'

'What the workers think is of no importance –'

'To you, perhaps, but not to me. Nor to Amelia, because what they thought and felt was always important to Martin, the best Master Potter this place ever had. In the whole of your life you will never learn as much about the craft as he did.' Anger drove her even as wisdom urged her to be silent. 'If you have brought me here solely to lay blame at *my* door, then be done with it. I have work to do. But before I go let me tell you this – putting an end to Amelia's museum will condemn you in the workers' eyes. They won't forgive you for treating her so high-handedly. How long did it take to have this place cleared?' Her glance went to the adjoining room and impulsively she flung open the door, revealing stacked hazel and willow crates which time had proved best for transporting pottery. In these straw-filled containers were already packed away years of diligent searching and restoring and identifying and labelling.

Tears stung Olivia's eyes. Slamming the door to shut out the unhappy sight, she then let her glance rove to her cousin's new furnishings. The desk with its splendid matching chair was as ostentatious as the stack of ornately framed paintings waiting to be hung. (And where had *those* come from – Carrion House or from an indulgent mama easily persuaded to part with them?) In one corner rolls of brand new carpet were propped.

'I suppose you are waiting for re-decorating to be done before all that can be laid,' she said, 'but I expect you will have it put in hand as speedily as you had this room emptied. The walls certainly testify to the good use they were put to; not even your fine gilt-framed pictures will obliterate the marks. But I'm sure your decorative taste will be excellent. How magnificent it will be, when finished! The most impressive master potter's office in Staffordshire, I shouldn't wonder.'

Anger suddenly choked her. She whirled to the door and reached it at the precise moment that Deborah Kendall walked in.

The girl stood still, glancing from Olivia's face to Lionel's and then, slowly, about the room.

'What is happening here? Where are all the exhibits?' Her eyes turned back to Olivia. 'And why are you looking upset and angry?'

'Because I *am* upset and angry – and I'll show you why!' She flung open the communicating door. '*There* is Amelia's museum – all of it! It seems impossible that so many rare and precious items could be crammed into things like that, but they have been – by order of our dear cousin, the new Master Potter who needs a bigger and better office for himself.'

Sparing no further glance for either of them, Olivia walked out of the place.

When she had gone, Deborah asked quietly, 'Is it true?'

'That I am relieving dear Amelia of much stress and anxiety? Yes. Why not? The work had become too much for her.'

'It never seemed too much. She loved it. And she was proud of the Drayton Museum.'

'I don't doubt it, but there is a time for everything –'

'Such as a time for her to retire, as you said the other night – speaking out of concern for her, of course?'

'I'm glad you remember that.'

She was looking at him searchingly, seeking reassurance; begging to be convinced that she had not been wrong in her judgement of him. 'Aunt Amelia will be hurt,' she said. 'I can't bear the thought of that.'

When he took a step toward her she imperceptibly withdrew and when he tried to take her hands she evaded him by clasping both about a roll of stiff paper she was carrying. It was the first time he had noticed it.

'Come, Deborah,' he said gently. 'You misunderstand. Let me explain.'

'What explanation is there? You said she should retire only when she was ready to, but now you seem to be speeding her on her way. Rob her of the museum, and what has she left?'

'A great deal. She is interested in the workers' children and can continue to occupy herself in that way for the time being. She also has a comfortable income from the pottery, which will continue to some degree when she leaves.'

'Pensioning her off, you mean?'

'Looking after her financially,' he corrected, then changed the subject. 'What is that you've brought? A picture of some kind?'

'A design of my own. I wanted to show it to Amelia and Olivia and – yes – to you, because you were encouraging.'

'Then let me see it.' He held out a hand. 'Didn't I promise to give you my fullest attention?' His voice dropped a note. 'I shall always find that easy.' When she made no answer he added, 'Why do you hesitate? Surely you aren't shy? Come, show me your design.'

'I'm sorry – no. I have changed my mind.'

She closed the door quietly, but firmly, as she left.

Although his talk with Olivia had not developed wholly as planned, Lionel was not displeased. Meeting his attractive young cousin again had been a welcome interruption, though it would have been more so at another time. He never liked being placed in a bad light, but was confident that he could overcome it.

But as for Olivia, that was a different matter. She had irked him throughout his life and seemed bent on continuing. For this reason he was determined to stress his authority. He would carry out the threatened investigation and if some broken pieces of her work could be justifiably suspect, so much the better. She would then have no choice but to resign and Amelia, in support, would follow.

The thought that he was several steps nearer to getting rid of the pair of them, restored his spirits. The sooner he issued orders to have every broken item minutely examined, the better. He could dismiss Olivia's nonsense about leeway having to be made up as rapidly as possible, for surely an established pottery like Drayton's had plenty of stocks in hand and therefore no need to worry about just one bad firing? More essential was the need to impress on every worker that their new master was a man to be feared and respected, like his father before him.

So resolving, he headed again for the kilns, but came face to face with Abby Walker immediately outside his door. He had forgotten the girl, but recognized her at once. Not even smudges of clay could lessen the enchantment of her face.

'And what are you doing here?' he asked indulgently. 'Why aren't you at your bench?'

'Why ain't everybody?' she quipped. 'Wot with all this huller-berloo, folks cain't be blamed fer sneaking off fer a few minutes. So I thought, Mebbe Master Potter'll be willing to spare a mite of 'is time fer the likes o'me.'

'And why should I?'

She wanted to say, 'Ye know damn well why! 'Cos ye eyed me good'n proper first time ye see'd me, so why pretend now?' But not for nothing had artfulness been instilled into her. She therefore answered guilelessly, 'Because I be Abby Walker an' ye spoke t'me kindly t'other day. So I thought ye'd mebbe spare time for a word, sir. Only a minute-like.'

The wheedling note was irresistible. A hasty glance round the potters' yard assured him that no one was in sight; even Peterson the gatekeeper had left his post to gather with others by the kilns. For that, the man could be taken to task later. For now, it amused the new Master Potter to casually reopen his office door.

Inside, Abby stood stock still.

'My, but ain't it *big*! Kinda empty too, with all Mistress 'Melia's treasures gone . . .'

'And is that what you want to talk about, Abby? I recall your threat of a battle between us.' He smiled. 'Have you come to wage it?'

'Well, since ye mention it, sir, it do seem kinda cruel an' folks is sayin' as much.'

'Are they indeed? Then they, and you, can keep their tongues still.'

The steel in his voice chilled her. It was a new experience. Men's voices were always warm when they spoke to Abby Walker and since this man had favoured her with approving glances she had anticipated the same from him.

The unexpected rebuff made her step backward, only to find herself up against a solid desk in the middle of the room, with his body confronting her. And the door shut.

'You understand me, Abby?' The tone was soft now, but the steel was there still.

'Aye – that I do, Master Potter.'

His hand reached out to touch her cheek, then halted. 'You're a pretty wench, Abby, but no man likes to kiss a dirty face.' A second later he was wiping it with a fine cambric kerchief which he then cast aside. The contact left her breathless, so that when his mouth came down to hers she made no resistance. In a remote corner of her mind the thought registered that she must have taken leave of her senses, but how enjoyable it was ... and mebbe he would want more ... and how pleased Mam would be!

But not Dave Jefferson. She thrust the thought aside and remained quite still as the Master Potter's hand slipped inside her bodice and fondled her small breasts. This too was something she had never experienced before, despite the number of men who visited her mother and tried to take liberties with the daughter when the woman wasn't looking. But Kate had eyes in the back of her head and would pounce, sharp as lightning. 'It be *my* services ye pay fer, ye randy bugger!' And off into the outside privy she would pack her daughter, hail or shine, summer or winter, hot or cold, and there Abby would huddle until her Mam's business were done with, hoping it would be quick this time and she'd let her back indoors. Kate would then give her a mug of tea laced with rum and be kind, in her rough way, until it was time for Abby to tumble into the rickety bed they shared. Then Kate would be off to the Red Lion to pick up more customers and go with them wherever they willed because, as she so often reminded her daughter, she was a good mother who didn't want to disturb her child's rest.

'Ye'll understand when ye're a bit older,' she would say, ''an that time ain't afar off, from the look o'ye.' And the painted face would smile as she scanned her daughter's rapidly maturing body.

Kate made it all sound enticing. ''Tis the easiest job in t'world an' the best paid,' she would say. '"The oldest profession", they calls it. *Profession*, mark ye, not a trade.' The pride in her voice emphasized the superiority of her occupation and the inferiority of women who were obliged to work in the pot banks. 'Lowest labour of all, that be, muckin' about wi' clay. Ye cain't git lower than the earth! But we'll git ye away from potting sooner than *I* did.'

'Meg Tinsley sez that if I stick at it I'll 'ave security an' a chance to marry a good man.'

'Marriage! Listen t'me, luv. I tried it once an' I don't reckon much by it. Ted Walker weren't no catch, I can tell ye. But I'll give 'im 'is due – 'e did the right thing by me when I told 'im ye were on t'way. Married me, but thought I oughta *thank* 'im! For wot, I wanted t'know, an' so I said when 'e lost 'is job at Drayton's just because 'is lungs give out. Joseph Drayton never kept anyone on when the coughing an' wheezing took over. That's wot the potteries do t'ye.'

'Not so much now. Meg sez Master Martin's got the right idea about them masks.'

'Fancy stuff! Ye don't see other pot banks using 'em. Ye listen too much to that Meg Tinsley. Ye should listen to yer Mam instead.'

'But Meg's kind t'me. Sez I'll be as good a turner as she is, one o'these days.'

''Aye – if ye works yer fingers t'bone, year in, year out, same as she do. An' why? 'Ave ye ivver thought about that, our Abby? *I* can tell ye. 'Cos men don't want 'er as they useter. I've 'eard tell that she was real beautiful once, with ev'ry man in Burslem after 'er favours. *Then* wot did she do? Upped an' quit fer a Liverpool docker! Rumours went around that she'd gone off to Lunnon with a rich client, though where she ivver met a rich 'un, God knows. Anyways, when she came back years later she were Meg Gibson no more, but Meg Tinsley, wife of Ma Tinsley's nephew, a seaman who'd come t'Burslem t'visit 'is old aunt an' stayed betimes as potman at t'Red Lion. Old Ma Tinsley were now't but a witch, but she 'ad 'er uses, I can tell ye. 'Tis a pity she's gone 'cos Burslem ain't got no one like 'er now, an' one day, Abby luv, ye'll mebbe be needin' summun with skills like 'ers. Careful as ye might be, these things 'appen. So 'tis a good thing ye've got a Mam like me t'teach thee 'ow t'dodge trouble.'

Kate had further sage advice: 'Don't give yersel' t'first man as comes after ye, our Abby. Learn from yer Mam's mistakes. If I'd waited afore startin' I might've bin noticed by summon like 'Igh'n'Mighty Joseph Drayton, who were Master Potter then. My, that would've bin a triumph! I swear t'God that man 'ad a rovin' eye, though nivver a breath o'scandal touched 'im. But I weren't so lucky as you be, m'gal. I 'ad t'make do with men who'd got nowt, but that won't 'appen t'thee. I were on t'game afore I were yore age, pleasin' any man as offered sixpence, but I've took good care *thee* won't start afore ye're ripe fer it. T'best fruit fetches t'best prices.'

Her ma's gems of wisdom were worth remembering, though Abby had experienced a flickering doubt about them when Dave Jefferson had kissed her beneath the mistletoe after the pottery closed last Christmas Eve. The way he had kissed her was warm, gentle and kind; not rough, the way Abby had seen men kiss her mother and which she had therefore assumed to be normal. For the rest of that evening she had been aware of Dave in a breathless sort of way, and he had never taken his eyes from her.

That had been a magical evening. Martin Drayton had laid on a feast for his workers, unlike other Master Potters for miles around who thought that a holiday on Christmas Day was generous enough. But at the Drayton Pottery an ox had been roasted on a spit in the potters' yard, with a broaching of more than one butt of Staffordshire ale.

But fond as she was of Dave, and even flattered by his attention because he was chief glazer, Abby had not experienced the feeling of triumph which now filled her. How could any wench withstand the attentions of a man so handsome and highly placed as the new Master Potter? It was an honour which went immediately to her head.

When he released her she felt something pressed into her hand. A coin. Looking down, she saw that it was silver. Never in her life had she possessed one. Mam was certainly right about not starting too far down the ladder.

Through a dizzy haze of success Abby heard the man saying, 'There will be more for greater pleasures. Our secret pleasures. You know what I mean by that, don't you? And you know what "secret" means?'

'Summat betwixt thee'n'me, sir . . .'

'Much more than that. It means that if you ever mention it to a soul, you will be punished. If you are good and pleasure me well, the coins will be gold, not silver, but one boastful word to anyone, one hint of betrayal, and punishment will be so severe you will never again be able to hold up your head in Burslem.'

Breathlessly, she promised to remember. 'But where'll ye want me, sir? Not 'ere at t'pot bank, surely t'God? Folks'd soon be whispering. They doan't miss nowt.'

'I will arrange things.'

Lingering only for his dismissive caress, Abby left. Not until she was halfway back to the turners' shed did she remember why she had gone to the Master Potter's office – to dare take up the cudgels for Mistress 'Melia. Her mischievous threat the other day had amused him, a reaction which had given her confidence. But now look what she'd done – forgotten all about it! Shame touched her, but the pressure of the coin in her palm was stronger and more persuasive.

CHAPTER 8

Not a worker in the place could believe it. After such a disaster no master potter would set a team to sift through a mass of breakages in order to pinpoint blame. Accidents were accidents and when they happened a quick search was made for undamaged articles, the rest were thrown away as shraff, and work started again. That was routine in a risky trade like this and the new master should be aware of it.

To make matters worse, the most experienced workers were drafted to comb through the rubble because inexperienced ones could overlook significant signs, but at a time like this it was the most experienced who were needed to start production flowing again.

The firers, too, were disgruntled because one kiln would now stand idle, waiting to be replenished, and others would follow suit if supplies were allowed to slow down. This would mean a rapid cooling of the bricks and a lengthier warming-up process; more delay, more disappointed customers, more frustrations.

Meg said as much to Dave Jefferson, adding that she could never remember such an order being given before.

'Nor me. Right daft it is. What's got into the man? What's 'e trying to do? Show us who be master now?'

'That's the sum of it,' Meg agreed, though inwardly suspecting much more. She had overheard Lionel Drayton summoning M's Olivia to his office and concern had sharpened when he commanded the searchers to save every item from the modelling shed – a clear indication that he believed the cause of the trouble to be from there.

'D'ye know what *I* think, Dave? That for reasons of his own the man's out for blood – first Mistress 'Melia's an' now M's 'Livia's.'

'Why the hell should 'e be?'

Meg shrugged, but reminded Dave of the museum's quick closure. 'Didn't waste no time getting every single piece packed! The crates are waiting to be shifted right now. They'll be gone afore the pottery closes t'night.'

'Not after a blow-up like this, with every man jack of us at work! And where can they go? They can't just be dumped outside the gates.'

Nothing would surprise me, thought Meg, and went back to work. She had something else on her mind – Abby. The girl had been absent from the turners' shed a bit too long for her liking, and when she returned she'd looked like a cat that had been at the cream. One hand had been hidden in the pocket of her hessian apron and before she picked up a turning tool it had emerged tightly closed. Then she had slid it into a deeper petticoat pocket, as if transferring something, and all the time there had been a smile on her face, sort of secret-like, relishing something. But when Meg had said, 'Where've ye been, Abby?' the girl's big eyes had turned to her, full of innocence.

'Why, t'see wot were up, same as ev'ryone.'

'I didn't see you near the kiln.'

'I were there orlright.'

'But not for long, or I'd've noticed, so where else did ye go?'

'No place, 'cept to talk t' Sadie Fisher. She called me over. Ye must've seen 'er. She were standing near ye.'

That was true. Sadie Fisher had been there when Meg arrived and still there when she left. Then it were mighty strange I overlooked Abby, thought Meg, but felt happier with this confirmation that the girl had been close at hand all the time.

'Well, I'm glad ye cleaned up your face afore going there. I like my workers t'take a pride in theirselves. Sets a good example. Muck on t'face be all right here in t'shed, but not outside it.' Meg finished casually, 'Did Sadie give ye summat?'

Abby grinned. 'Don't miss nuffink, do ye? Saw wot I slipped in me pocket, eh? Well, I'll show ye . . .'

From the hiding place in her petticoat she drew forth a small hunk of cheese. 'Swiped it from t'scullery, Sadie did. Don't tell on 'er, will ye, or she might lose 'er job there. That Ma 'Awkins wot doles out t'food be a right tartar. Nobbody can 'ave a crumb more than they be entitled to – that's Sadie's word, "entitled". I didn't know wot it meant 'til she told me. "It means 'aving no

89

more than wot ye've a right to," she said, which were a right giggle considerin' she'd swiped enough fer two!'

Abby's pretty white teeth bit into the cheese. Then she held it out. 'Wanta bite, our Meg? Not goin' t'tell on us, are ye?'

'Of course not. But one o' these days that Sadie'll fair cop it. She pinches more than cheese, that I know. I saw the neck of a stone ale bottle sticking from under her shawl t'other day, on the way home. I reckon t'weren't no gift from Ma 'Awkins, neether.'

Abby flung back her young head and laughed. As always, it was a happy sound. After the prevailing atmosphere of disaster, it sounded even happier than usual. Almost excited.

Amelia heard nothing of the kiln disaster until after the children's lessons. Promptly, she went to see her nephew.

'You are making a mistake, Lionel. And I am not referring to those crates in the next room, or to how I feel about them.'

'I should hope not, my dear aunt.'

If there was anything Lionel disliked it was being dictated to by a member of the opposite sex – the lesser sex. To be lectured by one of them, as if he were an errant schoolboy, was not to be tolerated. His aunt should have been relegated to hearth and home long since and the time had come to enforce it.

'My dear Amelia, if you are concerning yourself with matters here, please stop. You must realize that your usefulness has come to an end.'

'Not entirely. I still teach the children.'

'Educating children is not part of a pottery's function. I intend to get rid of all superfluous activities, *and* all superfluous people.'

'Such as myself, I know. But beware of losing Olivia, and beware of antagonizing the workers in your determination to blame her for an accident which can happen in any thriving pottery. Wasting time in hunting for the cause is a big mistake.'

'Wasting *my* time is an even bigger one.' He crossed to the door and opened it. 'Next time you come to call, do choose a convenient moment.'

She didn't budge. She even smiled, as if amused. 'You never change, do you, Lionel? You were a stubborn child and you are still the same. Do some men never grow up?'

'And do some women never stop interfering? Your husband may have tolerated it – perhaps he had no choice? – but not I.'

'To you, even your mother's attentions are interference. Poor Agatha. She waited ten years for your return, and now you are home you brush her aside.'

90

'You seem to have been listening to her plaintive grumbles. My mother is a very fortunate woman, living in luxury, well looked after, denied nothing . . .'

'Except her son's affection.' Amelia moved to the open door, then stopped in front of him. 'I came here to warn you, to plead if necessary.'

'To tell me how to run the pottery, you mean. How to handle the workers. How to be a master potter who can be bent to their will.'

'No. How to avoid losing valuable men and women who have served Drayton's loyally and well, winning the respect of fellow workers in the process. People like Olivia. My days here may be finished, that I know, but not Olivia's. Lose her, and you will regret it. Martin always said her work was outstanding, and time has proved him right.'

'There are other skilled modellers.'

'All trained by her.'

'And therefore capable of carrying on after she has gone.'

'So I'm right – your aim *is* to get rid of her. By blaming her for bad workmanship? If you hope to do that, you will fail. And if you succeed for any other trumped-up reason, Drayton's will be the poorer.'

'You are wasting my time,' he said again.

'I can see that.' Briefly, Amelia's shoulders drooped. He actually felt a faint twinge of guilt, but when she straightened up the dangerous response subsided.

He said briskly and not unkindly, 'I have a suggestion to make. A good one. Since you are a woman who likes to be useful, why not teach those children in your own home? You could start a Dame School. Medlar Croft must surely have room to spare and since you and Olivia are so obsessed with ideas of equality your own children could share the lessons.'

She answered serenely, 'I have already thought of that, but I'm sure you would never be so foolish as to jeopardize the Drayton Pottery's good name.'

'Meaning?'

'That the children should at least be transported from the pottery to Medlar Croft after their parents have brought them here each morning, otherwise how will they get there? It is a considerable distance. Arrange transport for them, and Drayton's good reputation will be preserved.'

'Countrybred children are accustomed to walking.'

'And the same distance back? Unfortunately, the only transport

91

I now have is a carriage for four, whereas the pottery has plenty of wagons capable of holding a much larger number. So I will strike a bargain with you. Put one of those wagons at the daily disposal of the children and I will "interfere" no more. You have defeated me, Lionel. You have succeeded, and I have lost.'

'Come,' he said generously, 'you mustn't look at it like that. You have served the place loyally and well, all of which is appreciated and will be financially rewarded.'

'Martin himself took care of that. I have no financial cares, thanks to him, and fortunately I am able-bodied and not yet senile. And while I think of it, I will relieve you of more than those burdensome crates in the next room. There are volumes there, records I have kept for many years, all out of date, all obsolete and, I am sure, of no interest to you. Of what use can ancient history be to a progressive young man like yourself?'

'Certainly you may have them. I will set them aside now. As for a wagon for those children, I will make one available when you open your Dame School. You see how willing I am to help you?'

To that she said nothing. He crossed to the adjoining room, only to find the entrance blocked by crates, stacked high. Craning his neck to see over them, he said, 'The shelves seem to be empty, so your precious volumes must also have been packed. I'll have everything delivered to Medlar Croft today.'

'Can you spare the time or the men? With all this frantic scratching around among rubble, I don't see how you can. Draytonware sells as rapidly as it is made, so kilns must be idle only for reloading. All the workers know that and will be none too pleased about the delay.'

He said with an elaborate show of patience, 'Believe me, I appreciate your interest as greatly as I appreciate your loyal service here, but I have no need of either. You may now go home and forget about the pottery. Enjoy your –'

'– advancing years? Thank you, Lionel, I will.'

At last she turned away, betraying no sign of the effort it cost her nor how desperately she wanted to repeat her warnings.

'About those crates,' she said as an afterthought before walking out into the potters' yard for the last time. 'Olivia tells me that arrangements have been made for them, so there's no need for you to take even one man away from the important job of probing for guilt just to satisfy your personal desire for power – or is it revenge? Revenge against Olivia because she always spurned you? And don't imagine that the workers are fools – they come of stock similar to your own. Do you know the origins of the Draytons?'

He shrugged indifferently.

'Then let me tell you, nephew. They can be traced back to the sixteenth century, a family of itinerant potters who peddled their wares up and down the country, setting up their stands on village greens or any other convenient spot. The ancestor who first came to Burslem in 1581 and settled with his family in a disused barn, had pitched his cart on any suitable site, erected his ancient potter's wheel, dug clay from the highways and byways and riddled it in any nearby stream with his wife and children helping him. They kneaded it and wedged it on convenient stones, just as potters did in these parts as long ago as the thirteenth century, and then his family turned the handle of a massive wheel that revolved a leather belt running to his turntable. They had to take it in turns because the wheel was heavy and the task was hard, while he threw pots for villagers for as little as a penny a time. At night, they slept beneath the cart, so the unclaimed barn which became the first Drayton pot bank was a godsend. It's from such stout yeomen stock that your workers come. They have the same courage and determination. So don't cross them, Lionel, or I repeat – you'll regret it.'

The news of Amelia Drayton's abrupt departure from the family business, and the circumstances of it, spread through Burslem as rapidly as a bush fire. Some said she had rushed out of the Master Potter's office in tears; that she had raged and ranted and abused him loudly; that she had wept on Meg Tinsley's shoulder in full view of the other turners and that Meg had broken down and cried with her; that she had ordered the items from her precious museum to be burned in the middle of the potters' yard, to shame her nephew in front of everyone; that she had vowed vengeance; that she had behaved as no one had ever seen her behave before – and, less excitingly, that she had held up her head and walked quietly across the yard to the modelling shed to see her niece before departing.

Every report varied in the telling and, but for the last, was laughed to scorn by people who had known Amelia Drayton all her life, but that didn't halt the rumours and speculations. Was it true that workers were rioting at the Drayton Pottery? Was it true that a mob was throwing stones through the Master Potter's window and that M's Olivia was inciting them to vengeance on her aunt's behalf? And was it true that she had produced faulty pieces deliberately, to explode in the kiln? Serve the man right, if so! Serve him right, indeed. What would happen next?

Many a woman on her way home from market made a deliberate detour past the pottery's gates in order to regale others with highly embroidered versions of the truth, one of which was that 'that-there Abby Walker' had been seen in the cobbled yard, loudly defying Meg Tinsley. 'Sticking up for the Master Potter, she were, bold as brass, an' Meg berating 'er and ordering 'er back t'work, an' young Abby taking not a blind bit o'notice. Going 'er mother's way, is that one.'

But Abby Walker was of no interest to folk who only wanted to know the truth about Amelia Drayton's abrupt departure. That she had walked quietly across the yard to the modelling shed to say goodbye to her niece was not nearly as exciting as the other variations, but on reflection seemed the more likely. And that Olivia Freeman had then been seen crossing resolutely to the Master Potter's office, only to emerge a minute later looking just as resolute and perfectly calm, seemed equally likely. And when one of her modellers reported, when reaching home that night, that when Mistress Drayton came to the shed wearing her outdoor cloak and spoke in a low voice to her niece, M's 'Livia had put down her modelling tool without a word, shed her hessian apron and wrapped all her tools in it, rolled down her sleeves, smoothed her hair, told her aunt to wait and then departed to see Master Lionel herself – well, all that had a distinct ring of truth about it and certainly seemed in character.

After that the two women had driven away from the pottery in M's Olivia's gig, leaving Mistress Drayton's carriage to be sent back to Medlar Croft. Gatekeeper Peterson had watched them go, and reported how they had headed in the direction of Fletcher's Forge.

'And afore she left, M's 'Livia said goodbye to each of us and told us never to forget all she had taught us and that she hoped we'd all be successful and happy under the new management. But I doubt we will be. Things'll never be the same again in the modelling shed.'

By noon, echoes reached Tremain, where Max Freeman stumped along to his sister's apartments demanding to know what the hell her son was up to now. 'And don't tell me you don't know what I'm talking about, Aggie. That Frenchie of yours gets every bit of gossip from the village, even at this distance. Talks to every tradesman who brings goods to the service door and invites the

94

most obliging to linger for a tipple – and then relates to you only what he thinks you should hear and keeps the rest to himself. You're a fool, Aggie, but I am not, so whatever Lionel is up to now won't surprise *me*.'

'I have no idea of what you are talking,' Agatha said loftily, 'and I do wish you would cease using that abominable abbreviation of my name.'

'I am talking about Lionel's sacking of Amelia. That's what the workers call it when someone is turned off or got rid of on some pretext or another, and from all accounts that's what Lionel has done to our sister, though I've no doubt he will have some plausible excuse which you will accept and I will not. If it's true, there'll be trouble and not only I will make it. Others won't take it lying down, either.'

'Meaning?'

'Meaning the Kendalls and the Fletchers.'

'They are *not* the "Fletchers". Olivia's name is still Freeman. Oh, you may wave that aside, but I do not. As for all this other nonsense, from where did you get it? From one of the footmen, or your valet, or from that chief steward of yours who, no doubt, had it from an estate worker or one of the coachmen. Servants' gossip! Always the worst kind. You shouldn't listen to it.'

'I'll listen to anything concerning the family. So should you.'

'Not to untruths about Lionel! He harbours only the kindest thoughts for Amelia.'

'Such as it being high time she quit the family business? Jessica herself told me when Miguel drove me over to Ashburton the other day. That boy of mine always seems to know when I need a jaunt and a change of scene, but I suspect he decided on Ashburton not merely for that reason.' Max finished on an indulgent note.

Agatha sniffed. 'He did it out of no thought for you at all, brother, only for himself. He's in love with that girl.'

'Meaning Deborah? And why not? And don't try to dodge the issue – what *is* that son of yours up to regarding our sister?'

'Only what is best for her, I'm sure. He has her welfare at heart. It's true that he believes she should retire, and I agree.'

'And when did you hear him say that? He rarely comes to see you and you rarely visit Carrion House.' Max finished cruelly but thoughtlessly, 'Doesn't he invite you?'

Ignoring that, Agatha continued, 'Amelia can no longer be useful at the pottery. I doubt if she ever was very much, but Martin doted on her and humoured her in all sorts of ways – like that museum, and teaching the potters' children to read and

95

write and other subjects, too, until they are old enough to become apprentices. She should now settle down to sedate widowhood, as I have done. So if my dear boy has persuaded her to do so, I am glad to hear it.'

At that, Max Freeman snorted and stumped back to his own quarters.

When Miguel heard the news he ordered a curricle to be harnessed and drove off to Ashburton at speed. He had to see Deborah. He had to be with her when she heard the news for, remembering Lionel Drayton's disparagement of the Mexican pots, he knew there was now little hope of her enthusiasm being rewarded. Without Amelia's persuasion coupled with Olivia's there would be no new ceramic line with a Mexican influence produced at the Drayton pottery. Only he, who understood her better than she suspected, knew how fervently she wanted to contribute to what she and others believed would be a new and exciting line, for which she had now produced a highly decorative design. During his visit to Ashburton with his father the other day, she had shown it to him, watching for his reaction with a certain anxiety.

'Your opinion is important because of your Mexican affinity,' she had said. 'If my drawing passes such a test I shall take it along to the Drayton Pottery with more confidence.'

He had truthfully told her that it was delightful, which made it even harder now to dash her hopes. So it had to be done in the right way and by the right person. Himself.

But the moment he saw her, he knew it was too late. Her normally sunny face was grave.

'I was there this morning,' she said, 'so it must have happened after I left. Sarah came back from market with the news – it was all over Burslem by that time. Someone told her that someone else had seen Meg Tinsley and a group of workers in the yard, shouting protests outside the Master Potter's office. Not that that will do any of them any good, even if true – which I doubt. You know how rumours and gossip spread.' She hesitated, then finished, 'I find it hard to defend Lionel even if he did do it for Amelia's sake, as he claims.'

'Do you believe that?'

'I want to, but how can I? My mother wants a council of war between ourselves and the Fletchers and is going to enlist Papa's help as soon as he finishes his day's work.'

'And what do *you* want?'

'I want to see Amelia as soon as possible.'

'Then you shall. I've heard that she drove away from the pottery with Olivia, heading toward Fletcher's Forge. Come – I'll take you there.'

When Damian saw Olivia driving up to the forge he knew at once that something had happened, and when he saw Amelia beside her, he knew what it was.

Promptly, he went to meet them.

'So you have left the pottery,' he said, helping them down in turn.

'How did you guess?'

'For no other reason would either of you turn your back on the place in the middle of a working day. I take it you resigned from choice?'

Amelia, who looked pale but composed, told him that it had been Olivia's choice, but not her own. 'I was given none. Now I wish I had gone straight home without letting her know.'

'Dear Amelia, that would have done no more than delay me,' Olivia declared, 'for I would have packed my tools the minute I heard. I could never have continued there without you. The place has been important in our shared life. Take the sharing away, and that part of it is over.'

Putting an arm about the shoulders of each, Damian led them away from the din of the forge. As they went, Olivia continued, 'I've brought Amelia to see the building you've set aside for her. The crates are ready to be dispatched, so the sooner she sees where they are going, the better.'

'I'm sure that wherever you store them will be very satisfactory –' Amelia began.

'Not stored – displayed.' Damian turned to Olivia. 'Haven't you told her, my love?'

'Not yet. I've been waiting for the right moment and this is it.' When Amelia looked puzzled and inquiring, Olivia raced on. 'It will make a splendid setting for your pottery museum and Damian has all sorts of plans for it – good display shelves, enlarged windows, and stronger flooring because the present boards won't stand up to the wear and tear of many feet.'

Seeing the mixture of hope and disbelief in her aunt's eyes, she chattered on in an attempt to help her through an emotional moment, and in this she succeeded until they reached the shed and Damian opened the door and led Amelia inside.

'Welcome to the new Drayton Museum,' he said gently.

Amelia tried to speak and failed. The huge area, emptied of its cargo of scrap iron, spread out before her like a promised land.

'And Damian is having a sign made, for all the world to see,' Olivia continued. 'It will hang outside, with another by the gates bearing an arrow pointing to the entrance.' Seeing now a definite threat of tears, she finished softly, 'Dear Amelia, don't be sad.'

'How can I be, with such generous friends? Not sad in the way you mean, at least, but – yes – a little sad that you should both be so sure the end was coming.'

'Not the end, the beginning,' Damian said briskly. 'Now, about that sign – I propose to make it in wrought iron, of course, and to hang it from an ornamental iron bracket, projecting like an inn sign to attract travellers along the road. You can choose the design while you are here, and the style of lettering too. And would you like "The Drayton Museum" set in a triangle, or all three words on one line? The choice is yours.'

'Four words,' Amelia said quickly. '"The Martin Drayton Museum". That is my choice – with "Martin Drayton" dominant.'

'Then that is what you will have. And the length and width and number of display shelves will also be to your choice and since there is plenty of room here for big display tables running the full length, the angle of the new windows must be calculated to shed the best light on them. Between us, we will turn this place into the finest artisan museum in Staffordshire.'

An hour later they were still discussing plans, heedless of the noise of wheels and hooves entering or leaving the cobbled entrance yard, until one of the double doors opened and Jessica Kendall's voice said, 'We thought you must be in here because there is nowhere else to look! Olivia's gig is still outside and reports said that Amelia was with her –' She broke off to embrace Amelia and then her niece. 'As soon as I heard the news, I knew something had to be done and Simon agreed. So here we are, both of us; Deborah and Miguel also.' To Damian she added, 'We must hold a council of war at once. We can't allow Amelia to be treated in such a fashion. And you, Olivia – I hear you promptly resigned. Well done! But now we must all decide what steps to take –'

'They are already being taken,' Amelia told her. 'This splendid outbuilding is to house the Martin Drayton Museum –'

The news met with enthusiasm and when Olivia suggested continuing the discussion at home, the party proceeded to the cottage which had once belonged to Damian's parents and in which she and Damian still lived.

It was more than a cottage now. An additional room had been built for Damian, as a sanctum in which he designed new projects away from the noise and interruptions of his ironshops; kitchen quarters had been extended and additional bedrooms added – one for Hannah, her mother's former maid, who had welcomed the chance to become their housekeeper, and others as guest rooms. Since Burslem's only hostelry was the Red Lion on Cobbler's Green, offering rough and ready accommodation, the Fletcher bedrooms were frequently occupied by Continental clients who came to England to discuss their requirements with the ironworker whose reputation had quickly spread across the Channel.

But the heart of the house was still the low-ceilinged living room, lined with Damian's treasured books, and as Deborah and Miguel followed the others indoors the girl felt her usual rapport with the place and wondered why she experienced it here but not always in the homes of many a respectably married couple. The same feeling had reached out to her at Medlar Croft when her Uncle Martin was alive, and despite his death it was there still. Both cases seemed to prove that love within marriage or outside it could be strong and binding – as with her parents. Glancing at Miguel she reflected that he too must have known it when young, warmed by his mother's devotion to his father – but now? In that vast, silent house in its vast, silent grounds was there an emptiness in his life despite his father's affection for him?

Impulsively, she reached out and touched his hand. Seated within a window, they were isolated from the rest. His palm upturned and the fingers curled close, covering hers, and something she had never felt before flamed through her. She withdrew because she felt it wise to, not because she wanted to, and forced herself to listen to the conversation – not because she wanted to, but because she felt she had to. She could not look at Miguel, and the reason puzzled her.

Old Hannah had plodded in with one of Drayton's largest teapots, a plentiful supply of home-made scones, and an admonishment to eat the lot because she 'didn't want no left-overs in *her* kitchen'.

Plans for Amelia's museum were well underway. It was all very exciting and splendid, of course, but Deborah did wish she could listen as attentively as Miguel. Glancing sideways, she saw that he was missing nothing. Naturally she was glad – or was she? And why did she regret withdrawing her hand? And how quiet he was – saying nothing, listening intently. He didn't contribute a word until at last a lull came when everything seemed to have been thoroughly discussed. Only then did he lean forward and ask, 'But what about Olivia – what is *she* going to do?'

'I?' echoed Olivia, surprised. 'Why, I'll be helping Amelia set up the exhibits . . .'

'And when that is done?'

'When that is done,' said Damian, 'she won't be cheated out of her talent or her need to express it. I have already thought about that. I shall see that she has her own workroom either here or wherever she wishes to have it. I happen to love and understand her.'

'Sir! I meant no offence – I wasn't implying – I mean, I just thought, wondered –' Distressed, Miguel stammered, 'Why can't they start their own pottery, the two of them? That's what I mean. With all their knowledge and experience – why not? Why should a new and ignorant Master Potter put an end to all that?'

There was a moment's silence and then Simon Kendall echoed, 'Why not, indeed?' and Jessica rose and came across to Miguel and kissed him soundly on both cheeks and said, 'Bless you, *bless* you! *Of course* they must!' And Damian was saying, 'Forgive my reaction, Miguel – I'm somewhat touchy where my wife is concerned,' and everyone took it for granted that he should refer to Olivia that way because they, too, thought of her as his wife, and Deborah danced across to her and hugged her, declaring that Miguel was absolutely right and they must waste no time . . .

'And you don't want to, do you, either of you? We can get it started while you are setting up your museum, Amelia, and then we can *really* begin!'

'"We"?' echoed her father. 'So you intend to be part of the place, do you?' His eyes were indulgent. 'And why not? You've already made a start with that design for a sundial . . .'

Olivia and Amelia naturally wanted to know what he was talking about, but it was Miguel who answered, describing Deborah's pheasant-and-partridge drawing in such detail that she was struck silent. He had complimented her on it, but she had not realized how closely he had studied it.

'May we see it soon?' Olivia asked, plainly delighted, and Deborah willingly agreed, explaining that it was designed for a large wall sundial which would have to be made of stoneware to withstand weathering, and that of course it all depended on whether the design would be considered good enough.

'It *is* good enough,' said Miguel. 'Wait until you see it, all of you.'

But he was looking only at Deborah, who, in turn, was looking at Amelia and asking why she looked concerned.

'Something is worrying you. What is it?'

'The children and their lessons. I hate abandoning them, but with so much new involvement how can I possibly start a Dame School?'

'*I*'ll do that,' Jessica said promptly. 'Right in the centre of Burslem for children of *all* potters. And I know where I'll run it – at the Wesley Meeting House. Martin admired John Wesley from the day the man first preached on Cobbler's Green and was pelted by the rabble. Despite that, the Meeting House was built. The social room attached can be hired for useful purposes, and what could be more useful than this? Have no fear, Amelia – your Dame School will flourish.' She finished with elation, 'What a *wonderful* day this is!'

'I echo that,' said Simon Kendall, smiling. 'My wife and the two pottery ladies of Burslem are about to make history.'

CHAPTER 9

When Meg Tinsley decided to lead a protest delegation from the turners' shed and called for volunteers, Abby hung back. Not because she wasn't as shocked as everyone else by Mistress Drayton's sudden departure, but because she didn't want to offend a powerful man who was showing such an interest in her. Kate would say as much and warn her to keep out of trouble, and mothers were supposed to know best, weren't they?

So Abby kept her head down over her wheel, pretending not to hear. She didn't like the guilty feeling it gave her, but what else could she do? Line up with the others and she'd surely be seen, even if she tried to hide behind them. From the top of the steps leading to his office – for it was certain-sure he wouldn't admit any of them – he would look down on everyone and even the smallest wouldn't be overlooked.

Some of the other turners eagerly lined up with Meg, but some hesitated. On those she cast a contemptuous glance and called them cowards.

'Afraid he'll send ye packing, are ye? Well – listen t'me. He daresn't. If everyone downed tools an' he sacked the lot of us, he'd get a nasty surprise if he thought we'd be easy to replace. You lot are the best turners in Burslem – *I*'ve see t'that. So what are ye worriting about? Think of M's 'Melia and all she's done for us all these years. Don't *that* make ye angry?'

There was no hesitation then. The clatter of shoes trooping through the door was followed by silence, Abby's whirring wheel the only sound.

Minutes later, the door flung open again.

'Well, Abby Walker? Why ain't ye out there with t'rest of us?'

'I've this pile o' pots to finish –'

'An' plenty of time to do 'em when we come back. Wot's got into ye, our Abby? Only t'other day ye were challenging the man, vowing that if he hurt Mistress Drayton he'd 'ave a battle on 'is hands – with *you*. Seems ye didn't mean it, after all. Shame on ye, Abby Walker!'

Without warning Meg seized the girl by the rolled collar of her potter's slop and half dragged her to the door. 'Aye,' she stormed, 'it's a coward y'are!'

'I ain't, I *ain't*! It's jest that –'

'That wot?' Meg demanded, releasing her but looking so threatening that Abby knew she would renew her grip if provoked.

'It's jest that I wanted t'get on wi' me work. *Summun's* gotta.'

'We'll all get on with it when we've said our piece, an' don't think the turners are the only ones rarin' to do it. There's men an' women from other sheds lining up out there, so come *on* wi' ye!' D'ye want me to drag ye? I'll do it – that's a warning!'

The group in the yard was larger than Abby expected, and was swelling as men and women emerged from all quarters. Then someone raised their voice and shouted, 'Master Potter, we'd like a word with ye!'

There was no answer until Meg mounted the steps, knocked on the door, then rejoined her fellow-workers who were now chanting in unison. At that, the door opened and Lionel Drayton, immaculate in a high-collared longcoat of dark green velvet – with matching knee breeches, white hose and tall cravat, satin waistcoat and silver buckled shoes – stepped through the doorway and looked down on them. His hair, tied back with an immaculate bow, made every man before him look unkempt. Standing there, he surveyed them; unruffled, calm, amiable.

'And to what do I owe this massed delegation?' he asked.

102

'There are too many of you to invite within, but perhaps a single spokesman –?'

'We're all here to say our piece, sir, so by your leave we'll say it here, together.' This was Dave Jefferson, standing in the foreground, and although his words were courteous enough there was nothing humble in his tone. 'It's about Mistress Drayton. We be concerned, Master Potter. Gravely so.'

'Indeed? And for what reason?'

'Because we hear she's gone, sudden-like,' Meg called out. 'We'd like t'know why.'

'Would you, indeed? And since when have workers had the right to question their employers?'

'We've allus been able to, at Drayton's,' said Dave. 'Master Martin useter say, "Come t'me any time there's summat on your mind," an' we allus did. So here we be. We want Mistress Drayton back, Master Potter. And M's Olivia, too. Folks say she left alongside her aunt, and the loss of either ain't to our liking.'

Their new boss remained unruffled. Concealed in the middle of the group, thankful that she was not as exposed as she feared, Abby gazed up at him in awe. He was an impressive figure – handsome, elegant, debonair even when faced with hostility – and her desire to retain his interest and approval increased. Meg Tinsley was a fool to antagonize him. They were all fools, the lot of 'em, even Dave who, she had always believed, had his head screwed on the right way. T'weren't the business of clay workers to argue with the bosses. Their lot was to get on with their jobs and mind their own business, no matter if they did feel badly about something. She felt badly herself when she thought about M's 'Melia, but what could she do? What could any of them do?

She turned a willing ear to what the Master Potter had to say.

'My aunt left of her own choice. That is the truth of the matter and because I respect you as workers I am taking you into my confidence.'

(*There!* Y'see, the lot 'o ye? Ye be wrong about 'im, dead wrong . . .)

'An' did she ask ye to close down the museum and shove everything into crates and get rid of 'em?' Meg demanded. (Right angry she sounded – more fool she.)

A glint of anger flashed in the Master Potter's eyes. Abby shivered faintly. Get on the wrong side of such a man, and Meg would surely regret it. Abby marvelled now that she had ever had the courage to speak up to him the way she did that first time, and all on account of Mistress Drayton. But she'd meant it at the time.

103

So why didn't she now? Guilt stirred again, but died when the Master Potter continued, speaking so quietly, so politely, so convincingly that it was quite plain that he spoke the truth. It had all become too much for his aunt, he was saying. She had worked hard for Drayton's throughout the years, but had earned her retirement. Indeed, she had sought it. Since her bereavement she had struggled on, but without her husband at her side it had all become too much for her.

'To let her go was the least I could do, the least you would all have wanted me to do. I know how greatly you all cared for her. You will therefore be glad on her behalf.'

'An' M's Olivia?' called someone from the modelling shed.

'Alas, my cousin has behaved foolishly, but I have no doubt she will be back.'

'Even though she were blamed for the blow-up in the kiln – according t'*thee*?' Meg blazed. She was being reckless now. Abby tugged at her sleeve to silence her, but it was pulled away angrily. 'Why else did ye set all those men scrabbling around among the shraff?' she went on. 'An' now she's quit Drayton's too, d'ye mean t'let 'em go on wasting their time and everybody else's?'

Dave added his voice just at the moment when Abby thought the Master Potter was going to lose his temper.

'Meg's right, sir. Some of our best men are still at that job, including three of my finest glazers. With respect, it be getting us nowhere. If everyone don't get back to work, and soon, it'll be more than one kiln coming to a standstill.'

Dave could speak reasonably and calmly even when he wasn't feeling that way. Meg knew this and envied him the ability. She glanced toward him, caught his eye, and signalled the thought. Others were thankful when the words brought a much hoped for result.

'Then the operation will cease forthwith, and so will this meeting,' Lionel Drayton announced, and when Abby whispered, 'Wot do that mean, our Meg?' she was glad to hear that it meant everyone was going back to work again. The danger she had sensed was past and when the Master Potter bowed to the group and thanked them politely for coming, then went back into his office and closed the door, she, like many, sensed no irony in his words or his manner.

Only Meg, once back in the turners' shed, voiced any criticism.

'Smooth-tongued bugger!' she exploded, and snatched up her turning tool.

*

104

Leaving the turners' shed that night, Abby saw Master Lionel, as she now thought of him, lingering outside his open door. This was not unusual; many pottery owners stood at their office doors at night, watching their workers depart, bidding some good night, nodding to others, occasionally calling one aside for a word or two, either to voice approval of their work or to utter reprimand if necessary. She hoped he would notice her, but not if he was angry with her for being among that mob today.

To avoid walking home with Meg, who had established the habit a long time ago, Abby had lingered to finish a batch of pots which, she had pointed out with not a little satisfaction, had been delayed by all that to-do. Abby was beginning to chafe against Meg's supervision. It seemed that the woman was forever watching her and tonight she felt she'd had enough. So not until she estimated that the chief turner would be well on the way to her cottage in Larch Lane did she decide to leave.

By that time almost everyone had departed and the few stragglers were too intent on doing likewise to notice the imperceptible nod the Master Potter bestowed on Abby. It was a beckoning gesture, a summons, imperative and to be immediately obeyed. After it, he turned casually and re-entered the building, and Abby, slowing her steps, pretended to have forgotten something and went back to the turners' shed to await the moment when the yard would finally be empty and she could slip across unseen. She was surprised by her own sagacity.

Minutes later she flitted across the yard and through the Master Potter's door, conveniently left ajar. Quietly, she shut it. He was stooping over his splendid desk, apparently absorbed in a pile of papers, but she knew he was aware of her, standing there waiting, and a quivering excitement stirred within her. It was a breathless sort of game, an enjoyable game, and she was content to let him make the next move. It was his place to, wasn't it, not hers? Besides, prolonging things made it even more exciting.

She knew what to expect, or thought she did. He was going to do to her what her mother said was much better than working for a living, something a woman with sense enjoyed. So she was going to enjoy it too.

Even so, her expectancy was tinged with fear. No – excitement, not fear, she insisted in her mind. How could fear be part of a game? Keeping her waiting like this was all part of it and she knew she had to play it his way because he was the master. Standing there quiet as a mouse, she wondered when he was going to make the first move.

With the door closed and the night darkening outside, the room was heavily shadowed. A single oil lamp burned on his desk, but light also glowed from an adjoining room – the room in which M's Amelia's precious things had been crated and stored.

She wished she hadn't thought of Mistress Drayton right now. It brought uncomfortable feelings of guilt and regret. She thrust them aside, along with the thought that her Mam would have said she'd acted the right way. 'Never get mixed up in other folks' business,' she would say. 'Keep yer mouth shut an' yer nose clean.'

Abby was clean in every way tonight. Remembering how he had said that a man never liked to kiss a dirty face, she had paid particular attention to it ever since. Her hands as well. In fact, all of her as far as she was able in the one-roomed hovel in which she lived with Kate. As often as possible, when her mother was out on business, she poured water from the big black kettle, which was forever on the hob, into a wooden washtub, then she stood in it and swished water all over her body, the way Meg had told her was good to do.

'I useter do it when I lived down by the marlpit, even though old Ma Tinsley useter say I'd catch me death. But that's how folk in big houses keep theirselves clean, Abby, by washing all over in tubs filled by servants . . . ye can pretend t'be a grand lady that way!'

But she didn't want to recall Meg any more than she wanted to recall M's Amelia right now. Both women seemed to be disturbing reminders of something she didn't want to think about.

At last he looked up. He crossed to the door, locked it, then came toward her and cupped her chin in one hand.

'That's better, Abby. A clean face and a pretty one – that's what I like to see,' and he kissed her on the mouth, not the way Dave had kissed her under the mistletoe – gently and softly – but greedily, his tongue thrusting and demanding. She was startled. When he released her she was breathless and a little bewildered, but even so she guessed why he then extinguished the lamp on his desk – so that when old Peterson went the rounds, checking that everywhere was locked up, it would seem that the Master Potter had gone. Then the gatekeeper would lock the main gates and go home and they would be alone, here in the Drayton Pottery, and no one would even suspect.

Silently then, he drew her into the adjoining room and shut the door. They were enclosed in a small world from which dim lamplight could not be seen from outside, and there he stripped her and fondled her and pulled her down on to the floor. In a remote corner of her mind she was surprised to feel the softness of carpet beneath her, and even as he began to caress the most intimate parts of her body and she quivered in response her startled eyes noticed, over his shoulder, a roll of carpet half undone, the rest of it spread beneath them, and the same remote corner of her mind registered that he had prepared this himself and that he must have done it as soon as Mistress Drayton's crates were out of the way, and that seemed so callous that suddenly she was crying . . . silently, helplessly, ashamed and regretful and wretched . . . hating herself for being disloyal to a woman who had always been kind to her and in whose defence she had once sprung and whom she had deserted . . . and she wanted to get away . . . now . . . *right now* . . . and couldn't because she was pinned down beneath the weight of this man and pain was piercing her as he penetrated her body, making her cry aloud.

Promptly, his hand covered her mouth and his voice, panting, hissed at her to be quiet . . . and on it went, and on, and on, until pain gradually became merged with sensations that drowned all others . . . and thought had gone, and shame and regret and sadness . . . everything had gone but this surging, overwhelming feeling.

It seemed to continue for a long, long time and when it was over she lay supine, spent, partially stupefied and partially radiant; partially happy and partially sad, though why she was sad she could not analyse and now had no wish to try. Then suddenly she was shivering, for when he had finished with her he simply rose and left her and without the heat of his body the chill of the room struck down on her nakedness. The light was very dim, but she saw his white form stoop and pick up something and throw it to her. It was a towel.

'Get dressed,' he commanded, and the curtness of his voice was a shock. No gentleness, no fondness, no feeling for her whatsoever. He had finished with her and now she had to go.

In the outer room he tossed a big iron key toward her. It fell at her feet. Leaving her to pick it up he said, 'You'll have to unlock the gates and let yourself out. Leave the key on the inside.'

'Why?' she stammered.

'So that I can lock the place up when I leave,' he answered impatiently. 'You don't expect me to be seen leaving with you, surely to God? Now away with you. And here's your reward.'

It was another coin. Larger this time, but still of silver.

'Ye promised gold,' she managed to say, but at that he laughed and casually touched her cheek.

'When you do better. Next time perhaps – *if* you do better. You've a lot to learn.'

Mam had never said anything about learning. Mam had always said it was easy. Puzzled, Abby said, 'Didn't I do right, sir? I thought I did right . . .'

He yawned. 'You will, in time. You're promising, but I won't put up with all that whimpering. Why in hell's name were you crying? You must learn to enjoy it. Now be off.'

Dismissed, she obeyed.

CHAPTER 10

Meg's favourite day was the Sabbath, the one day of the week when the pottery closed, unless firings were underway and therefore demanded the supervision of fire men. But for Meg it was a day of precious freedom and the highlight was the hour she spent at Ashburton, learning to read and write under Jessica Drayton's tuition.

She would hire the ancient nag from Joss Barlow, landlord of the Red Lion, and cover the distance impatiently, chafing at the animal's plodding pace – but what could be expected for five pence? The Red Lion's stables didn't boast thoroughbreds.

The lessons were progressing well. She could now write a weekly record of the number and type of pots turned in her shed, instead of making chalk marks on the wall and getting someone else to add them up at the end of the day so she could wash the wall clean again. Her pride in her new skill was immense. It had also been appreciated by Mistress Drayton from the time Meg made her earliest entries, but whether the new Master Potter appreciated it too was open to doubt.

Along with other supervisors Meg would hand in her record book at the Master's office every Saturday night, place it on his desk, bob the curtsey expected from a female employee to the overseer in charge (the men tugging their forelocks) and there the book would remain until she lined up to collect it when the pottery reopened on Monday. The pile of books always appeared to be untouched, which was scarcely surprising since Saturday was a holiday for the Master Potter and he never arrived on Monday until long after his clay workers had started and the record books had been handed back, again by a deputy. So it didn't fool Meg when Lionel Drayton pretended to have production figures at his fingertips.

It was now five months since M's Amelia and M's Olivia had departed. With them had gone the contented atmosphere that had prevailed under Master Martin. Looking back through the years, Meg saw life at Drayton's in a series of pictures, first of herself dragging at her mother's skirts or being carried in her mother's affectionate arms when her footsteps flagged, a toddler dumped with others on a few sacks in a corner of the earthen floor while their mothers worked non-stop over wheel or bench; women prematurely bent, prematurely aged. Then when tiny legs grew stronger their owners would have to earn their midday hunk of bread and their mug of watered-down ale by performing tasks for which they were usually unequal.

But not under George Drayton, that dear absent-minded old man who almost ruined the business by his inattention to essential matters. George Drayton had preferred the books of prose and poetry that he brought to work, daily, in his saddle bags. Near ruin had been averted by his eldest son, who promptly reinstated the child labour abandoned by his father and restablished the Drayton Pottery as a thriving concern.

But at that stage Meg stopped looking back over her life because there were slices in it that she wanted to forget. She preferred leaping ahead to the times when the young Martin Drayton, whom she herself had tutored in the art of turning, at last came into his own and undercurrents of resentment and hatred at the Drayton Pottery yielded to a wholly changed atmosphere; when the workers were no longer afraid of their master and no longer suspicious of their superiors or of each other, and the shed overseers became more trustworthy because they no longer had to spy on those beneath them and report their misdemeanours and mistakes. An overseer could then take his workers to task personally and the matter would go no further – unlike that brief and unhappy spell when Maxwell Freeman from Tremain Hall was brought into the place for no better purpose than to relay to Master Joseph every kind of goings-on.

Some had said he was there solely because he had married

Phoebe Drayton and a share in the family business went with her dowry, but that seemed nonsense since the Freemans were far richer. In any case, he didn't last long and there wasn't a worker who wasn't glad about that. Max Freeman had been an unattractive youth, over-indulged and self-indulgent, and no one had been more surprised than Meg when he came back to Staffordshire, a changed and far more likeable man.

There was time for these reflections, and others, as Meg rode to Ashburton on this particular Sunday afternoon. The aftermath of the Drayton upheaval seemed to be getting worse instead of better. Supervision at the pottery was rapidly deteriorating, despite intermittent demonstrations of the Master Potter's authority, which seemed to be his idea of the right way to go about things; a periodic round-up of overseers, chastising them or criticizing them, demanding greater endeavours, better results, more diligence, more attention to duty, when each and every one of them was doing his or her utmost already, and so were the workers.

'The man'll drive us to breaking point,' Dave Jefferson had declared one day in a rare bout of temper.

'Aye, but not himself,' Meg had answered. 'Haven't ye noticed that his rantings are allus followed by a lull, like he's run out of steam?'

'Until the next time.'

But why think about that now? Today was the Sabbath; the weather was fine. It was May and a balmy one, the hedgerows in leaf, apple and prunus in full bloom, hawthorn blossom burgeoning. Early spring flowers were over but carpets of bluebells spread richly in the woods and cottage gardens were bright with colour . . . and she was on her way to spend an hour with her lifelong friend and benefactress, Mistress Kendall. There was always a welcome chance to talk with her when the lesson was over and today Meg was anxious to discuss Abby, who had somehow changed and was slipping out of her reach. And that was frightening.

There were other things, too; not frightening but important and exciting. Ever since the news that Mistress Amelia's museum was to be re-established alongside Fletcher's Forge and that it was to be named after her late husband, Burslem had been agog. And when it actually happened, everybody sat up because it was far more splendid and far better situated, attracting passers-by as well as coach travellers who commanded their drivers to stop. Museums along the way were an unusual attraction, so the

110

Martin Drayton Museum won the attention of many folk besides dealers who were heading for the pottery on business. And how did the new Master of Drayton's like *that*?

Fletcher's Forge wouldn't be doing too badly out of it either, some said wryly, because it was obvious that the whole scheme had been aided and abetted by Damian Fletcher and the young woman he lived with. But more kindly folk said good luck to 'em, some adding that Olivia Freeman must feel lost with nothing to do but supervise her household. Meg thought the same and was surprised that she didn't appear to be helping at her aunt's museum. It was the other niece, Deborah Kendall, who was doing that. When M's Amelia was absent, the girl took over and the heir of Tremain would sometimes join her – which started tongues wagging, of course. He was very active about the place, putting finishing touches to this and that and doing anything else required by Mistress Drayton.

There was more local speculation when it was reported that Lionel Drayton, dropping in to see the place one day, had begun to repeat the visits whenever Miss Deborah was on duty. Not that he was interested in the museum. He had been heard to refer to it, contemptuously, as his aunt's little pastime, but Meg doubted whether he had uttered that remark in the young lady's hearing; he seemed too anxious to win her approval and to belittle anything associated with her aunt would never achieve that.

Meg's lessons took place in Ashburton's library, a room she had found awesome until Mistress Kendall had taken down volume after volume and introduced her to the marvel of illustration and lettering and the enjoyment of listening to words read aloud. She had a lovely voice, had Miss Jessica – even now, Meg sometimes thought of the mistress of Ashburton as the young lady she had once been. The most handsome in Burslem, in her opinion, though everyone had seemed to admire the golden prettiness of her sister a great deal more. Plump Phoebe. Pretty Phoebe. Pettish Phoebe. Spitey-Phoebe, Meg had secretly called her, because the rose-bud mouth could tighten spitefully if she were crossed. And yet she had produced a daughter like M's Olivia who, in character if not in looks, had resembled her mother's twin in many respects and Spitey-Phoebe in no way at all.

But today, on this ambling trot to Ashburton, Abby Walker began to dominate Meg's thoughts. Of late, the girl had taken to prettying herself up; new ribbons for her hair, new stockings too, and of white cotton so fine that Meg herself had never been able to afford anything like them. At least Abby had the sense not to wear them to the pottery, and Meg would never have seen them had she not forgotten her shawl one night and gone back to the shed to pick it up – and there was Abby, carefully rolling on one stocking and tying it above the knee with yet another ribbon and her other leg, bare and wet, waiting to be dried. A bowl of water was on the floor and a piece of scrim a yard long beside it, and a hunk of rough soap, used for scouring the work benches at the end of the day, was melting in the water.

The girl had been not in the least put out. She had smiled pertly and, extending the stockinged leg, said, 'Pretty, ain't it, Meg?' and laughed and picked up the length of scrim and dried the other leg with it. Meg had been struck dumb at first, and when she had found her tongue all she had been able to say was, 'That there soap's melting. We ain't allowed t'waste it.'

'I b'aint wastin' – wast*ing*,' Abby corrected hastily. She seemed very anxious, of late, to talk proper. 'I ain't wasting it. Soap's for keeping a body clean.'

'And who told ye that?'

'Me mam, o'course. 'Sides, ye've allus told me t'wash'n tidy meself after work.'

Her hands and face, yes. And her hair too. But not other parts of her body except in private.

'Ye should've locked the door, Abby. I s'pose ye thought everyone were gone. Next time, wait 'til ye get home.'

The fact that Abby made no answer and continued calmly with her toilet had told Meg that the girl was not going home and that all this preparation was for something, or some*one*, special. The freshly brushed hair, the white stockings, the removal of all signs of clay, even from beneath the fingernails where it lingered permanently with most potters, all indicated that Abby had remained behind to prepare secretly for an assignation.

'Is it Dave? I 'ope it be. He loves ye, Abby Walker.'

'Aye, I know that. 'E's told me often enough.'

Thrusting her feet into working clogs at which she glanced distastefully, Abby picked up the bowl and threw the dirty water out into the yard. The place was totally deserted and totally silent but for the distant roar of the massive kilns. Not even the brick walls shut out the sound; it was the hum every potter liked to hear and the lull following the blow-up had now mercifully passed; production was flowing again. But the comforting noise did nothing to assuage Meg's sudden unease. Something was wrong. Something concerning Abby.

112

'I don't see Dave,' she said, glancing through the open door. 'He's not out there, waiting for ye.'

'An' who said 'e would be?' Abby answered pertly as she turned back into the shed. Only recently had she begun to speak to Meg that way, with a touch of insolence, too confident by half.

'D'ye do this often, Abby? Stay behind to pretty y'self up?'

'I be only practising wot ye preach. Ye oughta be glad.' The girl picked up Meg's shawl and handed it to her. 'This be wot ye come back for?'

Meg had taken the shawl, saying awkwardly, 'I'll be off then. If Dave's walking ye home a second party won't be welcome. Don't forget to lock up afore ye leave.'

But there was still no sign of Dave. No sign of anyone but old Peterson locking up the gatehouse. Looking back as she walked through the gates, Meg had seen the flickering light within the shed snuff out as Abby prepared to leave. Meg had turned away then and headed for Larch Lane, not waiting to see the girl emerge because she didn't want to give the impression that she was spying. No doubt Abby would head for the glazing sheds to find out what was keeping Dave and old Peterson would see them off the premises, or leave the gates unlocked if firers were on duty through the night. Either way, it were no business of hers.

Feeling suddenly tired, suddenly aware that she was no longer young, Meg had gone on her way.

After the lesson, Jessica Kendall said, 'You've something on your mind, Meg. What is it?'

Were it that plain, then? Or was it just a way this lady had, sort've sensing when a body's thoughts were troubled?

'Come, Meg. Tell me. You've not been concentrating so well this afternoon.' When Meg hesitated, Jessica crossed to the fireplace and tugged a bell rope. 'We'll take some tea together and talk about things, and as it's such a beautiful day we'll take it outside. Remember how we sometimes did that at Cooperfield, when you came to turn my brother's pots?'

Meg remembered it well – and the small outhouse in which Master Martin had launched himself as a potter, thanks to the Kendalls.

The library opened on to a wide terrace flanking the whole of the south side of Ashburton, and here Sarah brought the tea. She showed no surprise on seeing Meg Tinsley, being accustomed to her mistress's varied assortment of friends, and her master's too. When the Kendalls entertained they did so in a variety of ways

113

with a variety of people. Sometimes they threw open the grounds for local fairs, letting the organizers set up maypoles and Aunt Sallys and coconut shies and Punch and Judys and anything else they fancied in whatever spot they chose, and when everything was over the weary helpers would be fortified with food from the Ashburton kitchens, washed down with mugs of strong tea or home-brewed ales, often imbibed right here on the terrace.

For miles around, the Kendalls were liked and respected, feelings shared by both their indoor and outdoor staff, so if her mistress wanted to take tea with someone as humble as Meg Tinsley, Sarah served it willingly. She also nodded and smiled affably at the guest because, despite all she'd heard about Meg throughout her lifetime, she liked her.

'Now tell me what is troubling you,' Jessica said as she took the silver kettle from its silver spirit stand and poured boiling water into the silver teapot in which Sarah had already put tea leaves. 'Is it the pottery? Aren't you happy there any more? Or is it some-one?'

'Aye,' Meg admitted, then with some hesitation added, 'It be young Abby Walker.'

'*Abby?* But everyone likes her. My sister-in-law once described her as very promising.'

'She be that orlright, if she sticks t'the job. Wot worrits me is – she mightn't.'

Jessica waited while Meg drained her cup, set it aside, wiped her mouth with the back of her hand and sighed appreciatively. Feeling much better for it, she went on, 'I'm afeared she'll go the way of 'er ma, Miss Jessica – beggin' pardon, mistress. Sometimes I think o'ye just as I useter.'

Jessica smiled, then said seriously, 'Tell me why you suddenly fear for Abby.'

'T'aint' sudden reely. I've bin afeared for a long time. With Kate for a mother, there be plenty o'reason. I useter hope that one day Kate'd clear off an' leave Abby, an' a good riddance it would be. Then I'd step in an' look after the lass an' one day she'd marry a good honest chap like Dave Jefferson, but now – yes, I be real worrit. She's changed.'

'In what way? Tell me.'

'She be allus prettying 'erself up –'

'That's quite natural in a growing girl.'

'Aye, if she earns the money t'do it on. But Abby's wages ain't enough for fancy new ribbons an' fancy new blouses an' other things besides. I caught 'er washing 'erself t'other day, after

114

everyone had gone an' she thought she was safe; 'tweren't just her face an hands, but way up 'er legs too. I remember well, 'cos I saw fancy frills underneath, the like o' which only come on costly garments.'

'Perhaps she had made them herself.'

'Not Abby! She's no great shakes with a needle an' these frills were made o' real lace – an' lying on the floor were her cast-offs – coarse cotton like us pottery women all wear an' no fancy trimmings. So she be getting money from somewhere else, an' I don't like it, mistress.'

'Did you question her?'

'I wanted to, but 't'were a waste o' time. She don't open up t'me no more. She's changed. More'n more she's beginning t'sound like 'er mother, an' t'look like 'er too, or trying to. An' all I can do is look on an' say now't, 'cos trying to talk sense into her be a waste o'time.'

'Meaning she won't listen?'

'That she won't.'

Jessica tried to lessen Meg's anxiety by reiterating that it was natural for a girl like Abby to take an interest in her looks, but when that met with only a distracted nod she knew that Meg's anxiety was too deep to be soothed by trite observations.

'You think there's a man. That is what's worrying you, isn't it, Meg?'

'Aye.'

'Some man providing her with these things, or the money to buy them, and for a reason.'

'That's the truth of it, mistress. An' it'll grieve me sore if Abby goes t'way of 'er ma.' She burst out passionately, 'For two pins I'd tan the hide off that Kate!'

'I shouldn't try it, Meg, since she's twice the size of you.' The light note Jessica forced into her voice did at least make the other woman smile. 'There must be some other way we can handle this . . .'

'Aye, there be, but whether it'll work, I don't know. I can but try, an' somehow I will. I want t'get that woman t'quit Burslem once an' fer all, an' then I want Abby along with me 'til such time as she be wed, an' that'll be young, being the way she's made. The sooner the better, then she won't be pleasuring the wrong men for the wrong reasons, 'cos mark me words, mistress, once started on that road it ain't easy to stop. I were lucky. I met Frank Tinsley an' 'e loved me just as I were –'

'As you always were at heart, Meg. Your circumstances were

different from Abby's. Yours were tragic and harsh. You weren't taught that taking money for satisfying men was an easy and therefore enjoyable way of making a living, as Abby has been taught by that mother of hers. I share your dislike of Kate Walker. Do you really think you can persuade her to leave Burslem? And how?'

'Leave that t'me,' Meg said darkly, and Jessica chose to, asking instead if Meg knew the identity of the man concerned.

'One of the overseers, perhaps? Not Dave Jefferson, surely? He seems a wholly honest and decent young man.'

'No – not Dave. It'd break his heart if 'e knew, though he ain't so dense as not to notice a thing or two.'

'Then another pot maker . . . surely not more than one, Meg?'

'Not yet, I be sure o' that. It be summun in the pottery, though, I'd take a bet on't.'

'If he is giving her money, he must be one of the top employees, otherwise he couldn't afford it.'

'Aye.'

Meg suddenly shut up like a clam, and that was when Jessica suspected that the woman had guessed the man's identity, but that nothing would persuade her to name him. There could be only one reason for that. No pot worker could afford to fall foul of the most important man in the place, their employer and boss, the Master Potter who could turn them off at a moment's notice without pay. The thought made Jessica run cold. Her brother had been that type of a man, and now his son had taken his place.

Something had to be done, not only about Abby but about Meg.

Casually, she asked what life was like at Drayton's these days. Was she still happy there? Were things as they used to be?

'That they ain't, mistress. How could they be without M's Amelia an' M's 'Livia? They kept Drayton's together, them two. But it's a living, o'course, an' I count me blessings.'

'And you still have the Tinsley cottage in Larch Lane?'

'Aye, thanks be t'God.'

'And you think you could manage there if Abby were with you? Wouldn't it be too cramped?'

'I'd fix things. I'd manage. She'd be better off an' I'd be a deal easier in me mind, an' though right now she thinks I be an interfering busybody, she'd feel different once we were t'gether again.' Meg finished sadly. 'We useter be so close, Abby an' me. Like me own child, she were.'

Jessica didn't know what she could do to help, but decided that she would definitely do something. She would consult Simon.

116

Deborah, too. Ever since Miguel had made that splendid suggestion about starting a new pottery, her daughter had been enthusiastic, full of bright ideas and agog to help. The two young people
had involved themselves in the project whole-heartedly.

The first question had concerned the situation of it. The location of a new pottery required considerable thought. There had
to be space in which to build the first kiln, space that could be
cobble-stoned or brick-set, with sufficient area to accommodate
at least one more kiln eventually, and there had to be worksheds
for throwers and turners and glazers and modellers and mould-
makers, although at the start the minimum would be employed.

There had been so many things to decide, so many things to set
in motion, and though Amelia had declared that the launching
of the pottery was of greater importance than re-launching her
museum, she had been unanimously overruled by the rest of
them. They were all in it together, united in enthusiasm.

Miguel had suggested Tremain. He was sure some outbuildings
there could be converted for use as a pottery and that his father
would give his consent. When approached, Max Freeman agreed,
providing the kilns could be situated far on the outskirts of the
estate, or Aggie would have the vapours – and he wouldn't much
like the sight or smell of belching chimneys. Wouldn't it be possible
to cart the stuff away to be fired down in Burslem? And mightn't
Tremain's inaccessibility discourage prospective customers – and
possibly the grandeur of the place even intimidate some?

The centre of Burslem was obviously the most desirable location, but with proliferating industry such a site was hard to find.
Then Deborah suddenly asked, 'Why not here at Ashburton?
With Papa's enterprises attracting more and more attention, and
the main road from Stoke-on-Trent passing right by our gates, a
bare six miles from Burslem wouldn't discourage clients. And
there are acres of space down in the valley, and still some
outbuildings that Papa hasn't put to good use.' Excitedly she had
cried, 'Seize them, Olivia, or he'll be using them for some other
project! And think of this – a new pottery established right here
would be on the spot to have first choice of the new ground flints.'

That settled the matter, and now preparations were almost
complete. The site was on a distant perimeter of Ashburton's
estates, but accessible to the Stoke road, where a new entrance
was being made. A bottle oven was having the final touches put
to it and draught-testing would take place within a few days. Earth-
floors in suitable outhouses had been flagged, work benches built,
kick-wheels installed, supplies of clay and grog and whiting and

117

rutile and manganese delivered. It was as exciting as dear Martin's early venture into independent production, but on a large scale, for Olivia and Amelia could fortunately launch the concern backed by years of experience and the support of men like Simon and Damian.

No one expected quick results. Potteries weren't established that way. It would take time and patience and dedicated hard work, slowly proving its worth, gradually building up individual lines which would become instantly recognizable as the work of the Ashburton Pottery. From the start, that name was the obvious choice; wise, also, for to involve the name of Drayton would instantly suggest rivalry. People would look on, waiting for the new Drayton establishment to founder and 'those two eccentric women' along with it. But a new industrial project alongside other Ashburton concerns would arouse neither criticism nor adverse comment; it would be accepted as yet another venture to which that experienced man, Simon Kendall, had given his approval, otherwise he would not have accommodated it.

Jessica now jumped to her feet, saying eagerly, 'Come, Meg, I want to show you something –' and from the terrace she led her across sweeping lawns toward a far distant screen of trees, heading for a path curving away between them.

As they approached it, a figure came walking toward them. It was Olivia. She wore the homespun working clothes she had worn at the Drayton Pottery and over one arm she carried the thick hessian apron she had always preferred to a potter's slop. Her hands were clay-soiled and she looked for all the world as if she had just walked out of the modelling shed.

She called, 'I'm on my way to the house to clean up.'

Her face lit up at the sight of Meg, and Jessica called back, 'And *I* was on my way to you because it's important that you talk with Meg . . .' When they came abreast Jessica finished, 'She's the very person you need, Olivia, and *she* needs *you*.'

CHAPTER 11

When Meg rapped on his door next morning and walked in without waiting to be summoned, Lionel Drayton was momentarily speechless. He didn't like Meg Tinsley; an uncomfortable woman, with an arrogant walk and a disconcerting glance which he chose to call insolent though secretly recognizing it as un-compromising. Such a quality he found baffling. Boldness he knew how to handle, but a cool and enigmatic approach he did not. Worse, he could hazard no guess for her unceremonious arrival.

'I'd like a word with ye, Master Potter.'

No 'please, sir'; no curtseying; no waiting to be spoken to.

'Did you seek it through the Overseer?' he answered sharply. 'You know the rule. No worker can approach the Master Potter direct.' Glancing at his desk, he added, 'Your name is not on this morning's list.'

''Cos there ain't been time t'get it there. Willis is away on canalside . . .' She almost added, 'bossing everybody around, like 'e be doing these days,' but managed to refrain. Willis, formerly chief thrower, had been newly appointed as overseer, but was not making a good job of it. He was more at home at the wheel. She reckoned Willis wouldn't last long and then the Master Potter would be looking around for someone else, but if any other man would willingly take on the job, she doubted very much. Still, that was no concern of hers. The realization that she could now put events at the Drayton Pottery right out of her mind left Meg with an exhilarating sense of freedom.

'Then find him, and leave it to him to arrange an appointment.' With this dismissive remark Lionel turned back to his work, though most of the accumulated papers on his desk were baffling and he was realizing, more and more, that he needed some knowledgeable person to rely on; someone better than a manual worker; someone with administrative experience, or a grasp of it. Even his mother said so, though her advice always jarred on him. Every time he paid a duty call she would start asking about affairs at Drayton's and expounding on how his father would have handled this or that situation. She had harped on things only last night.

'Although I don't like to say so, dear boy, I have to admit that Amelia, having worked so closely with Martin throughout the years, must surely be able to guide you – or could have done, had you not been so unwise as to let her go. Oh, I know you acted with the best possible intentions, and I commend you for it – but perhaps – a little too hastily?'

Damn his mother. He had fallen into the habit of taking supper with her once a month, partially to ease his conscience about neglecting her (it was Amelia who had accused him of that) and partially because timing a visit to coincide with one of Pierre's excellent meals spared him much tiresome conversation. His mother could talk even with her mouth full and all he had to do was pretend to listen.

Meg Tinsley's next impertinent remark jerked him back to the moment.

'There ain't no time like the present, Master Potter, an' it won't take long, neether. I've come to tell ye I'm quitting, an' since me wages are paid by the hour an' ye can lay me off at a moment's notice without pay, I can do t'same. But me new employers won't hear of it. "'T'wouldn't be fair," they said. "'T'wouldn't be right." So I'll tell you wot I'll do. I'll work the week out t'give ye time t'replace me. I've worked at Drayton's nigh on all me life an' I feel it only proper. So I won't pack up me tools 'til the week's out. An' now I'll get back t'me bench. Good morning t'ye, Master Potter.'

She had reached the door before he regained his breath. Then he exploded.

'You can leave this instant! Out you go – *now* – straight through this door and out through the gates. Whoever your new employer is, he may have you, and welcome.'

Impudently, she curtseyed. 'Thanks, Master Potter, that suits me fine – an' good day t'ye.'

But he delayed her by declaring that if her new employer was known to him, there would be trouble.

'That ain't likely, sir. Ye've no indentures on me. An' it should be easy t'find another chief turner in a place like Burslem.'

'It won't be necessary to look even that far. There's a young woman under you who can take your place.'

'Which one d'ye have in mind, sir? Any of the women I've trained be good workers, some better'n others.'

'The choice of your successor is my concern, not yours.' As she opened the door he added, 'And let me remind you that all tools are the property of this establishment so if you remove any you will be charged with theft. You must look to your new employer to provide such items, which I hope will be as good as those supplied here.'

'Oh, they will be, sir. I be sure o' that. Only the best'll be good enough for M's Olivia an' Mistress Drayton.'

After a moment's stunned silence he wanted to laugh aloud, and did so as soon as the door closed. Then he sobered as something his mother had said last night filtered belatedly into his mind. Agatha babbled so much that he had schooled himself into ignoring most of it, but now memory dredged up some of her words.

'. . . it was Miguel's idea . . . Max will listen to anything he says . . . if you ask me, the whole scheme is too ridiculous to heed . . .'

What idea? What scheme? Being uninterested, he had paid no attention, but now he was alert and suddenly suspicious. Those two women were up to something – but what? They couldn't be establishing their own pottery. Whoever heard of a pot bank owned and run by women? So it could be no more than some trivial sideline connected with the new museum. That was it, of course! Olivia was planning to make those figurines of hers that people liked so much, getting some local potter to fire them and then selling through Amelia's new venture. Bird life, animal life, flora and fauna, and those delicate figures of dancers that went so well in exclusive galleries in London and New York and which, as yet, none of the other modellers at Drayton's had produced quite so exquisitely.

He admitted that now, but reluctantly. Whole consignments of what he considered admirable replicas, made since her departure, had been rejected by more than one long-established dealer and the only thing to do with them was to sell them off cheaply to lesser ones. The financial loss didn't bear thinking of. Nor could Drayton's now continue with that new line of character figures Olivia had launched shortly before he took control – Nelson, Napoleon, the Kings and Queens of England and Scotland, men of renown and women of fame forming a whole pageant of history. The last batch had been snapped up and orders had poured in from all quarters. None could now be fulfilled because no one could equal Olivia's brilliance. On top of this, there was unrest amongst the modellers because he complained incessantly that their work no longer came up to scratch.

But perhaps there was a ray of hope after all. If Olivia's work was to be sold through the agency of the Martin Drayton Museum, which would no doubt be glad of additional finance, it would be a source of supply ready to hand. He wouldn't reveal he was the buyer, of course; the purchasers could be made through a third party. Orders substantial enough to cover her entire output would safeguard against rival purchases. He would have a monopoly. The idea pleased him so much that he wanted to shout to the world, 'Who says *now* that Lionel Drayton doesn't know how to run a successful industry? Who says he isn't astute?'

121

Excitement was deflated when Meg Tinsley's voice echoed in his mind. '... *it should be easy t'find another chief turner in a place like Burslem.*' Turners were only needed in potteries. Their services were confined to receptacles. Models of any kind had no need of them so, plainly, Meg was going to work in a rival pot bank, an enterprise in competition with his own. How typically cunning of those two women to entice Meg Tinsley away from her secure job at Drayton's ... secretly ... furtively.

The thought outraged him, and anger gathered momentum even though he reminded himself that two women setting themselves up as potters were doomed to failure, particularly when only one could rightly call herself that. The ceramic trade was a man's world in which women were predominantly labourers, such occupations as modelling and decorating being the only spheres offering other opportunities. They might rise to being in charge of individual sheds, as Meg Tinsley and that tiresome cousin of his had done, but never to the rank of employer; never on a par with master potters. Amelia had only achieved her former position through her marriage to Martin Drayton. She had made herself indispensable to him; her husband's shadow, his devoted wife.

As for Olivia, she must have played on Damian Fletcher's feelings to have won his support for this new and ridiculous notion – if indeed Meg Tinsley's hint was founded on fact. He found himself snatching at straws, telling himself that the woman might have been bluffing, blurting out the words to conceal the identity of the rival potter who had really lured her away.

But what if it *were* true? If Oliva had persuaded Amelia to join forces with her, and then persuaded Damian Fletcher to back them, the man could only be humouring her. Surely he must realize that the idea could only be a whim prompted by pique?

He decided to dismiss the whole thing with amused indulgence. And yet ... if it *were* true ... how well the secret had been kept! The sheer audacity of it re-sparked his fury. Unlike the reopening of the Drayton Museum on a prominent Burslem site, this other venture had been launched so quietly that no one knew a thing about it.

Except his mother. That must have been what she was babbling about last night! But how had she found out, living her isolated life amidst the isolated splendour of Tremain Hall?

He wished now that he had heeded her prattle, tedious as it always was, because he might have learned a thing or two and been spared the shock of losing a highly skilled turner. Although disliking Meg Tinsley, he knew it would be difficult to find someone to equal her. Abby had a long way to go before reaching Meg's standard, although he had had her in mind when declaring that he would have to look no further than this very pottery for a successor.

And of late Abby had not been concentrating on her work as formerly, so it had suffered. He knew the reason for that and it pleased him rather than concerned him because it was entirely due to her obsession for himself. The termination of his present dalliance rested entirely with him and he had not yet tired of her. She was an obliging little thing, a lusty little thing, and a few baubles, a few trinkets, and an occasional silver coin, kept alive her devotion. The gold coin could wait until he decided to end the affair; a final reward, a last generous gesture. She would accept it in ecstasy and tears, and he would be rid of her.

Meanwhile, he now had other things to think about. He had to find out what was going on – and where. The only way was to visit the new museum and, if Amelia were there, question her point blank. If she were not there then perhaps Deborah Kendall would be, and that would be even better. After losing ground with his pretty cousin, he was anxious to repair broken bridges.

His impulse was to go there at once, but ever since the kiln disaster and his subsequent insistence on tracing the cause and the person responsible, he had become aware of the watchfulness of his workers. It even seemed to border on antagonism. Although he had called a halt to the abortive search the minute Olivia had left the pottery, this attitude seemed unchanged. Even Dave Jefferson, that able young man whom he wanted and needed as an ally, had become guarded in his manner; civil, speaking when spoken to, but nothing more than that.

He had had his eye on Dave from the beginning, seeing him as a possible candidate for the position of deputy, a much-needed manager to run the place in his absence. As yet, he had had no opportunity to absent himself at all, no chance to indulge his taste for horse-racing and bear-baiting and cock-fighting, all of which were well catered for throughout the surrounding countryside. To be so bound to a trade for which he really had little taste was becoming irksome, and to be aware of surly acceptance rather than respect from those under him was something he had not anticipated and was now increasingly resenting.

In see-saw fashion he had fallen into the habit of alternately seeking to placate or bully his employees, playing the part of either a kindly patron or a stern master. Either way, he was left with a sense of failure and then arrogance would drive him to demonstrate that *he*, Lionel Drayton, was lord and master here. *He* was the one and only Drayton left to rule the famous Drayton Pottery and they had best remember that. This establishment was his by right and *his* will had to be obeyed.

And obey it they did, but mutinously, which indicated how unwise his late uncle had been in indulging them and, even worse, how badly the subsequent womanish rule had undermined his own.

Everything, always, came back to Amelia and Oliva. Even though they were no longer part of the place, their influence lingered. And now they were robbing him of competent workers. Meg Tinsley could be only the first. It had to stop.

Without warning, his mother's voice echoed again. Through a mouthful of Ratafia Cream she had mumbled, 'Can you *imagine* such an idea, dear boy? Can you *imagine* pottery workers here at Tremain? Without wishing to be the least unfair to Miguel, the fact that he should even suggest such a thing indicates that he doesn't *truly* comprehend what it means to be an English land-owner. Needless to say, I refused to countenance it and Max had the good sense to agree – well – to declare that he knew I would be a stumbling block. He even turned to Miguel and said, "Didn't I tell you so, my son?" . . .'

And on she had gone, and on, her words floating over his head but leaving an unexpected imprint which now came to life. Obviously, she had been talking about some ridiculous enterprise for which those two women had enlisted the help of his uncle's bastard in finding premises. And that only showed how absurd the whole idea was. No pottery hidden in the wilds of a vast country estate could hope to thrive. How many customers would take the trouble to search for it, how many would travel so far? For once, he applauded his mother's wisdom. She had been right in opposing the idea.

But in that case, where *had* the women set it up?

He wasted no time in finding out.

Fortune favoured him. Amelia was at the Martin Drayton Museum.

Grudgingly, he conceded that they had made a splendid place out of what was, to him, a very ordinary outhouse of ancient stone and timbered ceiling. He had never realized that rafters could be architecturally effective. The natural oak had bleached throughout the years to a mellow tone which harmonized, and yet contrasted, with the weathered stone walls and floor. Against this ancient background the displays of multi-hued pottery stood out dramatically.

Despite the early hour, visitors were already there. A stage coach stood outside, London-bound, and not a single passenger remained seated. The vehicle carried six within and eight back-to-back on the ham-boards outside, a top-heavy arrangement which travellers were beginning to protest against, but to which drivers turned a deaf ear. The important thing was to pack the coach to capacity, with sometimes four squashed each side within and five-a-side on top. He had heard that nowadays drivers were supplementing their takings by halting to show passengers a few interesting sights *en route*, in exchange for a good tip or for financial encouragement from the owners – or both. Doubting whether his aunt would be astute enough for that, he was forced to attribute the attraction of the Martin Drayton Museum to the splendid sign created by Fletcher's Forge. No passer-by could possibly overlook it.

When he entered, Amelia was talking to a small knot of well-dressed people. He heard her expressing regret that she was unable to sell replicas of the exhibits, but that perhaps in the future it would be possible. Naturally, she would be only too happy to please them. Perhaps if they ever passed this way again?

Irritated, he turned aside. Why had Drayton's never thought of doing that? The only function of the original museum had been to preserve the pottery's history. Dealers had chosen new lines from the showroom, and even that had seemed unnecessary since a tour of the establishment displayed the latest products – and, of course, still did. The thought mollified him slightly, but left him resolved to do something about re-establishing a room where Drayton's latest products could be shown to advantage. The right place would have to be found for it, because of course he could not sacrifice his splendid office again. Perhaps one of the larger store-rooms might suffice. But that would mean finding further accommodation for stock ... which reminded him that Martin Drayton had had some notion about building a storage cellar. He had even had plans drawn up, details worked out.

That was it! He would go ahead with the scheme. No one would be able to consider him inept once he took that first step in extending the premises.

By the time the visitors had left, Lionel's equanimity was restored. He turned then to Amelia and kissed her hand.

125

'My dear aunt, you look remarkably well.'

'Thank you, Lionel. I feel so.'

'Much less tired and far less haggard. No longer jaded, no longer worn out. You see, I was right, was I not? Rest was what you needed. No more work, at your age.'

She smiled.

'And yet I have been working very hard, as you can see. Setting all this up was quite demanding. Of course, I did have help – Damian and Olivia have been wonderful. But so has everyone . . . the Kendalls . . . and dear Miguel. But you know that. Deborah told me that you called when she was deputizing for me one day, so I'm sure you heard all about everything.'

'Not *every*thing. Not about the other scheme which you and Olivia have been keeping so secret. The pair of you have been hatching plans and putting them into operation. That is why I am here. To wish you all possible success. You will obviously need it.'

She answered calmly, 'You refer to the new pottery, of course. Success will be ours if we work for it – as we intend to.'

'By pilfering my best workers?'

'You mean Meg Tinsley? We are delighted to have her. As yet, we have approached no one else, though of course we will be looking for good and experienced workers. None will be persuaded to leave their present employment, but if they approach us we will naturally give them fair consideration. But I am sure you have nothing to worry about. Workers who are content will not be looking elsewhere.'

'And how do you propose to combine this place with a pottery? I assume it is to be established here. A clever idea of Fletcher's, to expand his own trade? Or a whim of Olivia's which he, besotted as ever, cannot refuse her?'

'All your assumptions are wrong,' she said coolly. 'The Ashburton Pottery, as its name implies, has been established –'

'– at *Ashburton*? So the Kendalls are behind it!'

'We are all behind it. And now, if you will excuse me, I have work to do.'

He wanted to say, 'Do you call it work, dusting your precious exhibits and mooning over the past in a place designed to immortalize the name of your dear departed and to dramatize your widowhood?', but she forestalled him.

'Sometimes your thoughts are very obvious, nephew. In your view a museum doesn't represent work but, believe me, a place the size of this requires supervision and attention. Already it has attracted more interest than I expected. We have had to draw up a timetable, attending here in shifts. Until the outside help I am engaging – Maude Barlett, the lawyer's widow living close by – starts working full time, I come daily, with Miguel and Deborah giving as much time as they can spare. Olivia is already hard at work at Ashburton, building up stock, and Deborah will soon be fully employed there. She has talent. You should have paid attention when she brought her design to show you. Luckily for us, the Ashburton Pottery is producing it instead. And we have other plans, other ideas.'

'Such as making replicas of these ancient relics?'

'I hadn't thought of that until those people wanted to buy some, but I shall certainly suggest it.' The sound of approaching footsteps and the lifting of the ancient latch cut into the moment. More visitors. He wasn't sorry. He was ready to leave, even impatient to, for he knew exactly where he was going next.

Impeccably mannered, he again touched his aunt's fingers with his lips. Above his head, she murmured, 'Thank you for wishing us success, Lionel, but it would be more acceptable if you meant it.'

He drove furiously to Ashburton, uncaring when the pair of greys arrived in a lather. Nor did he spare time to present himself formally because he had no wish to be hindered by Jessica Kendall, who would no doubt try to prevent him from visiting what he had already dubbed 'Olivia's hideaway'. No one was going to stop him now.

He guessed that the pottery would be situated far from the house, down in the valley along with Si Kendall's workshops. He had only to leave his curricle at the stables and proceed on foot, so he drove straight round to the coachyard, shouted for a stable lad, tossed the reins to him and dismounted. Then he headed briskly for a bridle path which, he remembered from his boyhood days, descended to the valley.

He had scarcely reached the complex of workshops when Kendall himself emerged through a pair of oaken doors leading from the interior of a windmill, built on to an ancient barn. Within, Lionel glimpsed an immense circular vat from which came the noise of water-driven power and the thunder of tumbling stones.

Kendall greeted the visitor with characteristic courtesy, asking if he had come to see how the flint-grinding mill was progressing.

'If so, you have timed your visit well. It is undergoing its final test at this very moment. Come – I will show you.'

127

For a moment Lionel was nonplussed. He had forgotten all about Kendall's latest whim, but now he recalled Olivia's enthusiasm for it and how she had declared that it would result in the whitest stoneware ever seen. Alerted, he followed the older man and stood with a line of silent and appreciative workers, all watching giant paddles pushing blocks of Derbyshire chert stone round the circular drum. The bed of the cylinder was covered with the same stone.

'Why so much water?' he asked, wondering how anything of value in the making of pottery could come out of a pile of wet boulders.

One of the workers suppressed a laugh, but the rest were too absorbed in the operation to heed the question. Satisfaction was on each one's face. They had done it. It was working. The master's hand and the master's mind had guided them and the result was good.

'Why so much water?' a voice echoed – not the voice of a worker, not a voice with a dialect, but the voice of a young man who plainly did not belong to a gang of labourers. Annoyed, Lionel turned and faced his uncle's half-Mexican son. Lionel wanted to ask what he was doing here, but ignored him instead. Unperturbed, Miguel continued, 'An exact amount is needed to smooth the passage of the stones so that they are ground evenly and finely. The result is a liquid containing ground flint that can be reduced by heat to the form of a fine powder.'

'Obviously. I can see that.'

'Not yet,' said Si Kendall with a smile. 'The grinding process will continue for a long time before the liquid and the residue form the first grit, which must then be ground again into an even finer quality . . . and so on until the power is produced.'

'But the stones are black.'

'Chert stone is naturally black, and becomes even blacker when burned. After quarrying, we burned it for many days while the final engineering work was being completed. Black flint-stone, when burned, produces a powder whiter than any other. Ostlers mix it with water to poultice their horses' eyes.'

'And *we* will mix it with clay to produce the first truly white stoneware.' This time, to Lionel's surprise and pleasure, it was Deborah's voice. 'Miguel,' she continued, 'I came in search of you. I want you to see my sundial – it's finished. Olivia says we must allow some weeks for it to dry out before bisque-firing.' To Lionel, she added graciously, 'You may come too, if you wish. I imagine that is really why you are here – to see the new pottery, not my father's grinding mill. The news had to reach you some time and I'll be happy to show you everything – including my wall sundial. My very first. I used a basic Mexican design combined with wild game. I brought it to the Drayton Pottery to show you. I think you may be sorry you didn't see it.'

You pretty bitch, he thought. You taunting, teasing, tantalizing bitch.

He smiled. He said, 'What a pity you won't be able to make it in the fine white stoneware you're all so excited about.'

That startled her. It startled the others too, but Simon Kendall regarded him inscrutably.

Deborah declared, 'I certainly shall, sir! In fact, I have already done so since a wall sundial is made for outside use. *And* we will use it for other outdoor items.'

'Only with my permission. It was agreed that the new grinding powder was to be produced exclusively for Drayton's.'

His triumph was curtailed when Simon Kendall said quietly, 'There you are wrong. I agreed to supply it to Martin Drayton personally. The agreement was signed in his name, not in that of the Drayton Pottery.'

Shortly after he heard the news, Dave Jefferson knocked on the door of Meg's cottage. She steered the conversation to the subject of Abby.

'Talk to her, Dave. Make her see sense. She'll listen t'thee.'

'I doubt it. Abby ain't got eyes nor ears for nobody but the Master Potter these days.'

Meg didn't want to believe it, but she had a sickening feeling that Dave was right. The girl was besotted by the man, flattered by his passing glances and the smile he seemed to have for her even when everyone else was out of favour. The poor dear dolt – couldn't she wake up, couldn't she *see* what he was after? And didn't she know what would happen to her if she were so foolish as to give in?

'Look at your ma,' Meg had wanted to say when the girl refused point blank to listen to her. 'D'you want to finish up like her, cheap as they come?'

But things like that couldn't be said; not to a girl who had been brought up not to recognize the difference between a way of life that could be full of promise and one so precarious that it could land her in the gutter, old before her time? (But for Frank, dear God, that might've been me . . .)

Meg had even told herself that Abby's admiration for the new

Master of Drayton's would peter out quickly enough, that it was no more than a young girl's romantic dream from which she would soon awaken, but Dave's words were alarming. Plainly, he viewed Abby's infatuation as serious.

'Ye don't think she's given in to him already, do ye?' she asked anxiously.

'How else does she come by all them fripperies and gew-gaws? Not out've wages, that be sure. I saw 'er swaggering by Cobbler's Green t'other Sabbath, wearing a gown that must have cost more than she earns in a year. Y'know what it be like down by the green of a Sabbath – everyone taking the air. There she were, showing off 'er new finery. All eyes were on 'er and well she knew it. Nor could she have missed the things they shouted. "Goin' the way o'yer ma?" some woman yelled, so up I went to Abby and said, "'Tis a fine day for a walk, Abby lass –" "Aye," she sez, "it is that," an' keeps right on, so I falls into step an' asks where she be going, quiet-like so folks can't hear, an' all of a sudden she rounds on me and tells me t'mind me own business.'

Meg frowned. 'That ain't like our Abby.'

'It be like 'er now. Prickly as a hedgehog an' hoity-toity with it. So what makes ye think she'll listen to me? An' what d'ye want me t'say?'

'That she'll be far better off along o' me, working at the Ashburton Pottery. 'Specially the way things are going at Drayton's nowadays.'

'She won't believe that because she don't want to believe it.'

'Then make her! 'Sides, it be true. Master Kendall be doing all sorts o' fine things, like putting labourers' cottages in fine shape so folk can live decent in 'em. One is t'be mine soon as ready, cos I'm t'be M's 'Livia's chief assistant.' Meg grinned. 'Sounds grand, don't it, but that's wot they're calling me, she an' M's Amelia. You'll've heard by now that they're in partnership, with Mistress Drayton running the management side –'

'As well as the museum?'

'She did both at Drayton's, didn't she, after Master Martin went? But this one's bigger so she's taking on a full-time worker – that well-spoken widder from yon by the green. Things be really getting going, Dave, an' Abby could come with me and share the cottage when it be ready an' I'd take good care of her, like I've allus wanted.'

'What o' this place, Meg? Ain't ye going t'miss it?'

' 'T'ain't mine. 'Tis one of Tremain's tied cottages, but Master Maxwell's let me live in it since Frank's pore old auntie died. I've bin grateful for that, but somehow I've never bin able to shake off Ma Tinsley's shadder. I've often wondered when the time would come for me t'leave, an' where I'd go. Well, now I know and it's mighty pleased I be. 'Til then, the distance ain't important. I useter walk it when Master Martin started in that shed the Kendalls set 'im up in at Cooperfield; went there as often as I could, turning pots for him. But this time I'll be hiring Joss Barlow's old nag an' if she could be persuaded t'come too, Abby could perch up behind me. Ninepence for a whole day's hire won't make a hole in t'good wages I'll be earning at the Ashburton Pottery. M's 'Livia offered to pay, but no thanks, sez I. I have me pride, same as thee, Dave. Fair wages means a fair return, an' that's wot I'll be giving. Works t'other way round, too, so keep your eye on that Lionel Drayton and make sure of it.'

'I'll be watching more'n that. But I'm right glad you be fixed up so well, Meg, an' though I'd miss Abby at the pot bank, I'd be glad t'see her safe away from it.'

Meg urged, 'Come too, Dave! I don't doubt the two ladies would gladly take ye on. The pottery's small right now, but it'll grow quick-like. Ye should see it! Lacks for now't and lots o' room for growing.'

'As long as Abby stays at Drayton's, I'm staying too. I take it ye've asked her t'go along wi' ye?'

'That were the last thing I did afore I quit. She said no, point blank. She likes it at Drayton's, she sez. She can't see nothink wrong wi' t'place. Said she were reel sorry about the two ladies, but not so much now everything seems t'be going fine for 'em – "An now I'd like t'get on wi' me work, if ye don't mind, our Meg?" Just like that she sez it, an' I snaps back, "Well, I 'opes it turns out better'n of late, Abby Walker, 'cos your work's gone right off, that it has!" I shouldn't've said that, true though it be. And that be another worriting thing, Dave. She ain't giving 'er mind t'the job no more.'

'All the more reason for me t'stay on at Drayton's. I can't do nothink about her work, but I can keep me eyes open. That's why I said yes when Master Potter sent for me t'other day an' made me Overseer. Willis be right glad t'be Chief Thrower again, an' I'd be glad t'go on being Chief Glazer, but in the new job I'll be able t'see a lot more an' find out things . . .'

Things he didn't really want to know, but which had to be faced. What puzzled him was where and when Abby obliged the Master Potter. Although finding out would be painful, he regarded Abby as his love and therefore his responsibility and

131

until she told him to get out of her life he was determined to remain in it. But that was something he didn't want to discuss, so he turned to the new development at Drayton's. The Master Potter had sent for him not merely to offer him promotion.

'You have been here a long time, haven't you, Jefferson?'

'Aye, sir. Man an' boy.'

'And you were taken into the late Master's confidence about many things?'

'No more'n anybody else, sir. Master Martin never had no secrets.'

'I don't mean secrets. I mean matters pertaining to the pot bank: plans; schemes; developments. Like new extensions, new buildings . . .?'

'He were a very open man, were Master Martin.'

'So you knew about the storage cellar he was planning?'

' 'T'were already planned, sir.'

'Drawings? Costs? Full details?'

'I believe so, sir.'

'Did you ever see the drawings?'

'Aye – once. Master Martin showed 'em t'many of us, wanting to know what we thought o' the scheme.'

'Then why did he abandon it?'

'Master Kendall advised agin it. Risk of flooding from the canal during heavy rains. We gets a lot of 'em in these parts, sir.'

'I know, I know – but as for flooding, safeguards could have been taken.'

'Aye, sir, but not worth t'cost. Leastways, that's wot I 'eard tell.'

Lionel Drayton had dismissed that as unnecessary pessimism.

'Perishable goods could be damaged by water, but not pottery. In any case, properly built and properly protected against seepage, the risk would be minimal. We must find those drawings, Jefferson. What my late uncle was afraid to do, *I* will do. This pottery will have the best underground storage in Staffordshire, thus releasing buildings above ground to be used beneficially.' He had then asked casually whether Dave knew what had happened to the drawings.

'Last time I seed 'em, sir, 't'were in that small office Master Martin used. He were paying out our wages an' I were last in line. Master told me to bide a bit because he 'ad summat to show me. 'T'were Master Kendall's plans. Not that I understood 'em much; a maze of lines 'n figures they were. "All that work for nothing," Master Martin said, sounding disappointed, "but

Simon Kendall never minds how much work he puts in an' won't take a penny payment for all this. I'd go ahead, but he warns against it."'

'And did you see what he did with the drawings? Was he still looking at them when you left?'

'No, sir. He'd rolled 'em up and put 'em in a drawer of that old desk 'e allus used. "This desk has belonged to the Drayton family for centuries." Master Martin useter say that often, proudlike –'

'Yes, yes – and thank you, Jefferson. That will be all, and good night to you.' Looking pleased, Lionel Drayton had then finished, 'Stay with me, Jefferson, and we will go a long way together.'

Stay with him? Why had the man said that? Was he afraid that other valuable clay workers would be following Meg Tinsley's example?

Now the cellar construction was already being put in hand. An even larger one. Only this morning a new designer had been summoned from Stoke and plans were afoot for an additional room down there. 'Can't see the sense in that, I can't,' Dave told Meg as he related the tale. 'It's t'be a smaller room with a lock on the door. I wonder what 'e be planning t'use *that* for . . .'

CHAPTER 12

It seemed to Miguel that although he now saw more of Deborah, he actually saw less. There were no more accidental meetings in the early morning, but plenty of contrived ones because he always knew where he could find her. This was a big advance in one way, but frustrating in another since he never saw her alone.

He was aware that she was the first to arrive at the new pottery each morning because she had only to head for the valley as soon as she had breakfasted. This brisk walk had replaced her customary early morning canter. Soon after Deborah, either Olivia or Meg would arrive, Olivia driving her spanking little gig and Meg on Joss Barlow's plodding mare. Either simultaneously or hard on their heels would come the nucleus of workers now employed at the Ashburton Pottery, whose number would plainly increase.

This new routine meant that Deborah now had little time for

cross-country riding except on the Sabbath when the pottery closed. It was then sandwiched between family prayers and other Sunday rituals and therefore unpredictably timed, which meant that Miguel had no way of knowing what direction she would take, or at what time, or whether she would ride near Tremain at all. The anticipation of waiting for her and sharing uninterrupted moments with her was now lost to him. He had to be content with seeing her only in the presence of others.

But he had acquainted himself thoroughly with the new routine of her life. He knew that she unlocked the pottery each morning and then allocated the morning's quota of clay for various requirements. By the time this was done Meg would have arrived and together they would start wedging it. As additional workers were recruited and the pottery's payroll extended she was able to delegate this preliminary work and to concentrate more on her own, with Olivia equally absorbed at her modelling stand and Amelia arriving from Medlar Croft mid-morning to deal with office demands. All Miguel had to do was to indulge his interest in the pottery by dropping in at various times, but he had to suppress the temptation to do it too often. He could then linger in Deborah's vicinity, watching as she worked. And with that he had to be content.

It wasn't enough, but even reminding himself that any other man would press his attentions without fear of rebuff failed to overcome his shyness. Deborah liked him, was perhaps even fond of him, and he was afraid of jeopardizing that tenuous relationship by trying to force it into something more. He could only console himself with the thought that at least he had no particular rival, that none of the men who pursued her at local events and monopolized her at hunt balls had a prior stake in her affections. So he must continue to wait, and hope.

Two months after the pottery opened, sufficient stock had been built up for a full earthenware firing. Stoneware, requiring as high a temperature as porcelain, had to wait until a requisite number of stoneware pieces had been produced. This meant that Deborah's wall sundial, even after it reached the bone-dry stage, still had to wait. Meanwhile, she was developing other ideas, encouraged by Olivia who had no doubts about the appeal of these primitive designs with their pronounced Mexican influence, but other people, especially dealers who expected to see repetitious conventional ware, viewed this new line with mixed feelings; puzzled, intrigued, or frankly not in favour. Who, they said, would want to buy what they considered to be crude symbols of some ancient culture?

Others disagreed, arguing that sophisticated taste would be delighted with them and that artistic circles in London and major cities would welcome them. All were agreed that they would certainly be a change from mass-produced designs of flowers and fruit and the usual emblems.

If it had not been for Olivia, who countered criticism with: 'Wait until they are glazed, wait until they are fired, wait until you see the rare whiteness of the clay . . .', Deborah might well have lost heart. She was too new to the work to be confident of her talent.

Then Jessica offered further encouragement by suggesting that she and Miguel should browse in Ashburton's extensive library, where they could study volumes on anthropological art which could supplement the designs gleaned from his mother's domestic items and her few pieces of native jewellery.

'I well remember coming to Ashburton to catalogue the Armstrong library, and the valuable research Martin put in there when he began as a lone potter. That was one of the several ways in which dear Sir Neville helped my brother to get started. The volumes on oriental ceramics that inspired him are still there, and there are others on South American cultures that could do the same for Deborah, with your help, Miguel.'

He thought it incredibly fortunate that her mother should unintentionally give him this opportunity to spend time alone with her daughter, and when Deborah joined him one day – the first time they had been alone together since the Ashburton Pottery was launched – he felt, for the first time, that she had joined him because she wanted to and that the study of Mexican motifs was not the only reason.

Miguel was determined to become the owner of her sundial, and knew exactly where he would place it at Tremain – on a wall beside the entrance to the Heir's Wing, his own. There he would be able to see it every day and reach up and touch it, tracing the intricacies of a cylindrical border from Guerrero, featured on a copper necklace of his mother's, into which Deborah had skilfully interwoven the mask of Ehecatl, the wind god, and Tlaloc, the rain god, with wild game birds on the wing as a centrepiece. The combination made an original and somehow apt design for a sundial and although she would undoubtedly produce better work with experience, he would treasure this one not only because it was her first, but because it had brought them together, if not in the way he desired.

The association was better than nothing, however. She now

135

sought his opinion on preliminary sketches, some of which she discarded and some of which she saved for further development, with still others set aside to feature in future projects.

'But only if *you* like them will I use them,' she said one day.

'Surely the test is whether others will like them enough to buy them?'

'Don't you think they will?' she asked anxiously.

'How can I say? It may be because I am half Mexican that these designs appeal to me.'

'But whether they will appeal to the English is another matter? That is what some think; I have seen it in their eyes, hastily concealed for my sake.'

'Someone specifically?'

'Cousin Lionel. I'm quite sure he doesn't like it, though he declares that he does. He is very amiable these days. He makes me feel almost guilty for turning against him.'

Had she really turned against him, or had her swift resentment over his treatment of Amelia been overcome by his determination to win her over? His frequent and apparently casual visits to Ashburton had not escaped Miguel and made him wonder how many other times he passed this way. He could not resist asking.

'Does he come here often? I would have expected otherwise following your father's refusal to supply Drayton's with the new grinding powder.'

'Lionel seems to have forgotten that, and I must say he accepted the decision very well. Not a word of reproach, no hint of resentment. He seems incapable of harbouring malice. Perhaps he isn't as bad as we think. Perhaps we have misjudged him. He has behaved thoughtlessly, yes, but he does have much to occupy his mind these days. Have you heard that he is building a storage cellar at Drayton's? Papa declares that it is folly, but Lionel insists that a new set of plans overcomes earlier uncertainties.'

'And what does your father say?'

'That to be convinced he would have to see the new plans and that anything redesigned at such speed must be suspect. I felt quite sorry for Lionel when Papa said that.'

'I would back your father's opinion.'

'All the same – poor Lionel. One must admit that he is trying hard to make a success of things.'

'By getting rid of people who have devoted their lives to the place?'

'Miguel! I have never heard that note in your voice before. He insists that he had no intention of hurting Amelia but acted in

136

what he honestly believed were her best interests. I think we should give him the benefit of the doubt.'

'And what of Olivia?'

'She seems to have forgiven and forgotten.'

And have you? he wanted to ask but, fearing that his voice would betray him, Miguel said nothing. When Deborah made a list of page numbers, closed the volumes, and rewarded him with a brilliant smile, his depression lifted slightly; even more when she kissed his cheek spontaneously and declared he was the best friend she had, then danced away, saying over her shoulder that he absolutely must stay to supper and looking quite disconsolate when he declined.

Much as he wanted to accept the invitation, he felt that he was perhaps neglecting his father a little too much these days. Sometimes the old man was quite tetchy when he returned after a long absence at Ashburton. 'It's nice to know I have a son after all,' he would growl, and Miguel would make up for his neglect by playing endless games of backgammon with him – taking care to let him win – and then lull his sense of duty further by visiting Aunt Agatha to say good-night. Sometimes that made her quite tearful and he felt then that she was wishing he were her son . . . that dear, devoted son who was plainly pursuing Deborah and to whom Deborah, in return, was seemingly too forgiving.

Although Olivia appeared to have forgiven and forgotten, she had not, and Lionel was well aware of it. He had only to meet her in passing to realize that despite her polite and amiable greeting she disliked him as much as she had done from childhood. When he troubled to reflect on it, it amused him, but these days he had little time in which to think about anything other than the cellar construction that he was hastily putting in hand. No time had been wasted in approving the new plans; he had scarcely glanced at the details, so impatient was he for completion. The builder from Stoke obviously knew what he was doing and, being newly launched as an independent contractor, would be doubly conscientious because he had his reputation to think of. All this, to Lionel, was reassuring.

And really the plan was so much better than the one drawn up by Simon Kendall, who must be getting past things, at his age. The new one was so simple, too; just one single drawing instead of all those unnecessary ones from a variety of aspects and angles, showing varying levels and elaborating on details and measurements. All that was meaningless to a layman, and in this respect

Lionel freely confessed to being one. He was therefore a great deal happier dealing with a builder who didn't expect him to ask questions, much less to understand the answers. Each man to his own allotted task, Lionel thought complacently. That made life much simpler.

It seemed that in no time at all the area was dug out and the foundations laid. Naturally, since he was paying the bill, Lionel inspected every stage and it all appeared to be satisfactory. The builder assured him that great care was being taken to fortify the walls with doubly strong brickwork, so there could be no doubt about the safety factor.

Everyone took an interest in the procedure, including Dave Jefferson who, to Lionel's surprise, made no comment at all. When the steps were built – wooden, to save labour and costs, but of course guaranteed to be sound – Lionel invited his deputy to descend with him and inspect the whole area. Still silent, Dave did so, pausing only to ask what the smaller room was intended for.

'For storing the most valuable pieces, of course. The finest Draytonware will be locked in there.'

'But no piece is more valuable than another, sir. Not at Drayton's. We make utility products –'

'And fine china. And porcelain. You should be proud of our finest products, Jefferson.'

'I am, sir. But since no one's ever pilfered them why expect it now? And locks can be broken, sir.'

'Not the one I have chosen for this door. Wait until you see it.'

With that, Lionel ordered the man back to work. Sometimes he sensed, or suspected, an underlying note in his foreman's manner, a veiled suggestion of criticism or even dislike, but the latter idea was immediately dismissed. Lionel decided that he was becoming too sensitive, imagining hostility where none existed. He had overcome all that earlier trouble and could now forget it.

Turning to more pleasurable things, he thought of Abby and how surprised she would be when she first visited that inner room. For a long time he had been pondering on the best place to rendezvous with her. Once or twice he had allowed her to visit Carrion House, but only when the servants were abed, when she could slip down the side lane and through the kitchen entrance. Even that was risky. Although the domestic staff slept in the attics, one never knew; sounds might be heard and an inquisitive or apprehensive servant creep downstairs to check on the cause.

Besides, his home was really too good for the likes of Abby, the daughter of Burslem's loosest woman. Kate was a familiar sight to Lionel, as she was to all the men around, her raddled face, coarse manner and gaudy clothes plainly advertising her trade. Lionel had no desire for a woman like that to present herself at the door of Carrion House, demanding money for her daughter's services or threatening to tell the world about the girl's secret visits there. Not even that shabby garden house in which his father had met his death was safe enough.

And, illogically, there was another reason for disliking the thought of Abby Walker becoming a familiar guest in his home – it was the thought that she would be preceding Deborah Kendall who, he was beginning to hope, might occupy his bed permanently. There was no law against the marriage of first cousins, nor did the Church forbid it although, illogically it seemed to him, it forbade the union of some less close relationships.

There was something challenging about Deborah; her insouciance, her independence, her charm, her casual air, her occasional flares of defiance, her impetuosity, her warmth, her gaiety – all these characteristics suggested passion. Making love to her would be very different from satisfying himself with a silly little whore who was pleased with a few baubles.

But silly little whores could get above themselves if allowed to imagine that they were good enough to enter a man's home. It was therefore wiser to keep Abby well away from there. So far, that small room off his office had sufficed, but could not continue to. Too many people called on a master potter, and although he continued to excercise care by admitting Abby only when everyone had gone home, if she lingered too long and too often her fellow-workers could begin to wonder why. They would notice if she persistently stayed behind. Perhaps they had done so already, but as long as they didn't see her hurry across the yard to his door, no matter. They could imagine she lingered for different reasons, for a different man.

But there was the additional risk of a late worker encountering some emergency that would bring him hurrying to the Master Potter's office in the hope that he had not gone home, such as a fire man appointed to keep his eye on an overnight firing. And although Lionel made sure that the place appeared to be dark and empty, one never knew . . . a chink of lamplight might filter through the cracks of that inner door.

But the cellar room was a different proposition. Not only could he keep it locked, but access to this new basement area was out of sight, situated round a corner away from the worksheds. Abby was a bright little thing, sensible in her way, quite capable of making sure that she slipped along to that entrance, not only when the coast was clear but speedily and nimbly. The distance was less than crossing the potters' yard.

The new room fulfilled all his expectations. So pleased was he with the builder's work that he even added a bonus. 'That's for your diligence and the speed at which you completed the job,' he said, promising to call the man again if and when he needed further construction carried out. There was mutual satisfaction on both sides and Lionel wasted no time in preparing the room and introducing Abby to it.

'My!' she breathed, inspecting it thoroughly. 'Carpet'n all! An' them cushions – look at the size of 'em! Pity it can't be a bed though. I likes it better in a bed.'

'One can't have everything, Abby. It was tricky enough to explain the need for a carpet in a cellar. Tiresome, too. A master potter shouldn't have to make excuses for anything.'

'Then why did ye? An' wot did ye say? 'An who wanted to know about it, anyways?'

'Young Jefferson. He seems to think his new position entitles him to probe where he has no right to probe.'

'Well, I dunno about that, but I do know Dave ain't young. Rising eight-an'-twenty.'

At that the Master Potter laughed and told her to strip and be quick about it. 'You'll find those cushions just as comfortable as a bed . . .'

And she did. And everything seemed fine until, when it was over and she lay naked and unabashed she gazed around and said, 'Feels kinda shut in, don't it? Needs a winder or two, don't it?'

'You can't have windows in cellars.'

'Well, *I*'ve seen 'em. When me mam's bin broke she's gone scrubbing at them big 'ouses of rich folk, an' when I were small she'd take me along with 'er, an' down in them coal cellars there'd be bars up near the ceiling for vent – venti –'

'Ventilation. That has been taken care of in the main cellar here.'

'Then why not in this 'un?'

'It wasn't practical.'

Surely she was bright enough to realize that light would penetrate through an open-barred ventilator and shine across the ground outside? He hoped she wasn't going to be tiresome. He hadn't gone to all this trouble and expense for nothing.

140

Abby retorted, 'Then we'd best leave the door open next time so's this ventilation ye talks about can come in 'ere too. Then 't'won't be so stuffy. I don't like that funny smell, neether. Musty-like.'

'That's due to the newness of the place. When thoroughly aired, the mustiness will go.'

''T'won't air if no air can get in.'

'The whole place has to dry out,' he answered irritably.

'Then it'd best dry out quick, Master Potter, or this fine carpet'll be ruined. Real damp it is. Take a feel.'

She had rolled off the piled cushions and now jumped to her feet, rubbing her body and then reaching for her clothes. Looking down at him she said cheerily, 'Don't worry, Master Potter. I don't mind if we do it with t'door open. Nobbody's like t'come down 'ere, so I can't think why ye've locked it.' She was dressing hurriedly. For the first time in his recollection, she was eager to be gone. To demonstrate his annoyance he took his time, keeping her waiting for the customary reward.

Feeling the damp carpet beneath his feet, he regretted not waiting until the place had thoroughly dried before having the floor covered. If he now took the precaution of leaving the door ajar during the day, the additional comforts he had installed would arouse comment. His excuse – that the carpet was a precaution against breakages should any fine porcelain be dropped while being stored here – would then cease to pull the wool over Dave Jefferson's eyes.

Perhaps he should think of getting rid of that young man, or at least of promoting someone less alert in his place. Or perhaps he should have retained the less observant Willis?

'Oh sir, please 'urry. I wanta get 'ome. Me mam'll be wonderin' where I be.'

'She will be wondering nothing of the sort. Your mother, at this moment, will be occupied with her own trade.'

Abby exploded.

'"Trade", d'ye call it! Let me tell ye, Master Potter, it be a profession. She told me so, years ago. "The oldest profession in the world," she said. An' that ain't low, like a trade, sir. No ways it ain't.'

She couldn't understand why he laughed. She didn't like being laughed at. Sulkily, and without even pausing to see what it was worth, she pocketed the coin he tossed her.

A ripple of interest ran through Burslem and its environs when it

141

was heard that the ladies' pottery at Ashburton had completed its first earthenware bisque-firing. Fifty-four hours of cooling, and then the kiln would be broached and the results known. Meanwhile, a stock of stoneware items was being built up. One of the clay workers employed there, a villager from Cooperfield, bragged about it in the Red Lion on his weekly outing one Sunday night.

People from outlying villages were often patronized by the natives of Burslem. 'Come t'see a bit of life, eh? A nice change f'thee, likely, buried out there 'midst t'pigs!' But the minute he mentioned the Ashburton Pottery, folks pricked up their ears and he enjoyed some rare attention. Everyone, it seemed, was eager to hear how the two eccentric ladies were getting along.

'Lucky for them they've got money to back'em,' someone said sourly, to which the Cooperfield man retorted, 'Lucky for they as are working for'em, y'mean! There be four full-time pot workers there now, counting in Meg Tinsley – and *she* wouldn't't've quit Drayton's if it 'adn't been worth 'er while! An' mark me words, there'll be many like Tinsley as'll be willing to trudge a few miles t'work at the Ashburton Pottery. Treats ye well, they does. Reel ladies, they be. An' ye never seed stoneware the like of Ashburton's. Whiter than any *I*'ve ever seed! Next firing'll make all the potteries sit up.'

It was a wild claim that no one believed. Stoneware was never white. It was greyish, dun-coloured, strong, the colour of stone – which was why it was so named. But here was this man, talking freely after a few pints of Staffordshire ale, bragging about Ashburton's being better than any used elsewhere. A man spoke the truth when in his cups; that was the time to listen. So everyone listened.

'Wait 'til ye sees it! Even M's 'Livia's using it now.'

That aroused only derision. Everyone knew that stoneware was rarely used for modelling – at least, not the kind of modelling Olivia Freeman was renowned for. Porcelain was her favourite, or fine china, or – if requested – good quality earthenware. Apart from stout kitchen and oven pots, stoneware was used mainly for exterior stuff like garden urns and statuary because it could withstand the elements. None of that was Olivia Freeman's field.

Muttering into his glass darkly, the villager from Cooperfield told them to wait and see.

To Lionel, when he paid one of his now regular courtesy calls, it seemed that there was nothing outstanding about the Ashburton earthenware product, nothing to represent competition. He was surprised to see none of Olivia's fine modelling. In the main, the stock consisted of the usual domestic ware produced by most pot banks. There was no likelihood of any rival establishment being eclipsed by it.

He judged that the stuff would sell well enough in surrounding towns and villages, but would have to be packed and taken there because dealers would be disinclined to journey out to Ashburton specifically to buy it. Curiosity might persuade some to go and see the first firing results, but these would not encourage them to return. Dealers and traders liked to go from pottery to pottery, loading up with supplies. Any journey to outlying pot banks was not worth the trouble unless the ware was outstanding or unusual or other potteries were within reach. Time was time and money was money – so went the saying in Staffordshire – and few had much of either to waste.

With her customary perception, Olivia knew what her cousin was thinking.

'A first firing needs to take no chances,' she said. 'Until it is known how a kiln behaves, a good potter doesn't risk more valuable ware. Hence this conventional load. We can be more venturesome next time. Meanwhile, it's good to know that the chamber is reliable, though we expected as much from something designed and built by Simon Kendall. Everything has fired evenly and well. At this stage, we ask for no more than that. In an average firing a measure of wastage is expected, but in this one it was minimal.'

'Then you have done well, Livvy. I congratulate you and wish you many substantial orders.'

There was no need to congratulate Amelia, who contributed nothing to the creative side, so he merely greeted her with the dutiful respect of a nephew. Meg Tinsley he acknowledged with nothing more than a curt inclination of the head, though he could have complimented her on the excellence of her work. Every Ashburton pot was faultlessly turned. At least no purchaser would have to examine each one to make sure of that.

Courtesies exchanged, he then sought out Deborah, and found her totally absorbed. She scarcely raised her eyes when he greeted her, but when he stooped over her shoulder to see what she was doing, and remained with his face close to hers, she said calmly but not ungraciously, 'I find it disconcerting to be watched, Cousin Lionel, and I dislike people breathing down my neck.'

He withdrew, laughing and apologetic.

'Forgive me, but you know what a boor I am, dear Deborah!'

'I know, and *you* know, you are nothing of the sort. You are a sophisticated man and sophisticated men pride themselves on their good manners, so when I ask you not to hinder me at work, I know you'll heed it.'

'But I may browse awhile, may I not? That is what customers like to do and you would surely not discourage them.'

'But you aren't a customer.'

'Am I not?' he murmured with a secret smile, deciding there and then to surprise her. Glancing round, he added, 'And there is so much her to browse amongst! How busy you've been!'

'The majority is Olivia's work, not mine. I have produced only a few pieces so far, but she set to work long before the pottery was launched.'

He scarcely heard that because his attention was caught by the surprising number of large pieces, the like of which had never featured in Olivia Freeman's work. There were large-scale models of wildlife and an even greater amount of garden statuary. He was particularly struck by their whiteness, which indicated that nearly all were ready for bisque-firing.

Strolling from piece to piece he commented, 'White earthenware, I take it . . .'

Deborah neither confirmed nor denied it. To all intents and purposes she was unaware of him again. He looked at her bent head and wondered what was going on inside it. Could she be so totally absorbed in the slab of clay on which she was building up a bas-relief apparently inspired by a drawing propped up before her?

'Did you sketch that, pretty Deb?'

She nodded and indicated that he could examine it, if he wished. He did so, and was baffled. Art in any form was beyond him so he could not imagine what this maze of geometrical lines, embellished with what seemed to him to be hieroglyphics, was supposed to represent.

Deborah smiled. For the first time, he had her attention.

'It is an idea of my own, inspired by a primitive Mexican design from Oaxaca coupled with another from San Andres and a sun motif from Chiapas.'

At his expression, she burst out laughing. The sound delighted him but failed to quell a spasm of jealousy. That half-Mexican outsider had plainly been influencing her.

A moment later even that was forgotten when he halted beside a trestle table bearing a large square slab of finished work slowly drying out. From the look of it, it was almost ready for its first firing. It was plainly a wall sundial with a border surrounding a central motif of partridge and pheasant. That part, at least, he recognized, but the border was unlike anything he had seen before. Whether he liked it he was unsure, but he found it compelling.

'Is this yours, Deborah? Is this the design you brought along to Drayton's and I was fool enough to let you take away?'

She smiled.

'The very same. The outer area is Guerrero-inspired, and the masks are of the Mexican gods Ehecatl and Tlaloc.'

'My dear cousin, that sounds very impressive but such unpronounceable names are foreign to me.'

She laughed. 'So they were to me, at first.'

'I suppose Miguel soon put that right.' He regretted saying that. Even more he regretted the tone because it betrayed how he felt, so he hurried on, 'I would like this for the wall at Carrion House. I'll buy it as soon as it's glaze-fired.'

'I'm not sure that it will be. If it is, then salt-glaze will suffice. Much depends on the bisque-firing. If hard enough to be weatherproof, it will be left in its natural state so that, in time, it will blend with surrounding stonework.'

'Then I take it this is the new stoneware clay that Drayton's originally commissioned . . .'

She didn't want to discuss that and was sorry he had mentioned it. The atmosphere had been amiable until then. Anxious to restore it, and refusing to discuss her father's refusal to supply Drayton's with the new flint powder, she said hurriedly, 'Please don't buy the sundial because you want to let bygones be bygones. I am sure everyone wants that.'

I doubt it, he thought, but said, 'I want to buy it because *you* made it, because it is your very first piece –'

'I shall make better ones.'

'I want this one.'

'You have sundials at Carrion House already.'

That was true. He didn't need another, didn't really want another, but because she seemed reluctant to part with it he was immediately more determined, so he pointed out that those he already owned were freestanding and were already there when he inherited the place, and therefore not of his personal choice. 'I have no wall sundial and this would look extremely well above the main door of the house . . .'

But not too high above; near enough for him to be able to

145

reach out and touch it when he felt so inclined, tracing the ornamentation she had created, following the lines her fingers had touched. No, he didn't need it and had it been for sale in any other pottery he would not have considered buying it at all, but here was a chance to forge a new link in their relationship, a chance to repair one broken bridge. And it provided an excuse for more contact with her while waiting for delivery; he could call to inquire about it, to find out when it was being fired, to be there when it came out of the kiln. So buy it he would.

'I insist on your reserving it for me, sweet Deb. Tell me the price and I'll close the deal at once.'

'I don't know the price. That has nothing to do with me. To reserve it, you must see Olivia and for the financial side you must see Amelia.'

'Then I shall do so at once. But if you were to put a word in for me, I would surely be less likely to miss it?' Standing close to her now he sensed that she was excited about the sale of her first piece of work, and trying not to show it. 'Dear Deborah, you won't mind my having it, surely?'

'Of course not. Why should I?' She smiled suddenly. 'How can I pretend? It would be unnatural for me not to be pleased.'

'About the sale, or because the sundial will be mine? The latter, I hope.' He put out a hand and touched her cheek. 'Dear Deborah, please say it is the latter; say you *want* me to have it . . .'

'If you genuinely want it, of course I do. Come, I'll take you to Olivia. Her new modelling room will interest you, I'm sure.'

'I'm damned if it will. I'm interested only in *your* work . . . in you . . . in us. Come to Drayton's, sweet Deborah. I want you there.'

Before she could draw away he seized both her hands, kissing each in turn. He was gratified when he felt a slight trembling in them, but not when he looked up and she burst out laughing. Clay from her fingers was imprinted on his mouth. Shaking with mirth, she pulled a kerchief from the pocket of her hessian apron and held it out. 'Oh, Lionel – I'm sorry – but if you could see your handsome clay moustache!'

The intimate moment was gone. He took it well. Wiping his mouth carefully, he then thrust the piece of cambric into his pocket. 'You won't get this back, my tantalizing cousin. I shall keep it as a souvenir to remind me of the day we did our first business transaction, though actually it will remind me more vividly of something else. I see you're not going to ask me what that is, so I'll tell you. It will remind me of my admirable self-restraint.'

Puzzled, she asked, 'In what way?'

'In resisting the temptation to kiss you. At least you have no clay on your mouth and *I* would have had no false moustache. What a pity I resisted!'

Skilfully, she avoided him. 'Come,' she said, 'I'll take you to Olivia . . .'

'I would prefer Amelia. And I'll pay in advance to ensure that the sundial is mine. And furthermore I'll tell her that you want me and no one else to have it. That is the truth, I hope.'

'Since I know of no one else who wants it, the answer, I suppose, can only be yes.'

Her voice was light and that pleased him because she plainly had to make it so.

CHAPTER 13

'Why do you visit that silly pottery so much, dear boy?'

'Perhaps it isn't so silly as we imagined, Mama. It's small, but efficiently run. Amelia appears to be coping well and, although there's no love lost between Olivia and myself, I also have to admit she is skilled. And since you are a woman yourself, isn't it illogical to call it "silly" because it's run by women?'

Agatha dodged that. Chewing contentedly on pickled pigeon stuffed with hard egg yolks, marrow, sweet herbs and spices, she insisted that he was being very forgiving, though how he could be, she couldn't imagine . . .

'. . . nor how you can wish them well, even though one *is* my sister and your aunt, and the other my niece and your cousin. I can only think that blood is thicker than water after all, but even so I consider you are being *most* charitable. Who else would hold out the hand of friendship to people who turned their backs? That is what they did to you, the pair of them. *And* worse. Setting up in opposition to their own kin, indeed! Yet you visit there often, Max tells me.'

'And how does he know? From that son of his, I suppose. He is forever hovering about the place, currying favour.'

'Miguel – currying favour? I've never known him to do that.

Quite the reverse. Sometimes I think he is too retiring by half. *Much* too shy. I have told him so very often.'

'Have you, indeed? You sound fond of him.'

'He has been very kind to me over the years.'

'Currying favour with you too? But as for my visiting the Ashburton Pottery, why shouldn't I? You once hinted that I had made a mistake in persuading Amelia to leave Drayton's. Have you forgotten that? And aren't you attaching too much importance to this new venture? With so much opposition in the potteries, how can the pair of them possibly succeed?'

Agatha pursed her lips, her tier of chins settling in folds beneath, and said reflectively, 'We-ell . . . perhaps you're right . . . but with those two men behind them, two influential men let me remind you, their chances of success may be greater than you think. Can you afford to encourage them with friendly visits?'

'My dear mother, friendly visits are a far better way of finding out what is going on, than relying on rumour or gossip.'

At that, she beamed.

'My *clever* boy! So that's what you're up to! And there was I, fearing your generous nature was likely to rebound onto you, biting the hand of friendship.'

Sometimes his mother's metaphors were singularly inept, but in this instance Lionel knew what she meant. But how tedious she was! And what a twittering fool! And he couldn't take his leave for at least another hour . . .

Stifling a yawn he said, 'You look tired, Mama.'

'Dear boy, I am not in the least tired. Not with you for company. Do have more of this excellent Carrier Sauce, so delicious with pigeon despite the conventional idea that it is only suitable for mutton – dear Pierre can prove the best cooks in the world to be wrong! And that's right, help yourself to another glass of Burgundy. And you'll be pleased to hear that Pierre will be sending up some of his splendid Souster because he remembers how much you loved it as a child –'

'I am not a child now,' he interrupted impatiently. He was glad she had dismissed the hovering servants and that the Burgundy had been left close at hand. In getting through a wearisome evening it helped considerably. And when at last he made his escape he would head straight back to Drayton's and let himself in with his master key, leaving the gates unlocked so that Abby could do the same shortly after.

Her agreement had been somewhat reluctant because she disliked going down to the cellar. 'Why can't it be somewhere else?' she had demanded fretfully. 'Why not same as afore? Or why can't I come to Carrion 'Ouse when everybody's asleep? You've let me, once or twice.'

'Only as a temporary measure, until I could make these better arrangements.'

'I don't like 'em,' she had answered mutinously, to which he had replied that what she liked or disliked concerned him not in the least. She could accept his conditions, or not at all. At that, she had begun to snivel, complaining that these days she wasn't a bit happy and that nothing was turning out the way she had expected and even her mam wasn't the same to her any more. 'I can't think why. I ain't done nuffink but what she wanted me t'do.'

It was all becoming rather tiresome. Abby herself was becoming tiresome. And he hoped she wasn't going to drag in that dreadful mother of hers. If so, he would send the pair of them packing.

But he had not finished with Abby yet; he still wanted her, still enjoyed her, so it wasn't yet time to end the affair. Nor did he regret the installation of that secret room, which would no doubt prove to be useful in other ways if and when it ceased to serve its current purpose. Meanwhile, it was comfortably furnished and very handy, and why silly little Abby had taken such a dislike to a room which was better than anything she had known in her life, was beyond his comprehension.

Ah well, he thought as he refilled his glass, she would get over it. Meanwhile, his thoughts turned to Deborah, as they were doing frequently of late. It might please his mother to learn the real object of his visits to the Ashburton Pottery since she was forever harping on the question of his marriage. Either she was lecturing him on his duty to beget a son and heir, or saying simperingly that she yearned to be a grandmother with children clustering at her knees. Dear God, what a bore she was!

At last the meal was over and he could conveniently take his leave. When his mother embraced him it was like being enfolded in a mound of billowing bolsters, but he endured it. The dribbles of gravy and sauce on the cascading lace of her bodice heightened the illusion that she had been dining in bed, but he tolerated that too. Even when her plump, beringed hands patted and mauled him, he made no attempt to evade her. If Aunt Amelia could have seen him now, never again would she have been able to accuse him of not being a dutiful son.

The last test of endurance came when Agatha ran her hands

over his shoulders and sleeves, down the front of his elegant brocade coat and even inside the wide, buttoned-back cuffs to see if his valet was caring for his clothes properly.

At last she said grudgingly, 'We-ell, he's improving, I'll grant him that. Those buttons are sewn on better than the last time I examined them, but only a mother can really care for her son's wardrobe. I will come to Carrion House one day soon to check on the rest of your garments.'

'My dear mother, you do that so regularly that you scarcely leave the man anything else to do!' And it annoys him as much as it annoys me, he wanted to add, but commendably refrained. He was being remarkably stoic and courteous tonight.

On an impulse he decided to extend his courtesy by visiting his uncle before leaving. It could be interesting to learn just how much Maxwell Freeman did know about his visits to Ashburton and how and why Miguel had commented on them. Secretly, he was rather pleased about that. If the youth was jealous, so much the better.

Leaving the West Wing and entering the main part of the house, he came face to face with Miguel descending the impressive staircase which, as a boy, he himself had found awesome in its grandeur. He had never tired of gazing at it and of secretly ascending and descending, imagining himself as lord of the manor, when no one was about. In this way he had indulged one of his strongest fancies. Another had been to picture himself standing at the head of this staircase, receiving guests; Master of Tremain, monarch, ruler, king absolute.

It was a dream he had fully expected to be fulfilled. Instead, he thought bitterly as he halted at the sight of Miguel, that enviable role would be inherited by this half-breed, to whom it would mean nothing. What sort of a creature *was* he to be content with the life he now led, alone in this vast place with a couple of ageing people? Dear God, what a *waste* it was that Tremain should come to such as he, when all that had come his own way was the Carrion bequest and a family business that was proving to be nothing but an anxiety!

Managing an affable smile, Lionel said, 'I was on my way to see your father. I thought a visit might cheer him.'

'He has just retired. But it was good of you to think of it.'

'Pray remember me to him.'

'I will do so, most certainly.'

The ensuing pause was awkward, both trying to think of something to say.

'Then I'll take my leave . . .'

Miguel accompanied him. The youth was always so damned *polite* . . .

Lionel said, 'I take it you've been to Ashburton today?'

'To the pottery – yes.'

'You go there frequently?'

'As often as I may. I don't like to intrude.'

'My dear fellow, don't be so damned humble! That's always a mistake.'

'It's also a mistake to interpret reticence as humility,' Miguel retorted sharply.

That startled Lionel, who had never credited Miguel with much spirit. It also vexed him. He wanted to retaliate, but could think of nothing suitable, so he said smoothly, 'You saw Deborah, I take it?'

'Briefly. She was hard at work.'

They had reached the main entrance. Without summoning a footman, Miguel lifted the heavy iron latch and opened the door. Lionel ignored it and said, 'I expect she was working on another sundial. The sale of her first one must have been encouraging.'

To his satisfaction, it was Miguel's turn to be startled.

'The *sale* –?'

'Haven't you heard? Did no one tell you, not even Deborah although she herself sold it?'

'To whom?' It was plainly an effort to ask.

'To me. Only a few days ago. She was delighted to let me have it. I too am pleased. It will look well above the door of Carrion House.'

'I don't like it, Meg. I don't like any of it.'

'From the sound o'things, I don't neether.'

And that was putting it mildly, she thought. If what Dave said was true, she hated everything about it. The awful thing was that she felt no surprise; only a terrible sadness, a despair.

'You be sure that cellar be where they meet?'

'I'll wager a week's wages on it. Why else has it been done up the way it has? Real carpet, and stacks of cushions . . .'

'In a *cellar*?'

'Aye. He explained that the carpet is to safeguard against breakages. The best porcelain and china is to be stored there – leastways, so he sez – an' some might be dropped by accident. But that don't explain the cushions. He don't know I've seen 'em, o'course. I'm keeping mum about that. But the door were open a

151

crack when I went by one night. I'd stayed on purpose, I were that determined to take a look down there when nobbody were around. It looked as if it'd bin left ajar on purpose, so's summun could get in. Through the crack I saw all them cushions piled on the floor. Like a bed. I got outa that cellar quick, not just because I weren't supposed t'be there but because there'd've been hell t'pay if I'd been caught. It were after hours an' I'd no cause t'be down there – but there were another reason. If Abby were heading that way, I didn't want to meet her – didn't want *her* to see *me* or it'd be the end between us. Such as there be to end,' he finished unhappily.

'So ye went there 'cos ye guessed wot were going on . . .'

'No. For summat else. It were after that heavy rainfall awhile back an' I were worrit. I remembered Master Kendall's warning about the risk of seepage from canal an' Master Martin deciding not to go ahead for that reason. It would've had to be extra fortified, an' a long job an' a costly one that would've been – but this cellar's been dug out an' constructed in no time at all, an' I tell ye straight, Meg, I don't like it. The place ain't safe. If Abby does go down there –'

'She won't, lad. She's got more sense than to head for trouble.'

'She's taken leave of 'er senses. She's besotted. Why else do she linger after everyone be gone? More'n more folk are noticing that, 'specially the turners. Things in that shed ain't wot they useter be when it were yourn. Them women quarrel an' wrangle one with t'other –'

'*My* girls? There were now't o' that in my day, so why now?'

Dave rubbed a tired hand across tired eyes and Meg's heart went out to him. This was the first time they had met since he had declared his intention to continue at Drayton's for as long as Abby remained there. And all he had reaped for his pains was anxiety.

'I'd like t'shake some sense into the girl,' Meg declared hotly.

''T'wouldn't do no good. She be stubborn as a mule, these days. But for all that, she ain't happy. I can tell. We've gotta do summat, Meg. You'n me.'

'Sounds like ye've tried, lad – an' got nowhere.'

'Aye. That be true. I just thought mebbe if we put our heads t'gether we might come up with an answer. Remember how you wanted her to go with you to Ashburton?'

'That can't be done by snapping our fingers and saying "Hey, presto!" The first thing is t'get Abby away from that ma of 'ers, because so long as she's under Kate's influence she'll follow her lead . . .'

'I'm afeared that once started she'll continue that way even if the woman does go out of her life. Left alone in that hovel, the coast'd be clear for Abby t'do wot she liked.'

'Seems *I*'ve got more faith in 'er than you, Dave lad.' Meg gave him a friendly shake. 'Ye wouldn't talk that way if ye weren't unhappy. I'll grant that left on 'er own Abby could be fair game for any man, but she's that right now. But she don't have to stay that way. Without her ma, I think she'd willingly clear outa that dump, and that'd be where *I* come in. Ye know I've allus wanted Abby to live along o'me 'til such time as she be wed, an' the new cottage at Ashburton would do us a treat. *And* 'tis almost ready. "Only one more thing needed," Master Kendall told me t'other day, 'an' wot d'ye think it be, Dave? A real cooking range, oven an' spit an' all! So now I can do summat, now I can act.'

When Dave asked what she planned to do, Meg gave him her wide, warm smile and said, 'Wait'n see, Dave. Wait'n see . . .'

'Good day to ye, Kate Walker.'

'Well, if it ain't 'igh'n mighty Meg Tinsley! Ain't ye too good for t'Red Lion since ye turned respectable?'

'I still enjoys a noggin now'n then, Kate. An' Joss Barlow's a good friend.'

'But not *that* kind, eh? Got none o'*them* now, 'ave ye?'

'Not since I were a wench.' Meg added proudly, 'Not since I wed. After Frank Tinsley there were no other. After such as he, there never could be.'

'So wot are ye doin' in t'Red Lion?'

'I were passing through Burslem an' thought I'd drop in an' see old friends.'

'That don't include me and well I knows it, tho' ye've no cause to go lookin' down on the likes o'me. I remember well wot ye were once upon a time.'

'I remember too,' Meg answered serenely. 'That's why I can count me blessings now.'

After that there seemed to be nothing more to say. Kate eyed Meg indifferently and Meg eyed Kate assessingly, thinking how much worse the woman looked. In a year or two she would be even more raddled and gin-soaked. Vindictive. Horrible.

'An' how be you faring these days, Kate?'

'Grand. Can't ye tell?'

Meg studied the tawdry finery. Becoming confidential, she said, 'Aye – anyone can see you be doing fine, but ye deserve

153

much more than a place like Burslem can offer. Ye be wasted here. I've allus thought that. I'm surprised ye've never packed up an' headed for the big cities, like Liverpool with its ship-owners, or Leicester, full of wealthy industrialists – or Nottingham. Now *there*'s a place! Lace factories.'

'Factories! *Me*? *I* ain't workin' in no bloody factory!'

'Who's suggesting it? C'm *on*, Kate, ye know wot I'm getting at. Men are men wherever they be, an' the rich ain't no different from the rest. I spent enough years in Liverpool to see how the rich ship-owners lived *and* how they amused themselves. It'll be the same in Leicester or Nottingham or Birmingham. Or how about Lunnon?'

'Too much competition there. Actresses an' the like.' Kate gave a knowing wink. 'D'ye think I've never 'ad a chance t'go there? Or other places too?'

'So why don't ye?'

'Desert me dear daughter? *Me*? Never! Abby be the apple o'me eye. I've allus done me duty as a mother. I could've gone to any big city in England an' done well for me'self, but not with a brat t'look after.'

'She's not a child any more, Kate. She'd be no handicap to ye now. Leastways, not in the same way . . .'

'Wot d'ye mean?'

'I mean she don't drag at your 'eels no more. No burden to ye. No responsibility. So ye be free, Kate Walker. Free to go where ye like an' live where ye like – an' prosper. But with a daughter to rival ye, an' one as be sure to cut thee out –'

Startled, Kate demanded even more sharply, '*Wot d'ye mean?*'

'Wot I sez. Abby's a young woman now. A woman afore 'er time, some might think. Taken a good look at 'er lately?'

' 'Course I 'ave! An' mighty proud of 'er I be. Doing well, is my Abby. *She* won't stay in that mucky trade much longer.' Kate finished proudly, 'She's found favour already, an' mighty high favour let me tell ye!'

'That's what I mean. Soon *she*'ll be the one every man'll be after. Not thee.'

'Shut yer bloody mouth!' Kate took a deep swig of gin, braced her shoulders in a mixture of anger and pride and then said in maudlin tones, 'I'd never desert me own child. I've allus bin a dutiful mother . . .'

'But will *she* do 'er duty by *thee*? Children leave the nest, an' a pretty one like Abby'll go quick. Ever thought about that? What'll ye do then, Kate? What'll ye do when you're left alone in a one-eyed place like Burslem? We all grow old. Where would *I* be if I couldn't work in the pot banks? Where'll *you* be when men want your daughter instead of yr'self? Ye may be proud 'cos she's found favour so soon, but ye oughta be afeared.'

Kate scoffed, 'That shows 'ow little ye knows. My Abby's all set for a fine life, an 'er mam along with 'er. Ye'd be surprised if ye knew the truth!'

'Mebbe. An' mebbe not. Other folk 'ave eyes an' ears an' other folk gossip. An' news travels fast. An' things never work out the way we expect'em to. Young or old, it don't. Only it be worse when you're old. Ye can start again when young, but not when –'

Kate called loudly for another gin before rounding on Meg again.

'Ye'd best get back to your turning wheel, Tinsley. Trouble is, being old 'n past it, ye be jealous.'

'You an' me happen t'be the same age, but it be true that men don't come after me no more. But like I said, Frank Tinsley spoilt me for other men. Luckily, I can still make a living, but what'll *thee* fall back on when the time comes? Not that ye need to worry – yet. There be still time for ye to prosper, but not in Burslem, where all the men know you be old enough to 'ave a growed-up daughter rivalling thee – an' start coming after her.'

Kate bragged, 'Fat chances they'll get wi' my Abby! She'll be set up well afore long.'

'Sure o' that, are ye? Well, I 'opes as 'ow ye be right. But it ain't Abby I be thinking about – it be you.'

'Why me, all of a sudden?'

'There's never bin no need afore. Ye've bin all set an' doing fine, but nothink in this world lasts for ever, ye can take it from me.' After finishing her noggin of small ale, Meg added, 'My, I wish I were in your shoes, that I do. I'd be thinking of them lace merchants an' their like in Nottingham – all stinkin' rich an' partial to women. Famous for it, the place is. Did ye know that when the new French weaving machines were brought over from Calais, French operators came with'em an' took up wi' the local wenches an' even married some of 'em? Those Frenchies 'ave eyes for good-lookers like y'rself, an' so do factory owners an' rich merchants an' they'd fair go for thee, Kate. It be wonderful, the way ye've kept your looks. An' yet ye still be living in that poky place in poky Burslem! Mebbe Abby *will* get a chance to quit it soon, but will thee?'

Uncertainly, Kate muttered that she would make sure of that.

'Will ye? I wonder. 'T'aint so easy. If Abby's got 'erself a rich protector, ye can mark me words that the man won't be willing to take 'er kith 'n kin aboard too. So there ye'll be, out on your ear, still living in a shack wot's ready t'fall about your ears. Ye deserve better and what's more, ye could get it. Now. Afore it be too late.'

Influenced either by the gin or Meg's alarming picture, Kate became suddenly tearful.

'Eeeh, if ye did but know the nights I've spent, nagged at by all that stuff about the serpent's tooth an' ungrateful childer an' wot'll 'appen t'me when Abby ups an' goes! Wot if she does the very thing ye've bin atellin' me, after the way I've devoted meself to 'er all 'er life! The sacrifices I've made, the care I've taken of 'er' – Kate sniffed loudly as she added – 'an' she's not so much as *shared* them pretty things she's bin given!'

'If ye mean them new bodices and suchlike, would they fit ye, Kate? Abby's a scrap of a thing, but you be – well – what I once 'eard M's Olivia describe as "Junoesque". I didn't know what it meant 'til she explained it, an' d'ye know who it put me in mind of, straight off? Thee. Kate Walker. I said as much, too, an' meant it. So I be glad ye've been thinking about the future, an' I'm real glad I dropped in at the Red Lion today. I know ye've never liked me, but we've never really got to know each other. A pity, pr'aps.'

'Aye,' sighed Kate. 'A pity. Mebbe ye're not so bad as I allus thought . . .'

'Nor you, neether.'

Well into her third gin, Kate actually smiled on Meg, then instantly reverted to tears.

'Trouble is, Meg, I can't get away 'cos I ain't got money. An' I've nivver bin beyond Burslem. I wouldn't even know 'ow t'go about it. I can't afford stage coaches . . .'

'No need. I were penniless when I quit Burslem for Liverpool.'

'Then 'ow'd ye get there?'

'On a crateman's cart. There ain't so many about now, but in them days there were cratemen aplenty. They useter lie in wait for potters taking their loads to the big towns, an' set about 'em an' loot 'em. But Zach Dobson were different. An honest old man. He took me all the way t'Liverpool to join Frank, an' it didn't cost nothink like a stage coach –'

'Nor feel like one, I reckon!'

'Oh, t'weren't so bad. It got me there. Bumpy roads are bumpy any way ye travel. Cratemen turned to tinkering when the canals come along, because they couldn't jump aboard barges and raid 'em. There be a few bad 'uns among the tinkers still, but a woman like you knows how to deal with suchlike. Ye can halt a tinker's cart up by the Hiring Cross, same as ever. That were where old Zach picked me up that morning, long afore anybody were awake.'

Meg didn't tell Kate that Frank had paid the man in advance and instructed him to deliver her safely to the seaman's mission on Liverpool's docks. The woman would have to make do with a tinker and take care of herself if needful. Knowing Kate, she would probably render services instead of a fare, though tinkers nowadays were glad to pick up passengers because they needed the money. That would be Kate's problem and she would know well enough how to handle it.

'So all ye have t'do,' Meg continued, 'is same as I did. Find out where they be going, an' if it be the place you aim for – say Nottingham – jump aboard. Ye'd like Nottingham, I reckon.'

'I'd still 'ave t'raise the fare.'

Meg rummaged in her pocket. 'That should do it.' she said, slapping down a small bag of coins. They happened to represent her entire savings, but it was worth it.

Kate could never resist money. She gathered it up, saying off-handedly that she would make no promises. 'I'll think about it,' she said.

'Then don't take too long. Act quick. Time moves fast at our age. An' if ye don't go, I'll be after ye for that money, every penny of it, mark my words.' Gathering up her shawl Meg finished, 'Good luck t'ye, Kate. An' God speed thee.'

Deborah was disappointed when Miguel failed to arrive for the unloading of the first stoneware firing.

It was a momentous day for the Ashburton Pottery, the day on which the success or failure of her father's work was to be finally proved, for although the clay and powder mixture had been carefully monitored during its preparation and had dried to a satisfactory whiteness, a bisque-firing could sometimes change a colour unpredictably, enhancing it or diminishing it.

Meg and the other clay workers gathered round for this important event, and Si Kendall's men marched up *en masse* from the valley. Damian left his forge, Simon his projects, and Jessica her manifold duties. Everyone wanted to share these crucial moments with Amelia and Olivia – except, apparently, Miguel who not only failed to arrive but sent no message to explain his absence.

Deborah reflected that perhaps she should not have taken him

157

so much for granted. The thought reproached her and somehow worsened her disappointment. Even reminding herself that she had possibly expected too much of someone who had known her since her early childhood, and could therefore regard her as nothing more than a life-long acquaintance, did little to assuage it. He had played such a big part in fostering her talent that she couldn't believe he was not interested in the fruits of it. All along he had displayed such an interest in the progress of her sundial that she had thought he would be eager to see it when fired.

Her disappointment was doubled when it emerged from the kiln and proved to be all that she had hoped for and more than she had expected. The whiteness was splendidly maintained, the surface strong and unmarred. It would mellow beautifully. *He should be here to see it!* she thought passionately. *WHY isn't he here to see it?*

'One hundred per cent success for the first thing you have ever made is something to be proud of,' Olivia told her, well pleased. 'And this is only the first.'

The first, yes, but the most important. It had changed the course of her life, adding another dimension to it, and for this Deborah had to thank Miguel as well as Olivia and the others. His absence saddened and puzzled her, and the reaction was intensified by unfamiliar feelings that she failed to understand.

Somehow everything was made worse by the fact that no one remarked on his absence. She felt this was deliberate and out of consideration for herself. Disturbed, she went back to work without waiting to see the full load emerge, and here her mother found her.

Placing an understanding hand on her shoulder, Jessica said, 'He will be very proud of it when he sees it. Proud of *you*, my darling. Please don't fret.'

Deborah was sufficiently at ease with her mother never to feel the need to hide things. 'But *why?* she burst out. 'I should have thought . . . expected . . . that he would have been as anxious as anybody to be here . . . as Damian was for Olivia's sake . . .'

She bit back the words. The relationship between those two was totally different from the relationship between herself and Miguel, which was no relationship at all other than friendship . . . and friendship never insisted that a person should be at another's side at important moments.

Jessica smoothed back her daughter's hair, kissed her brow, then asked how long it was since Miguel had visited the pottery, and Deborah promptly answered, 'More than a month, Mama . . . a whole month . . . and I have only just realized it . . .'

'Then *I* should think there was a reason, and if it worried me I would make it my business to find out what it was. His father isn't ill, that I know because I paid a call at Tremain only the day before yesterday and found him in fine fettle. But there may be some estate problem with which Miguel is having to cope. It would be the easiest thing in the world to find out.' She finished idly, 'Don't you ride over to Tremain any more?'

'Not since we launched this pottery. I don't have time to go so far afield.'

'You must make time. The exercise will not only do you good, but lighten your spirits. Why not take a holiday this afternoon? Go to Tremain and seek out Miguel. Only shyness could prevent a young woman from presenting herself at a man's door, and I have never known you to be shy – certainly not with Miguel. And because the pair of you are just good friends he could not possibly suspect any underlying motive . . .'

Deborah was grateful for the maternal advice; also for the gentle smile accompanying it, though why she felt there was something more behind that smile she could not imagine and was now too distracted to think about. With characteristic impetuosity, she flung aside her hessian apron and went speeding back to the house to change, scarcely heeding her mother's reminder about the weather.

'The rains were so heavy last night that the valley is like a quagmire, your father says. So do take care . . .'

Deborah called back over her shoulder, 'Don't I always, dear Mama?'

'No, dear daughter, you do not!'

But the girl had gone. Smiling to herself, Jessica retraced her steps. The last pieces of stoneware were being taken from the kiln and everyone was gathered round, examining the collective results. Spirits were high. 'What a splendid day,' Jessica said to her husband as she joined him. 'And I think it might be even more so . . .'

On seeing Deborah, Miguel's feelings were mixed. Swift delight gave way to a regret that she had come. Having decided to put an end to his obsession, and believing that this could be achieved by avoiding her, it was disconcerting to see her come riding along Tremain Hall's three-mile drive.

Head down against the driving rain she failed to see him until they drew abreast, then she cried, 'A fine thing it is that I should have to brave weather like this to fetch you to Ashburton!'

'Then why do so?'

'What a question! Have you actually forgotten that the kiln was being broached today?'

Rain was streaming from the brim of her black tricorne hat with its swirling ostrich feather. She could feel rivulets trickling down her neck and sodden gloves made it impossible for icy hands to grip the reins firmly.

'I am furious!' she declared.

'Then you'd best come indoors. There's a good fire in the library and you can give vent to your fury in greater comfort there.'

'No thank you, I –'

But as he came alongside and seized her horse's bridle, the driving wind and rain flung her answer away, unheard. Without another word and without releasing her bridle he covered the long stretch to the stables, then helped her down. Wretched as she was feeling, she was nonetheless aware of how abruptly he let her go. It was as if he wanted as little contact as possible.

Silently they went indoors. Beside the blazing library fire she shed her tight-waisted redingote, untied her wet stock and dropped her hat before the hearth to dry. 'You shouldn't have turned out in such weather,' he admonished.

'It was fine when I set out.'

'I'll see about something dry for you to put on. Aunt Agatha is away on one of her visits to Carrion House, but no doubt Rose can produce something from her wardrobe, although' – he finished, with a wry little smile – 'anything of Aunt Agatha's will wrap around you like a tent.'

She smiled too, and the tension eased. Beneath her billowing riding skirt she wore pantaloons, tucked into elastic-sided ankle boots, a practical but revolutionary riding fashion much frowned on by people like Aunt Agatha, but thoroughly approved of by her enlightened parents. Without self-consciousness she discarded the skirt and spread that, too, to dry. The slender trousers and cambric shirt, with frills at wrists and throat, made her look almost boyish, an impression counteracted by the lovely sight of her young breasts thrusting beneath the dampened material.

Miguel wished she had not come . . . he was delighted that she had . . . he wished she would go . . . he couldn't bear it if she did . . . To cover his confusion he urged her into a chair and said, 'Off with those boots . . .'

He stooped before her, back turned, and she obediently thrust one leg between his knees so that he could pull the boot off. Then

160

the other. He examined her damp toes with one hand and ordered her to remove her stockings, but she held her feet out to the fire, saying they would dry in no time at all.

'In any case, I'll not stay long. I merely wanted to find out why you failed to come today. Everyone expected you.' When he said nothing, she burst out, '*I* expected you, and no wonder! Right from the start the sundial has been as important to you as to me, and yet you turn your back on it when at last it emerges from its final test – and that, let me tell you, it has passed superbly.'

'Congratulations. You must be well pleased. As will be its new owner.'

Arrested by his tone, she fixed a searching glance on him.

'I hope so,' she admitted, 'but why sound so angry?'

She was unpinning her hair and now it fell in a dark cloud about her shoulders. Stooping toward the fire she ran her hands through it, letting strands trail through her fingers, shaking them dry. To get a more direct heat she knelt on the thick hearthrug, stooping, and her shirt fell open at the neck. He saw the soft valley between her breasts, and could no longer avert his eyes. To touch there . . . to press his lips there . . . to explore and fondle . . . to pour out his love with his mouth against her flesh . . the longing was so great that the next moment he was on the rug beside her, gathering her close, his hand searching and caressing while murmuring inarticulately, 'I *am* angry! It was part of our coming together, and you let that damned cousin have it!' As she struggled to be free he gave full vent to his wrath. 'It meant nothing to you – you wanted to please *him*, and to hell with the Mexican half-breed who stupidly fell in love with you!'

'Stop! *Stop!*'

But he wouldn't. Couldn't. His tight control snapped and out poured the emotions of a lifetime, driven by passion and pain. Shock, more than the spate of words, rendered her speechless. This was not the Miguel she knew – or thought she knew – and when the weight of his body suddenly pinned her beneath him and his hungry mouth silenced her and one hand tore at her clothing, she could do nothing. And wanted to do nothing. She felt her own heartbeats respond to his and her senses stir in a way that bemused and yet threatened her. She was excited, but frightened. She was also saddened because the man who was about to rape her stripped away the mask he usually wore and hated her for making him do so. Had he told her as much, she could not have been more certain of it.

Suddenly his weight was gone, and the mask was back in place, and he lifted her to her feet and said abruptly, 'I'm sorry. I forgot myself.'

'Perhaps it is time you did,' she answered shakily, adjusting her clothes and haphazardly recoiling her hair. When he walked to the door she said, 'Don't go. There's no need.' She was pulling on her riding skirt, indifferent to its dampness, aware only that she shouldn't have come, but was nonetheless glad that she had. She picked up her scarlet redingote and went over to him. 'Help me into this, please –?' He did so, still avoiding her eye, and she reached up and kissed his cheek and said, 'Forgive me, Miguel . . . I didn't know . . . didn't realize . . .'

'Why should you? I am years older than you.'

'What has that to do with it? You are simply Miguel to me, however old you are. I would have you changed in no way at all.'

'But things between us have now changed and will never be the same again. That is my fault.' When she made no answer he added, 'You had every right to dispose of the sundial in whatever way you wished, but I didn't think you would be so eager to let Lionel Drayton have it.'

'And what makes you think I was?'

'You seemed to have swung round in favour of him, making excuses for him, suggesting that everyone misunderstood him –'

'Yes – I did wonder. I felt guilty for doubting him. He seemed genuine when saying that he had Amelia's interests at heart. Who was I to disprove that? I felt it was time to meet friendship with friendship.'

Miguel shrugged and turned away, reiterating that she had every right to dispose of the sundial to whomsoever she wished, but she guessed that he was making idle conversation to avoid any reference to his earlier behaviour . . . his betraying behaviour. On his part, he was convinced that she must consider him pettish over the matter of the sundial, like a child revealing jealousy over a coveted toy, but it was better to let her think that than to thrust on her his suppressed passion, which he was in danger of doing so long as she remained.

She said in conciliatory tones, 'I am already designing others. There may be one among them –'

The words died as she realized that, for him, the first sundial she had made was the most important because it had strengthened their friendship. It had united them in a common interest, discovering aspects of each other they had never seen before. It had brought them closer and no replacement would be the same.

'I have only myself to blame,' he said, making conversation as she picked up her crop and walked to the door. 'I should have told you that I wanted to buy it. Stupidly, I took it for granted that you would know, even that you would want no one else to have it. And now, of course, it's too late.' Wryly, he added, 'At least I won't be taunted by the sight of it on the wall of Carrion House, for I'm never likely to be a visitor there.'

'I have never know you to be bitter,' she said sadly.

'I am trying not to be.'

For the first time in her life she had an inkling of the pain that rejection could bring, and wondered if he had felt rejected ever since his arrival at Tremain Hall as the illegitimate offspring of the heir. She was distressed to think that the preference she had now shown for Lionel added to Miguel's sense of rejection. And he is *not* illegitimate, she thought indignantly. Not only had his father legitimized his birth, but the years had rooted him firmly in Tremain soil, in Tremain traditions. He identified with the place and all it stood for because he belonged there, and surely there was not a remaining member of the two linked families who still considered that he did not?

A thought halted her. Lionel did. Lionel had always regarded him as an outcast. Lionel had mocked him and would continue to. She even wondered if the man had guessed that Miguel wanted to own this particular piece of her work and for this reason had made first bid for it.

Anxious to atone, she said, 'It was a commercial transaction, Miguel, no more. It's true that I didn't object to Lionel buying it. I don't even know how much he paid for it. And you mustn't blame either Amelia or Olivia, because they, like me, had no idea that you had set your heart on it.'

'I set my heart on more than that,' he said cryptically, and hurriedly opened the door. Plainly, he wanted her to go.

'What can I do to put things right?' she pleaded.

'Only forget that this past half hour ever happened. Forget everything I said and did.'

'Is that what you really want?'

'It is. I've been talking a lot of nonsense. Meaningless nonsense. Meaningless to both of us.'

'And – what you did – was that meaningless too?'

'Of course. You didn't imagine otherwise, did you?'

He accompanied her to the stables, helped her to mount, but didn't even pause to watch her ride away. When she looked back, there was no sign of him.

CHAPTER 14

The rain had ceased by the time Deborah turned out of Tremain's gates and headed for home, taking the bridle path along the western side of the park. From there she could head down into the valley and through winding cross-country lanes, or take the open road leading to Cooperfield and thence to Ashburton. Either route could be approached from this point by riding across a stretch of Tremain's fields, now available for all, providing the tracks were adhered to and crops left unharmed – a concession in which, she suspected, Miguel had influenced his father.

She couldn't get Miguel off her mind – the new Miguel whom she had glimpsed for the first time this afternoon. She had always believed that the quiet manner he presented to the world was his real self, but now she remembered his passion and the urgency of his desire, and was less sure; less sure of herself, too, for her reaction to him had been bewildering. He had excited her, stirred her. She had not wanted him to leave her and when he did so, abruptly, her disappointment had been sharp.

She took the bridle path slowly, in the reverse direction from the one she had taken during her early morning rides. She found herself recalling how he would sometimes appear through the gap leading from the ancient gazebo in Merrow's Thicket where, according to local legend, trysting lovers had once met. Perhaps they did so still. If so, they could be only village lads and lasses who knew the secret byways, for high society was no longer entertained at Tremain Hall, balls were no longer held there, visitors no longer filled the guest rooms, youth no longer held sway. It was a lonely place waiting to come alive again, and within its quiet walls Miguel lived out his solitary life, hiding his feelings, his thoughts, his dreams, his hopes, his fears, his longings.

Not until this afternoon had she been fully aware of his loneliness. Because he was active about the estate, fulfilling all his duties, she – like everyone else, no doubt – had imagined his life to be full and satisfying. Why had she never realized that the library in which she invariably found him was his favourite room because it was a refuge, a place to which he could escape from his father's sometimes cantankerous company and his aunt's eternal fretfulness? He loved them, he cared for them, he listened to them, he sympathized with them – but did they do the same for him? She doubted it. Sometimes ageing people could be blind to the needs of the young. Miguel found solace in books while his innermost self craved the solace of love.

Deborah chose the longest way home because she wanted time for thought. She wasn't ready to return to Ashburton and her mother's inquiring glances. Jessica never asked questions, never probed, never interfered in her children's lives, which was why those who had flown the nest were ever ready to revisit it, but she would naturally wonder if her youngest daughter had seen Miguel and what reasons he had given for staying away from Ashburton, particularly today. To parry those questions she had first to compose convincing answers.

She took the bridle path slowly and when she reached the gap, she halted. It seemed very empty without him. She recalled how she had always looked out for him, hoping he would appear, looking forward to his company for the next mile or two and for their brief and friendly exchanges. She recalled how he always seemed to materialize just when she was reaching that gap, or be there already, stooping over boundary fences, intent on examining them. But had he been there for that reason? Had he really been there by chance?

She spurred onward and downward. The ford by Badgers' Brook proved to be swollen with rains, so she chose the right of way leading to the hill above Burslem where her mother had been born in a house called Medlar Croft, and in which Aunt Amelia still lived. The cutting emerged close to Carrion House, situated higher up. 'My brother Joseph lived there in splendour, looking down on us from above . . .' Jessica rarely mentioned her elder brother, but to Deborah that one remark conjured up a picture of the head of the Drayton family spying on their every action, sitting in judgement, passing sentence . . .

Rain began again as she reached the entrance to Carrion House. Tall gates opened onto a short and well-kept driveway. The whole place had been restored by her mother's twin sister, but Lionel's house-warming supper was the first occasion on which Deborah had ever been inside. The dining hall had been impressive, but the pink and gold withdrawing room, festooned

165

with flowers and birds and dimpled cupids high on walls and ceilings, and pink satin upholstery on sofas and fragile gilt chairs had seemed tawdry; its glittering ornaments reflected in glittering Venetian mirrors, and elaborate pink satin window drapes adorned with gold braid and ribbons, had seemed tawdry and garish.

'Like a brothel, isn't it, my pretty cousin? But of course you wouldn't know that, would you? You probably don't even know what a brothel is . . .'

Deborah had awarded him a disdainful glance. 'My brothers enlightened me years ago, when I asked what the word meant. They even enlarged on it. I'm sure brothels can be found in Stoke and Liverpool and Nottingham and all the big cities and towns, but I don't imagine they're so expensively decorated as this.'

At that Lionel had laughed, a note of approval in his voice. 'I'm glad you're not an innocent young miss – but I'm going to change this room entirely, get rid of all this gaudiness. I don't like it. Few people do, whatever compliments they may pay. I notice your mother avoids it. That's not surprising, since her sister died in this room . . .'

Deborah had suppressed a shiver then, and she suppressed it now.

Her brothers had never spared her anything. They were frank, boisterous, and affectionate, but boys the world over enjoyed shocking their sisters and hers had succeeded when telling her that their Aunt Phoebe had been strangled. 'In Carrion House, in her bee-ootiful withdrawing room . . . robbed of her rubies by some break-in thief . . .'

It was a horrible story set in a horrible place; a place with a violent history, some said, but the new Master of Drayton's lived there contentedly.

Deborah was about to spur her horse onward when the front door of Carrion House was flung open and a heavy figure lumbered down the steps. It was Aunt Agatha and the fact that she had given a footman no chance to open the door indicated uncharacteristic haste. Agatha always reminded Deborah of a placid cow contentedly chewing the cud, for that was how she mainly spent her days. To see her stumbling down the steps and across to her waiting carriage, not even sparing breath to call for her coachman's aid, was so startling that Deborah's immediate instinct was to go to her, but scarcely had she moved her horse forward than the man had leapt down from his perch and helped his mistress aboard and then, plainly obeying an urgent command, had whipped up the horses.

166

Deborah withdrew hurriedly, but as the carriage rolled by she caught a glimpse of her aunt's face. It was ashen.

Disturbed, she rode on. If her aunt had been taken ill, she would be immediately taken care of when she reached Tremain, but her haste indicated energy, not illness. The impression left on Deborah was that Agatha Freeman had wanted to get away from Carrion House as quickly as possible, that something had happened to speed her departure, that she was shocked and distraught and, in such a state, would not have welcomed anyone's attention – particularly the attention of anyone young. Agatha seemed to have very little time for young people, thoroughly disapproving of their manners and hinting darkly at their morals. Had she known, for instance, that Deborah had been alone with Miguel in Tremain's library she would have put the worst interpretation on it . . . and she would very nearly have been right, Deborah thought with wry amusement and a certain wistfulness as she turned up the high collar of her redingote as protection against a renewed spate of rain.

Far below, she saw Burslem crouched in the valley, the smoke from endless pottery chimneys drifting downward under the rain's pressure. Water appeared to be rising up the canal's banks, but there was no danger of flooding because her father had built it and anything he constructed was sound. But some of the mines farther afield might suffer.

Her route now took her past the gates of the Drayton Pottery, by which time the rain had become a driving force. Her already damp clothes were becoming saturated. Common sense urged her to take shelter and common sense prevailed. She turned through the gates and in the middle of the potters' yard she nearly ran down a flying figure . . . young, slight, plainly heading for the Master Potter's office.

It was Abby Walker and for a moment Deborah failed to recognize her. The girl had changed. There was a pertness in the way she looked up after dodging the oncoming hooves, a pertness quite unlike her earlier manner, which had been one of shy friendliness when confronted by those whom she regarded as her 'betters'.

Abby piped, 'Don't run me down, miss! I be wearing me new bodice an' Master Potter won't be pleased if it be dirtied!' Before Deborah could answer she continued, 'I'd best get back t'me bench if ye be visiting Master Lionel – ladies first, as they say, an' I ain't no lady. Not *yet* . . .' Swiftly, she changed her mind and with a toss of the head she finished, 'On t'other 'and, I were afore ye so *I*'ll see 'im first,' and with no further ado she knocked boldly on the Master Potter's door and walked in.

The girl's abrupt entrance annoyed Lionel. He scowled and ordered her back to work.

'But I've gotta talk to ye, Master Potter.' She had developed a way of saying 'Master Potter' that hinted at mockery. His annoyance became anger.

'You can have your say this evening; the usual time and place. Now get back to your bench.'

She burst out, 'It's me mam – she be off to Nottingham an' landlord won't let me live in t'cottage alone. Got to be shared with "re-spons-ible adults". Sez it's the law, but Ma don't believe it.'

'Then go to Nottingham with her.'

The unexpected idea presented him with a welcome and convenient loophole, free of dispute and with no lingering ties. The promised gold coin and a last hour of enjoyment and the baggage would be gone.

'*Go?*' she exploded. '*Me?* An wot would *I* be adoin' in Nottingham?'

'The same as your mother. I have no doubt you would be very successful. You have youth on your side, whereas she has none, and Nottingham is not only prosperous but renowned for its hospitable "ladies" and its wealthy gentlemen.'

Her confidence was shaken. Her eyes filled with sudden tears. 'Ye don't mean it! Ye can't!'

'I can and I do. There is a time for things to begin and a time for them to end. You must face facts, and an inescapable one is that your work has deteriorated – fallen off,' he explained, seeing her uncomprehending expression. 'That means you would find it hard to get work in another pottery, but in any case there are none in Nottingham. Lace is the main industry there, and you have no skilled training for that. On the other hand, I have taught you well in other ways and your mother will know how to get clients.'

'I won't! I WON'T! 'Sides, she won't take me. Sez it be *your* duty to set me up some place. Told me t'tell ye so, *and* that if ye don't, ye'll be sorry.'

There was a moment's deadly silence before he said, 'Get out.'

His voice was low and threatening. Abby backed to the door. This wasn't going the way her ma had predicted.

She quavered, 'If ye don't set me up, I got no place t'go. Landlord's got another tenant waiting –'

'He's sure to say that if he wants to get someone out. Who owns that row of hovels, by the way? They're alongside the Red Lion's livery stables, aren't they? That means they are tied and the Red Lion's owner is the landlord. You'll have to get out if he says so, though I should have thought one tenant was as good as another.'

'Not to Joss Barlow. Sez 'e won't 'ave no daughter o' Kate Walker living there on 'er own an' using the place for – you know wot.' Her voice became pleading. 'But if *thee* were to put in a word, Master Potter – if ye were to tell 'im, confidential-like, that ye want me t'stay there for good reason – then the man would be too afeared of offending the Master o' Drayton's to think o' turning me out. Or mebbe,' she finished, 'I'll get me mam to tell 'im, like she wants to.'

He stared. He half rose. He leaned across his fine desk and said in the same low voice, '*Get out* – you dirty little blackmailer. And stay out. There's no place for you in this pottery any more. If you come to work in the morning you'll find that the gatekeeper has instructions to turn you away.'

She retreated, shocked, sick with sudden hatred. She didn't believe this was happening. Her mam wouldn't believe it either – but her mam wasn't around to hear. She was on her way to Nottingham with a tinker who'd picked her up at the Hiring Cross and by now she wouldn't even be thinking of her daughter. Had she ever?

(Mam, you're a liar! All them things ye told me t'say, an' all them things ye made me do – where've they got me? An' where've they got *thee*? Nowheres! Ye said 't'were a fine way t'mak' a living – well, it ain't! It ain't even *nice* wi' swine like that. . . I *hates* thee, Mam, an' I 'opes as 'ow I never sees thee no more, ye dirty rotten baggage!)

Blindly, Abby stumbled down the steps and into the potters' yard. Rain was torrential now. There was no sign of the Kendalls' daughter, but her horse was there. Someone had flung a blanket over his haunches and led him under the shelter of an overhang. A bag of oats hung from his neck and he looked comfortable and content, which was more than she felt herself. She was lost. Stunned. She didn't know what to do or where to go. It would have to be back home – Joss Barlow couldn't turn her out until morning. But then? What then?

The door of the glazing shed opened and Dave Jefferson emerged, the young lady with him. Abby heard her thanking Dave for sheltering her, and at that moment both saw Abby, who promptly ran away.

169

She knew just where she was going – down to that cellar room – and exactly what she was going to do there. Wreck everything . . . rip those cushions to shreds . . . pour wine all over the carpet from that damned decanter he couldn't do without . . . then smash it and those fancy goblets too . . . destroy everything . . . leave nothing untouched – and *then* . . . what then? Scream to everybody to come and see what she had done and laugh for the joy of it, and laugh even louder when the Master Potter saw it too.

She plunged down the wooden cellar steps. They'd always seemed ricketty and more so today. Halfway down they were sodden. A tread broke loudly beneath her feet and the whole staircase came away, hurling her into a morass of water and mud. Silt filled her mouth and turned her screaming into terrified choking. Pain pierced her legs. Floundering, she tried to stand, only to plunge again into rising water. Dear God, she would drown! She would choke to death! She would be trapped – she *was* trapped! Wildly, she clutched at floating slats of wood and groped blindly for a foothold to climb out of this nauseous place. Pitifully, she continued with her futile screaming and in roaring ears her voice vibrated – unfamiliar, frantic, gasping on seering breaths but somehow producing a sound which was meant to be Dave's name, but only she, in this underground hell, could hear it.

CHAPTER 15

Lionel wasted no time in preparing to leave, although the pottery wasn't due to close for another two hours. No doubt there would be the usual sullen glances from workers who saw him depart, and the usual comment, from those bold enough to make it, that no Master of Drayton's had ever left so early, and he would resolve yet again that this increasing insolence would earn immediate dismissal, without pay.

He had already resorted to that in several cases and the only thing that made him hesitate now was his inability to find replacements. He had expected that to be easy, in the heart of the potteries, but the only ones he had been able to find were the idle or the inefficient, turned off by others. No expert hands seemed willing to work for Drayton's now, and those who remained resented the extra demands made on them. It wasn't their fault that production was falling off, they protested. Time was when every man and woman here was willing to work unflaggingly; time was when every extra hour put in and every extra load completed was appreciated and rewarded accordingly. Not now. The number of dissatisfied Drayton workers seeking employment elsewhere was increasing.

Thankfully, he reflected that he would have time enough to worry about all that when he reached home and relaxed with his customary glass of Madeira before changing into the fine linen laid out for him. As for what he would wear tonight – always an important consideration – there was his favourite ensemble of amber brocade with gold cloth lining and gilded buttons, and breeches of amber satin fastening at the knee above silken hose with a golden sheen. Such elegance was somewhat wasted when supping alone, but tonight he was in no mood for company and saw no reason why he shouldn't indulge in an elaborate toilet for the sheer pleasure of it.

He hoped his valet proved to be up to scratch this evening. If dear Mama had been on one of her visits, poking and prying into his closets in the hope of finding imperfections to which she could immediately draw the man's attention, then he would have nothing to worry about. He had to give her credit for knowing what she was about when it came to supervising his wardrobe. His valet resented her interference, but had to put up with it. He himself was well-content to let her meddle in that way – but not in others.

One thing he did *not* intend to do tonight was to regret his dismissal and keep his promise to that tiresome chit, Abby. Let her trot down to the cellar if she wished; it would do her good to wait in vain. It would drive home the fact that he meant what he said. There was a time to end things, and he had ended them, and felt remarkably free as a result. And he would make sure that she did go to join her mother. He would provide the fare, and a gift or two, and see that an inside seat was reserved on the next stage coach so that she travelled in style. The silly little thing would like that. 'Ever so grand!' she would think, prinking and perking all the way to Nottingham while he sat back and viewed his future with satisfaction – free and unfettered and with all the time in the world to turn his attention to pretty Deb.

The thought that he was rid of little Abby Walker was

171

gratifying. He had let the affair drag on too long, allowing her to become too sure of herself.

He felt singularly complacent as he prepared to leave the pottery. He could even smile at the thought of Joss Barlow believing that the Walker girl had been seduced by the Master of Drayton's and that a man of such standing would want her to be housed in that miserable shack to await his pleasure. Anyone would laugh aloud at such a tale and he had been foolish to allow it to cause one moment's apprehension.

No matter. The whole business was over now, and he could make his way home through this filthy weather and relax beside a fire, his bag wig thrown aside, his hair flowing free, a glass beside him and a well-cooked meal awaiting him. After that, he would turn his attention to the new plans for that tawdry withdrawing room which he could rarely enter without seeing his aunt's raddled face, with its dimples and its carmined cheeks and its kohled eyelids. Sometimes, but not often, he recalled it as it had been when he last saw it – staring up at him, eyes bulging, tongue lolling. Not a pretty sight. Phoebe, who relished her looks, would have hated it.

Perhaps, when the décor was changed, the picture would be finally banished and his increasing reluctance to enter that room would cease.

He pushed aside the ledger with which he had been trying to get to grips. He could try again tomorrow; similarly with all the others presenting the same depressing story. Orders were dropping and takings correspondingly diminishing. It was only a phase, of course. A temporary setback. No more than a taste of the doldrums. They occurred in all industries. Things would pull up again. A name like Drayton's could stand on its merits without fear.

As for heeding his foreman's tale about the success of Ashburton's new stoneware clay – how absurd! And how could Dave Jefferson, who reported that the kiln had been broached today, have heard about it? It was impossible to believe that within a few hours other Staffordshire potters were making inquiries about Ashburton's stoneware. How could the news have circulated so swiftly?

'Through Ben Fowler, sir – one of the Red Lion's ostlers. He were hired to give a hand at the Ashburton stables today, one o' their lads being took sick. Fowler bumped into Meg Tinsley. She's well set up there, in a cottage of her own an' a well-paid job into the bargain –'

'What concern is that of mine? Get on with your tale.'

'Well, sir, everyone's agog with the news an' Meg took Ben along to see some of the stuff. The man says it be like nothing ever seed in Burslem afore.'

'And how would a mere ostler know that?'

Ignoring the question, Jefferson had run straight on.

'Soon other potters were heading out to Ashburton to see it, and no one said them nay. All declared they'd never seen nothink like it. We'd best be thinking up some new clay mixture or some new glaze recipe if we're to hold our own. New glazes be what I want to specialize in, sir, as ye know.'

'Time enough for that. There's no hurry. As for this new stoneware, it may well be just a flash in the pan.'

Jefferson had donned his mulish expression, the one with which Drayton's Master Potter was becoming increasingly familiar, and said, 'I doubts it, sir. Master Kendall ain't prone to mistakes. Only successes.'

Insolent. Like so many more. Go home and forget about them, Lionel told himself. Deal with them in the morning. Show them then who is master. Meanwhile, put them out of your mind. And to assist in the process why not go to Ashburton to see the new sensation and assess the danger or competition of it? He had ample excuse – he would be calling to collect Deborah's sundial.

Pleased with the decision, Lionel donned cloak and tall-crowned hat and was preparing to open the door when a slowly gathering murmur swelled to a roar, culminating immediately outside. Voices were shouting his name – ugly, threatening. Something struck the door and bounced off. Other missiles followed.

Wood splintered as panels shattered. Stones and debris hurtled through. When a brick narrowly missed him, he backed away, uncertain what to do. He had to exit through that door because there was no other . . . but what sort of an escape would it be?

The door crashed open and on the threshold stood Dave Jefferson carrying a bedraggled body in his arms. Its slightness, its fragility, its thinness, all were sickeningly familiar although beneath a caking of mud and a tangled mass of wet hair the face was unrecognizable. Then he saw a broken bracelet clinging to a bloodied wrist . . . and the legs streaked with blood were also familiar . . . too damned familiar. And there was no mistaking that torn bodice . . . she had been proud of it, strutting up and down with her young breasts outlined through its thin fabric and her rough Midland voice piping, 'Why shouldn't I wear it t'work, Master Potter? Wot do *I* care wot folk think? I be sick o' potter's

173

slops. Make me look just like the rest of 'em, they do, an' *that* I ain't. Not no more!'

A voice said urgently, 'Put her here, Dave . . .' and through his bewilderment Lionel saw Deborah Kendall pull forward his splendid, comfortably upholstered chair. That startled him. What was his cousin doing here? When had she arrived, and why? And how did she come to be embroiled with the rebellious mob who now crowded into the room armed with sticks and anything else they could lay their hands on? One or two still carried heavy bricks and some even potters' knives, but once within the room their angry voices were hushed.

'Someone fetch a doctor – quickly. Take my horse. And bring the man back with you – tell him she is cut about the legs and feet and bleeding badly and she has plainly gulped a lot of water, but she's alive, thank God –' As someone dived for the door and raced off, Deborah turned to Lionel. 'I need bandages . . . water and towels . . . *quickly*,' and when he stood there ineffectively she threw him a furious glance. 'In God's name, have you medical supplies of *no* kind to hand?'

'Water's coming, M's Debra!' One of the women from the turners' shed pushed her way through, water spilling. Over her arm was a cloth of some kind. The well water was clean but the cloth was clay-soiled. Deborah wiped the heaviest dirt off Abby's face and pushed back the matted hair. The girl's eyes flickered. She whimpered. Deborah murmured, 'You're all right, Abby . . . you're safe . . . you're not down in that filthy place any more . . .'

The words jerked Lionel to attention. *Down in that place . . .?* Hell's teeth, what had happened there and who had found her?

Deborah cast the cloth aside and ordered her cousin to take off his shirt. 'If you can't produce clean cloths, then I'll use pieces torn from anything that *is* clean – and your shirt is obviously the only one to hand.' She waited, and when he tried to bluster she grew impatient. 'If you won't oblige, then I'm afraid these men will force you to.'

Clutching at dignity, he managed to say, 'Do you think a man in my position doesn't supply all necessities? Everything you need is in that cupboard over there.'

It was Dave Jefferson who fetched some of the Master's mono-grammed towels, carefully selecting a new one. After passing it to Deborah, his eloquent glance met Lionel's. 'When doctor's dealt with Abby,' he said firmly, 'we'll get round to dealing with thee. Ye've a deal to answer for and every man of us is here to see that ye do. *Then* we'll decide what's t'be done about it.'

174

'My good man, I haven't the faintest notion of what you are talking –'

A protest from one of the mob silenced him, a protest taken up by everyone within earshot and echoed by those who were not. The note of disbelief increased to a growl, stirring something stronger than uneasiness in the Master Potter's mind. Only now did he recall stories he had heard of rebellions in the potteries . . . of angry workers, who could stand no more, turning on their slave-driving masters and smashing wheels and modelling stands and tools of all kinds . . . of men and women driven by fits of demented rage . . . of mutiny when harsh punishments were meted out to those who fell asleep over their benches because they were un-equal to the excessive working hours . . . even the case, for ever to be recorded in the history of the potteries, of the woman who died after being flogged by her master because she had failed to produce the number of pots expected of her that day. That had led to unprecedented violence, total wreckage of the establish-ment, a near lynching of the Master Potter and jail sentences for all.

Lionel thrust down his sickening uneasiness with the reflection that such things had never happened at Drayton's and were never likely to. Conditions and wages here were better than any clay worker could get elsewhere. There wasn't a man in this room who would jeopardize his livelihood just because a stupid girl had met with a mishap.

But their mood was still ugly. Silence prevailed while Deborah tended the girl. Dave Jefferson cradled her head and when she tried to talk he said gently, 'Not yet, Abby luv. Not yet. When doctor's been, p'raps, but there's now't as can't wait 'til morning . . .' Then, beneath his breath to the Master Potter, 'Other things won't keep . . . other things'll be dealt with afore this night's out.'

The waiting seemed long, but eventually the doctor arrived. Lionel was relieved when the man ordered everyone out except Deborah, but not so pleased when it was assumed that he would go too. If he did, the mob would be waiting and they were still in a mood to carry out their own rough justice. So he insisted on remaining out of concern for the girl. 'I am her employer. I am responsible for everyone and I take those responsibilities seriously. When you have attended to her, I will personally take her home. My carriage is outside.'

So he remained, but so did Dave Jefferson who, after following the others to the door, then slipped quietly into a corner and remained there.

When the examination was over the doctor assured Deborah that the girl was young enough to recover speedily; the cuts, ugly as they were, would heal well.

'But I would like to know how she got them. Some were full of splinters.'

The Master Potter gave Deborah no chance to speak.

'She must have fallen down some wooden steps in the rain,' he said. 'No doubt they were wet and caused her to slip.'

'Dangerous things, wooden steps. I didn't know you had such things in potteries. I thought all workshops were at ground level.'

'So they are, but we utilize roof space for stores, so the use of ladders is necessary.'

'Then how did the child get soaked? She's been half-drowned.'

'Store-rooms are on the canal bank. The earth there is a quagmire since the rains came. No doubt she ran and slipped in the mud.'

'I thought you said it happened on wooden steps?'

'I can see no other explanation for the cuts and splinters, but what I am trying to account for now is her drenched condition. Mud and slime would soak anyone who fell while hurrying through torrential rain.'

The doctor pursed his lips thoughtfully and seemed about to nod his agreement when Dave burst out, 'It be a bloody lie! That damned cellar's flooded an' the steps caved in, but did the Master Potter trouble t'find out? That he did not!'

'Cellar?' echoed the doctor. 'What cellar?'

Dave blazed, 'The one the late Master wouldn't build because of the risk of seepage from the canal, but *this* man went ahead an' built on the cheap as a hideout! Called it a storage cellar, but *I* know what else were stored down there. *I* know what that extra room were used for an' why Abby went there! Take another look at her. Scarce fourteen she is, with a mother that's allus been bad an' now clears off, leaving 'er daughter for a Master Potter t'do what he likes with!'

Lionel Drayton threw back his head and laughed. 'You can't believe the prattle of a besotted youth –!'

The doctor, sensing something with which he had no desire to become involved, murmured something inaudible and tried to slip away, unnoticed, as Deborah demanded of Dave, 'Kate Walker has *gone?*'

'Aye, M's Debra.'

'Then who will look after Abby? She can't be left alone in this state!'

176

'Meg Tinsley, ma'am. She's allus wanted to. I'll be taking Abby there right away –'

'No. I will. You have unfinished business here.' With one swift movement Deborah wrenched Lionel's cloak from his shoulders. 'I'm taking your carriage as well. You can use my horse in exchange – when those men have finished with you.'

She wrapped Abby in the cloak and Dave carried her outside. Deborah thanked the doctor and reminded him to send his bill to the Master of the Drayton Pottery. At the door she spared one last word for Lionel.

'What happened to your mother at Carrion House today?'

He snapped, 'I don't know what you're talking about.'

'I'm talking about her hurrying away from the place, seemingly in a state of shock. I was riding by, and saw her.'

'Then why didn't you stop her?'

'I couldn't. She was quickly into her carriage and away.'

'And I was here, hard at work, so how could I even know she'd been to my house? If she'd been paying one of her busy-body visits, upsetting the servants, perhaps she'd got the worst of it. And serve her right.'

Deborah cast him a contemptuous glance, and left. The doctor was already driving away. Picking up the reins, she glanced back and saw Lionel Drayton standing in the open door, his way blocked by mutineering workers and Dave, with one strong hand, firmly propelling him back inside. The men followed. The door closed. She drove away as fast as safety and relentless rain permitted.

CHAPTER 16

On the following day, the whole of Burslem buzzed with gossip. Garbled stories passed from mouth to mouth, distorted in the process. The workers had gone berserk, some said. They had run amok, wrecking everything in sight. They had attacked the Master Potter, beaten him, injured him, kicked him and spat on him. They had smashed the latest consignment from the kilns and done the same to valuable loads bound for major cities at home and abroad. They had behaved like savages, charging through the place like ravening wolves and howling in packs. They had dumped sacks of glaze oxides in the canal and scattered rutile and copper manganese and other valuable chemical ingredients to the winds. They had set fire to bales of straw and hazelwood crates, then run with flaming torches through the whole place, setting alight storage sheds and workshops . . . and in the fracas people had been drowned in flooded cellars . . . Finally, the Master Potter's injured body had been thrown down there, with the pack howling for his blood. Jail cells would be full before this day was out.

Serve them right, said those who condemned such behaviour. They deserved rewards, said others who praised it.

The tales gathered momentum, spreading from village to village. Soon the curious were heading for the pottery anxious to see for themselves the damning evidence of violence and revolt.

They were disappointed to find the place looking just the same, with workers going about their business and the only signs of disorder being a stack of wet rubble in the potters' yard, brought up from some cellar. But it were strange stuff to come out of a potter's cellar; sodden carpets and cushions and suchlike. Must have been from the Master Potter's office. It were well known that Lionel Drayton had furnished that place in style. Obviously, the heavy rain had penetrated and spoiled all of them lovely things, and weren't that a crying shame . . .?

And old Peterson, the gatekeeper, wasn't much help. All he did was keep his mouth shut, or growl, 'Ain't ye got nothink better t'do than gawp? Folks in this pottery mind their own business, so why don't thee?'

But one thing everybody did notice and agree on was the absence of the Master Potter's carriage in the yard and the relentless look about his office door. Closed, it was, with that sort've locked look about it that doors have when remaining unopened.

Everyone went away dissatisfied and asking who started all them rumours anyway? Packers were loading their crates in the yard, ready to cart down to the barges on the canalside; women were seen going in and out of the turners' shed, carrying tray-loads of upturned pots to the drying-out quarters, and after the deluge of rain passed and the weather brightened other loads were lined up to dry in the sun. Rioting? There wasn't a sign of it.

But Drayton clay workers who dropped into the Red Lion for

178

their nightly swig of Staffordshire ale shut up like clams when folk asked questions. 'Now't t'say,' was their only reply when pumped, so that after a while the questions ceased. But that didn't stop speculation, especially when a servant from Carrion House responded to a round of free drinks by revealing that his master were laid low and were likely to be for several days. But as to his malady, no information was forthcoming.

To Meg, her new home at Ashburton was now sealed with contentment. To Abby, it was a refuge to which she felt she had no right.

'I'll be gone an' not bothering ye just as soon as me legs'll let me,' she said, sitting beside the window and gazing out on a scene more peaceful than she had ever imagined. The hovel alongside the Red Lion's livery stables had looked out on manure heaps and barrel stores, both smelly. Here the scent of the countryside drifted through the open window, sweetening the air, and on the hob one of Meg's stews, spiced with herbs, emitted an appetizing fragrance.

'Don't talk daft,' said Meg, bluntly. 'There be room for two of us in this place, an' work for us at the Ashburton Pottery into the bargain.'

'I'm no good at t'job no more. Told me so 'imself, when casting me off. Said me work 'ad dee-terior-summat.'

'Deteriorated?'

'Aye. That. Meanin' it'd gone off an' I were no use no more.'

'The man's a liar. Forget 'im.'

'I can't, Meg. I keeps remembering wot I were like afore I took up with 'im, an' wot I be now . . .'

'Ye've got to stop thinking that way, luv. Ye've got to do what I did – put it all behind ye. D'ye think I ain't gone through it, too? Ask your ma, if ye ever sees 'er again, which I 'opes ye never does.' Meg hesitated, then said resolutely, 'There be one thing ye'd better know, Abby. I'll tell ye now, then never again. *I* persuaded Kate t'go away.'

Abby swung round. 'I don't believe it!' She fell silent, looking at Meg's honest face. 'Why did ye? Why? Tell me.'

''Cos she ain't no good. She'd allus been bad for thee. I wanted t'take care of ye when ye were now't but a babby; told Master Martin so, I did. He wanted to help, an' so did Mistress 'Melia, but what chance 'ad anybody with that tartar Kate around? Nobody liked 'er, but everybody liked *thee* an' wanted to protect ye. Then when she were all cock-a-hoop and boasting

179

about the new Master Potter favouring thee, an' t'were plain as a pikestaff what'd happen t'ye when ye were cast off, I knew I had t'do summat, an' quick. So I did it. An' I ain't sorry.' She finished gently. 'I loves thee, Abby child. Everybody does. An' so does Dave.'

Abby said sadly, 'Now 'e knows wot I've become 'e'll look t'other way.'

'Like 'e did when getting ye out of that damned place? D'ye know 'ow he did it, yelling for help while 'e grabbed a rope an' got a coupla strong men to lower 'im on the end of it, then wound it around ye to haul ye up, an' then 'imself, an' wouldn't let nobbody else carry ye to safety? An' d'ye know how many times 'e's ridden out from Burslem t'see ye this past week alone an' ye've told me t'send 'im away? It be time ye stopped being cruel, Abby. Time ye saw how much he loves ye . . .'

Looking down at her hands, twisting them in her lap, refusing to lift her eyes to Meg's face, Abby whispered, 'I do see it. I do know it. But I ain't good enough for Dave. Not now, I ain't. I take after me mam.'

'That ye don't. You're Abby Walker, not Kate Walker, an' when the day comes that ye be Abby Jefferson ye'll put the past behind ye for ever. I be talking about what I *knows*, lass; what I've been through meself, so hark on it. You be still no more'n a child, a child misled an' ill-treated. Ye need to heal, an' ye *will* heal, an' Dave'll help ye. One day ye'll be ready to be loved the way ye should be. 'Til then, live like I've lived since I lost my Frank. Take each day as it comes. That way, things'll work out. But don't turn your back on Dave –'

'I tell ye, I ain't *good* enough for 'im now!'

'That be for Dave t'decide, an' for thee to let 'im. Now get this stew inside ye an' stop looking back over your shoulder. That never did nobbody any good. An' this afternoon I'll be taking ye down to the valley to visit the Ashburton Pottery, an' ye can sit on a stool an' pick up a turning tool again, an' I swear that with me around ye'll soon be good as ever. An' then ye can start working alongside me, just like the old days.'

'D'ye think they'll *reelly* tak me on – M's 'Melia an' M's 'Livia?' Hope shone in Abby's eyes.

'I knows they will. They've said so. Now shut up, lass, an' eat thy fill.'

News of the revolt reached Tremain Hall almost as speedily as it spread through the countryside. By mutual consent, Miguel and his father agreed to withhold it from Agatha, who had remained confined to her rooms for several days and, to her cook's concern, scarcely touched the food he put before her.

When visited by her brother, she was uncommunicative. With Miguel, she was slightly less so. She seemed to be touched by his concern. She even patted his hand and told him he was a dear boy and how fortunate his father was to have such a son, and tears filled her eyes as she said it. And then, even more uncharacteristically, she asked to be left alone.

'She's growing old,' said Max. 'Poor old Aggie. It's a bad sign when *she* has no fancy for food. Pierre told me she sent back some oyster-mouth soup today, one of her favourites, and only toyed with a dish of china chilo. I've seen her shovel *that* down and demand more on many an occasion. Must be sickening for something. Perhaps a doctor should be fetched.'

Agatha would see no doctor, but when Miguel suggested a game of backgammon she seemed almost grateful, so perhaps, he thought compassionately, the trouble is that she doesn't really want to be left alone; perhaps it's merely because the two of them, brother and sister, have never got along together.

He thought of the household at Ashburton, filled with family life and affection, where married sons and daughters and small grandchildren were happy to visit; Deborah had been brought up in such an atmosphere and when she married, she would create it about her because that was the sort of life she had always known and would always want. Tremain Hall would never have fallen into silence had real family life continued to fill it.

He remembered the affection his grandparents had given him and the devotion they had had for each other, and how greatly he missed it after they had gone. How sad that the happiness of such a marriage as theirs had been found by only one of their children, Amelia. If Agatha had found it, too, it had been curtailed by the death of her husband. And of course his father's had been an unhappy alliance lacking the love he had ultimately found in a far-off land.

Agatha couldn't concentrate on the game. She could make only monosyllabic answers and then drift into silence, her thoughts miles away. She had made valiant but pathetic attempts to preserve her looks, brightly rouging her cheeks and changing her gowns repeatedly, then summoning Rose to fill a hip bath for her and go through her toilet all over again.

'I don't know what to do with her, Master Miguel, that I don't. Nothink I do pleases her for long. "Do this, do that," she says, and "Get this, get that," and when I do, she don't want it. I wish Master Lionel could see how she is, but he hasn't visited her for weeks. I'd send for him if she'd let me, but she won't. Only this morning I suggested it, but "No!" she said, so sharp I were startled. Then she calmed down and said how busy he always was, and I fair wanted to cry because it seemed like she were pleading for him. "He has responsibilities, great responsibilities," she said, "running the Drayton Pottery like his father before him . . ." Well, Master Miguel, that don't stop the man from getting out and about and visiting other people in the neighbourhood. Many a supper party I've heard tell about from other domestic folk like myself, at houses in the neighbourhood and beyond, where Master Lionel's a frequent guest . . .'

While concentrating on the game and trying to get his aunt to do likewise, Miguel came to a sudden decision. He would drive over to Ashburton and confide in Jessica Kendall, ask her to come to see Agatha, seek her help. And perhaps he would be lucky enough to see Deborah, whom he was missing desperately and whom he had avoided since their last encounter. Was it really only a day or two ago that he had made a fool of himself down there in the library, complaining pettishly because he could not have something he coveted – like a child denied a longed-for toy – and then allowing his desire for her to overcome self-control? What a fool he had been . . . what a fool . . .

But there was no need to remain so. It was up to him to put things right. If he could only regain their earlier companionship, he would be partially content.

'You seem tired, Aunt Agatha. Shall I call for some tea? It always refreshes you.'

'So long as you stay and have it with me, Miguel, it would be very nice. Taking tea alone is such a solitary business . . .'

His hand was on the bell rope when Rose burst in, breathless and agitated.

'Oh, ma'am – dreadful news – down at the Drayton Pottery – terrible trouble, some say riots! Leastways, the knife-grinder who calls at the kitchens each month says so, but cook told him to stop talking nonsense and be on his way, but *I* thought you should know, ma'am, seeing as how 'tis said that Master Lionel hasn't been seen there since it all happened . . .'

There had been a time when bad news sent Agatha Drayton into hysterics; now she just sat there, pale and silent. Miguel went to her and touched her shoulder, saying gently, 'I'm sure it's exaggerated, possibly untrue, but would you like me to go there

182

and find out? Or would you like me to take you to Carrion House? Whatever I can do to help, you know I will.'

She put up a plump, beringed hand and patted his, but the gesture was automatic, puppet-like. She seemed unaware of what she was doing, and looked neither at him nor her maid. There had been several moments like this during the past twenty-four hours. It was as if a mental shutter had been slammed between herself and the world.

'Aunt Agatha – let me help you. Let me take you to him . . .'

Slowly, her head turned. Sunken eyes in a pallid face looked up at him.

In a dead voice she said, 'No. Let him come to me. He will. He will have to.'

CHAPTER 17

Olivia had arrived at Ashburton that morning looking singularly happy and had remained so throughout the day. Once or twice Amelia had been tempted to ask why, but the rush of visitors to see the new stoneware left neither of them much time for conversation. Within a few hours of the final piece emerging from the kiln, the curiosity of neighbouring potters had started the onrushing tide.

Scepticism had turned to admiration and admiration to envy when they saw the new clay. Few were surprised when told that it would not be marketed. This stoneware was to be the specialist product of the Ashburton Pottery, the cornerstone on which future success would be built.

But in the midst of this success, Amelia was troubled by reports of the deteriorating state of affairs at Drayton's. Her love of the place remained strong, for it had been a major part of her life, her husband's heritage and intended, eventually, to be her son's. Lionel could not deny young George his share even if he produced sons of his own. It was the *Drayton* Pottery, started by Draytons *for* Draytons, and her retirement from the scene did not alter that vital fact.

Her only fear was that in Lionel's inexperienced hands the place might fail – and from all one heard it seemed that the danger had already set in. Dissatisfied workers were seeking employment elsewhere. Many had called on her at Medlar Croft to beg for work at Ashburton and gone away disappointed because the new establishment was not yet big enough.

With the perfection of this new stoneware clay, however, the future was alive with promise. Until grinding mills on a par with Simon Kendall's could be built to produce ground flints of equal quality, there wasn't a pot bank in the country that could touch it. Deborah's attractive wall sundial, now on display, was a splendid example of its potential. There had been more offers for that one piece than Amelia could count, and her only regret was that the first person to bid for it was Lionel. He had even paid a substantial deposit to secure it.

Amelia had been surprised that he should want it. Somehow she had imagined that Miguel would desire it more than he, but Deborah had made no mention of Miguel. Surprise and pleasure because someone actually wanted to buy her work had been written all over the girl's face when announcing that her cousin Lionel was the purchaser. Reluctant as Amelia had been – Olivia also – they had had no choice but to agree a figure with him and to promise delivery when fired.

But now, unexpectedly, Deborah came to her aunt and asked for a word with her.

'It's about Lionel,' she said. 'I've been trying to put the whole thing out of my mind, but I can't. When I left the pottery, angry workers were waiting to deal with him. How they intended to I don't know, but their mood was ugly. If you're wondering why I didn't try to stop them, I can only say that even had I wanted to, I would have failed. But I *didn't* want to. Not when I learned why they were there, and what had happened to Abby – and where, and how, and why. Don't ask me, dear Aunt Amelia, because I don't want to talk about it –'

'Perhaps I can guess.'

'I would rather you didn't. What concerns me now is the fact that the last person I want my sundial to go to is Lionel Drayton. Can we stop it?'

'No. A promise is a promise, an agreement an agreement.'

Disappointment was evident on Deborah's expressive face. 'I am to blame,' she said remorsefully.

Olivia joined them at that point. She was leaving early because she and Damian had something to celebrate. 'You'll hear in all good time,' she said, smiling but revealing nothing.

When the two of them had departed, Olivia happy and Deborah saddened, Amelia had the sundial removed from its display stand, packed, and placed in her carriage. Then she too left for home, but instead of driving straight to Medlar Croft she headed for Carrion House.

The footman was sorry, but his master was unwell and not to be disturbed.

'You mean he is ill?'

'Not exactly, ma'am.'

'Off colour, then?'

'Slightly, yes, ma'am.'

'Has he had medical attention?'

'He says it's not necessary, ma'am.'

Amelia walked past the man and headed for the room she knew to be her nephew's study. It was the obvious place in which to find him, the place to which a man retreated when wanting to avoid company. When she opened the door she saw him sitting morosely before the fire, a glass in his hand.

He had the grace to stumble to his feet and to offer her a seat, which she declined.

'My business won't take long. I've brought your sundial. It's in my carriage outside. Your man can fetch it, but do tell him to handle it with care. However well-wrapped, accidents can happen, and to everyone at Ashburton this article is of particular importance, being the first wall sundial to be made in our splendid new stoneware. You are fortunate indeed to get it. There have been many offers since we put it on display.'

'Oh – that,' he said indifferently. 'I'd forgotten about it.'

Looking at him closely she saw that he was unshaven, his locks tangled and neglected, his shirt unbuttoned at the throat. He had plainly been drinking heavily.

'How are affairs at Drayton's?' she asked.

'Perfectly splendid!' He waved his glass. 'You are looking at the most successful master potter in Staffordshire, loved by his workers, admired by everyone, a man who inspires devotion in a pack of ignorant, uncouth animals lacking all respect for their betters! So why should *I* heed their threats?'

Slowly, she sat down.

'What sort of threats?'

'Nothing for your delicate ears; nothing a lady would care to hear.'

'So it's true then – that you were cornered by a group of angry men? I've heard rumours, but ignored them. Looking at you now, I think perhaps I should have heeded them.'

185

He waved her aside. He had said too much, and now regretted it. He wasn't going to confide in any female. Except his mother, perhaps. He had always been able to confide in his mother; when caught out in any misdemeanour he could always count on her support. The more he remembered that, the more he thought that perhaps, in his present predicament, it might be a good idea to take advantage of that maternal devotion again. But first he must get rid of this tiresome aunt.

'About that sundial,' he said, 'you can keep the payment.'

'Why? Because you now decide you don't want it? I find that odd because I thought your only reason for buying the sundial was the fact that Deborah had made it.'

'How very discerning of you,' he murmured, nose in glass.

Amelia said equably, 'If you really don't want it, then thank you, nephew. I accept your offer, and I'll tell you what I propose to do with it. I'll place the sundial in the Martin Drayton Museum as one of the first Ashburton stoneware artefacts, with the customary notice acknowledging you as donor. I'm sure everyone will admire your generosity.'

With that she rose. It was plain that whatever had transpired between the workers and this man, she was not going to be told. But she had learned enough. The time to renew her ties with the Drayton Pottery was drawing nearer. Hadn't Damian Fletcher and Simon Kendall predicted as much? She had not expected it so soon and, as yet, she would say nothing about it. Not even to Olivia, who was suddenly cherishing some secret happiness but was not yet ready to share it.

Dragging himself to his feet, Lionel bowed and said that a servant would show her out.

At the door she turned. 'If the time comes when you decide to abandon the Drayton Pottery, I pray you will let me know.'

'Why? You own another. A flourishing one, from all accounts.'

'A promising one, yes. But the two could merge. My ties are naturally stronger with Drayton's. I've already begun to regard the Ashburton Pottery as Deborah's, where she can devote herself to stoneware production, for which she has an obvious flare. Olivia agrees.'

She failed to understand why he laughed.

'Olivia! My dear aunt, she'll be crowing! She already has cause for that . . . Ah, I can see you don't know why. No matter. I imagine Jessica Kendall is crowing too. From what I hear, all is going well with the Dame School in Burslem. What a bunch of busy bees you are, to be sure . . .'

*

186

The more Lionel thought about it, particularly in a pleasurable alcoholic haze, the more sensible seemed the idea of calling on his mother. She would tell him what to do. She would know how to handle a bunch of threatening hooligans.

But before he did so he had to decide whether to take them seriously or not. *Would* they lay down tools if he didn't quit the place? *Would* they smash all the stuff now awaiting delivery to clients who had dealt with Draytons for years, and then tell the world why they had done it? *Would* they march to every respected potter throughout Staffordshire and report the truth about Abby Walker's accident and what had led up to it? *Would* they enlist men from other potteries – fathers and sons; men with daughters and grand-daughters; men with wives and young men with sisters – and organize a mass attack on himself, whether he were at the pottery or in his home, and drive him out of both if he so much as set foot in the Drayton Pottery again?

And *would* they report him to the magistrates, who were becoming rather more vigilant these days about sexual offences against young women, even though thirteen was the age of consent for girls and twelve for boys? Many people were agitating for further reform, demanding that the ages should be raised, and some magistrates were among them.

But *would* those howling men do all they threatened if he didn't stand down in favour of the late Master Potter's wife, whom they wanted back, and Miss Olivia along with her? *Would* they turn as ugly as they had been prepared to be before Dave Jefferson had finally halted them by saying that if anyone should have the pleasure of thrashing him half to death, that man was he, and after that they could tar and feather him and drive him out of Burslem for all the world to see?

At that the mob had yelled approval and, thinking they were coming at him to strip off his clothes and start the horrifying, degrading process, his stomach had retched so violently that he had vomited. Their yells had turned to laughter then and the names they shouted at him had been hideous, so that his stomach had retched again and he had sagged to the floor, weak with terror, and his fine desk had been overturned on top of him and the rest of his splendid office had been wrecked. Only now did he remember that it was Dave Jefferson who called a halt, pulled him out, and left him with a final warning not to forget every threat they had made because they were more than capable of fulfilling them.

'Show your face in this pot bank again, and see if they don't – and *I*'ll be in the thick of it!'

The thought of going near the place was intolerable. He hated the whole grubby business anyway; the muck and the mess, the anxiety and the harassment. Only the triumph of inheriting the Drayton legacy had kept him going. Now he scarcely cared about that. He had this house and enough money for its upkeep. He also had some money left by his father, thanks to his mother's diligence, though he would have appreciated more and felt she should have arranged it. The man had died without knowing he was to be a father. A child born to a fatherless estate deserved all the compensation he could get.

Such thoughts should have been comforting, but uneasiness remained. He was beginning to hate more than the Drayton Pottery and to fear more than the threats of those rabble-rousing men. He was beginning to hate this house and to be haunted by the sinister legends attached to it, even though he knew them to be nonsense and that to be influenced by them was beneath such an intelligent mind as his. But discard them as he might, the fact remained that both his father and his aunt had died at Carrion House in tragic circumstances. Tragic – and prophetic?

Not that his father's murder had ever touched him other than to make him wonder how it had happened, who had committed it, and why so respectable a man should have been lying naked in an exotic background clad in nothing but an exotic robe. At times, the thought had been amusing. The man couldn't have been the paragon of virtue his widow always claimed. Poor Mama . . . poor stupid Mama . . . Joseph Drayton had obviously duped her.

Luckily, she was still easy to dupe. That was one thing he himself could count on. Nothing would ever shake her belief in her son. He would always be able to fall back on her support. She would understand and condone anything he did or any decision he made – such as to sell the Drayton Pottery, pocket the proceeds, and settle down to enjoy life in his own way. Since he was officially Master of Drayton's he surely had the right to dispose of it?

And why not Carrion House as well, since he didn't really like the place? It was beginning to get on his nerves. Particularly that gaudy withdrawing room which he still hadn't got around to refurbishing. Whenever he tried to put his mind to it, he would thrust it aside. He would open the door and shut it again quickly – which was odd since no recollection of it had bothered him even during Phoebe's funeral service, which he had attended dutifully

188

and piously with both families. On that occasion his mind had been more pleasurably occupied with thoughts of Caroline Fletcher and how soon he would be able to join her in America.

And why not? After all, Phoebe's death had been an accident, so really he had nothing to reproach himself with. She shouldn't have refused to give him the ruby necklace; shouldn't have provoked him into seizing it. And if the damned clasp hadn't been so stubborn he wouldn't have had to use such strength . . . wrenching at it . . . twisting it. She shouldn't have resisted. She shouldn't have let her scrawny neck become so rigid that he had to use force until the ageing muscles slackened, gagging the hideous choking noise which made her eyes bulge from their sockets and her tongue loll out . . . swollen . . . hideous . . .

The wine was mellowing. Beneath its influence the idea of leaving Carrion House for ever became more and more appealing. He would sell it, and the pottery, and clear out of the country as before. He had enjoyed himself in America. Caroline had proved useful and, for a long time, accommodating. Why shouldn't she do so again – especially since, at long last, she had responded amiably to his letter?

Fletcher is now one of the most successful tradespeople in Staffordshire, he had written. *He ranks as an industrialist now . . . and he is still your husband, but richer, far richer, than he used to be. If you come to Burslem now, it will be well worth your while.*

His motivation had been simple. He had always wanted to put a spoke in the wheel of Olivia's happiness, and nothing could have achieved that more effectively than the arrival of Damian's wife to break up the domestic bliss. She had not come, but to his mind her reply could be regarded as promising.

But all that seemed unimportant after recent events. He had to think only of himself now, decide on the best steps to take. His mind had gone round in circles, searching for a solution and finding none. The only person he could rely on for that was indeed his mother.

He roused himself with an effort. Before calling on her he had to make himself presentable; eliminate signs of heavy drinking; wash, shave, and don his finest clothes. No hint of slovenliness must betray the despair of these past forty-eight hours. He must appear to be confident, buoyant, his usual suave self. He must be the charming son on whom she doted, and nothing would please her more than to see him in the suit of clothes she most admired – the amber brocade cutaway with enormous cuffs and matching pockets, all elaborately braided, set off with amber satin breeches and silken hose. This had always been his most admired and most fortunate ensemble, which was why he kept the ruby in a secret, well-concealed inner pocket; his talisman, his lucky charm, his insurance against misfortune.

He took his time over an elaborate toilet. To his valet's surprise, he was patient, polite and appreciative, even dismissing him before finally donning the long-skirted coat. Lionel detected the man's gratification and was amused by it. If the fellow did but know, he was anxious to be rid of him. Alone, he could turn to the secret pocket which he was always careful not to reveal in the presence of others.

A clever tailor had made it undetectable to all but the sharpest eye – or the most searching fingers. It was situated beneath the padded shoulder lining, impossible to reach when on the body and therefore safe from pickpockets. It was also skilfully concealed beneath a fold and imperceptibly safety-fastened. Even he had to search well for it, but he could always assure himself of the ruby's safety by feeling for it through the silken material without troubling to look further.

Spreading out the garment, his fingers found the spot – and felt nothing.

Jolted, he reached for the tiny hooks. They were undone, the pocket empty. He ripped the lining apart, but nothing had slipped down within it.

There was no sign of the ruby anywhere.

Trembling, his hands scrabbled within the clothes closet and amongst the rows of elaborate garments and the tiers of stylish shoes. They found nothing.

He knew full well that never at any time had he transferred the ruby to another hiding place except when travelling, when he carried it on his person. At home, its concealment never varied because no other item in his wardrobe had such excellent secret storage. Logically therefore, but uncharacteristically, he must have failed to refasten the pocket after last examining the stone; it had fallen soundlessly onto the carpet and rolled away.

The thought that it could be lying in a far corner of the room, or be lodged beneath the skirting, was reassuring, though for it to roll away seemed unlikely since its setting was flat and orna-mental, broken from the original necklace. So it must have bounced out of sight, not rolled. He accepted the solution with relief, and a conviction that the ruby would come to light. He would scour the room for it on his return. Meanwhile, he had to get a grip on himself and proceed with his plans as if nothing had happened. He must go ahead and call on his mother.

The sight of her was a shock. She was slumped in a high-backed chair, her fat body and billowing skirts overflowing the narrow seat – like an unset rice mould, he thought unkindly.

But it was her face that shocked him most. It seemed to have aged overnight, the contours sagging, the eyes shadowed, the skin sallow. And, for once, no tray was beside her; no fortifying glass of wine, no sweetmeats, no tempting tidbits.

Nor did she greet him with her usual joy. She stared at him dully, her mouth slack and her eyes blank, as if looking into a world that stupefied her. She looked ill, and that was a nuisance because sensible conversation with a sick person was impossible and he had come here solely for that; for a common-sense discussion of his future. Also, of course, for something as tangible as money to supplement the proceeds from the sale of Drayton's. He could then leave Carrion House to be sold by the best property dealer in Stoke and be on his way to America.

'If you're unwell, Mama, you should be abed. Shall I summon Rose?' When she made no answer, he said, 'Or Pierre, for a glass of Burgundy? That always does you good . . .' When she still remained silent he added, with a touch of impatience, 'Plainly, you are in no mood for company. I'll come back another time.'

As he made for the door, her voice followed him.

'So you came. I knew you would have to.'

He jerked round. She might look dull and spiritless, but there was emotion in her voice; something deep and terrible and accusing and frightening.

'I suppose you thought *I* would come to *you*, as always. You were wrong, my son.' Almost on a surprised note she added, 'You see, I still call you "my son". I can still do that.'

Her mind is touched, he thought. How can I talk sensibly to a woman who is touched?

The thing to do was to humour her. He said gently, 'And why not? I *am* your son.' He went back to her and, with a display of affection, kissed the sagging cheek.

No plump arms reached up to embrace him this time. Vaguely alarmed, but not deeply concerned, he said, 'Come, let me take you to your room. You shouldn't be sitting here, alone and neglected.'

'Oh, but I'm never neglected!' Her voice was suddenly normal. 'I have servants at my beck and call, as you know. And Miguel is

191

frequently thoughtful. No doubt you find all that reassuring, if you ever trouble to think about me.'

'Mama!'

This wasn't the reception he had expected, nor one he had ever met from her. The underlying note of anger, the disturbing accusation, the lack of warmth – all were startling and unfamiliar. He scoured his mind for a cause and grasped the obvious one.

'I suppose you've heard about the trouble at Drayton's? Don't worry – it was nothing important. Nothing I didn't know how to handle.'

'Ah yes – the trouble at the pottery. Rose was agog with it. It was even rumoured that a riot had broken out.'

'A riot!'

He laughed, a little too heartily perhaps because she said, 'You don't have to pretend with me, my son.' Her voice was chillingly sane. 'I know you well, alas. Your bravado is meant to hide something. Fear – or guilt? What had you done to cause the trouble?'

'Nothing many a man in my position hasn't done before.'

'Seduced one of the pottery women?'

He shrugged. 'She was a pretty little thing. And willing.'

'"Little"? You mean young? How young?'

'Not under the age of consent, if that's what you fear. The magistrates would have difficulty in arresting me, for that reason.'

'But still young enough for men to be outraged? And what was the accident? Rose heard about it. Even that someone was drowned.'

Nothing much ailed his mother, he thought, if gossip could occupy her mind.

'Ridiculous,' he said. 'No one was drowned. D'you think the pottery workers don't know where the canal is situated, and avoid falling in?'

It sounded convincing and she accepted it. Even so, she seemed strangely beyond him and suddenly he knew that, for the first time in his life, he was going to have difficulty in winning her sympathy.

'What's wrong, Mama? What's on your mind? It almost seems as if you've something against me.'

'And I shouldn't have – that's what you mean, isn't it? A mother should harbour nothing against a son – not mistrust, nor doubt, nor fear, nor horror.'

'Horror? Why should you be horrified? Because I amused

myself with a chit of a girl? Did my father never do such a thing?'

He saw her stiffen, and was pleased. He had touched her on some secret, sensitive spot.

'Your father,' she said at last, dragging the words out, 'was not perfection, and I knew it. He married me for my money – I knew that, too. but I loved him. Even when I suspected that morally he wasn't all I believed him to be, I still loved him. No other man ever looked at me before. I was fat and ungainly, so I was grateful to him. But not for long. Not when he ridiculed my appearance and deplored my taste in dress and enlisted dressmakers to take me in hand. But it was worse when I began to suspect that he had *affaires*, even that he went with that village whore, Meg Gibson as she was –'

'Tinsley! Good God – *Meg Tinsley!*' He laughed aloud. 'You've always held my father up as a pillar of respectability and now you admit his sins were as bad as my own!'

'No. Not as bad as yours.' She thrust a shaking hand into her pocket. 'This is the first chance I've had to give you this. I found it when examining your clothes for moths –'

'– which you didn't find, of course. That valet of mine is more conscientious than you think.'

'He is at least honest. He could have helped himself to this and sold it very profitably.'

He glanced at her extended hand. Something lay within the palm, silencing him.

'I – recognized it at once.' She continued with an effort, 'It was part of a ruby necklace of my mother's. She lent it to Phoebe on one occasion, and Phoebe never returned it. You know that, of course. You also know when she wore it last. So do I.'

The retching he had felt when those men threatened him was as nothing to what he felt now.

His mother laid the ruby on a table beside her, dragged herself from her chair, then lumbered to a side table. She returned with brandy.

'Drink this,' she said, 'then go.'

'I – I found it!' he blustered. 'I found it by accident! I called at Carrion House after . . . after she'd been taken away and the house searched . . . this one ruby had been overlooked, hidden in the carpet pile . . . His voice petered out. He gulped the brandy. He continued desperately, 'I was too frightened to admit it . . . I might have been suspected!'

'Even though you found it *after* the murder? After her body had been removed?'

He gulped more brandy, then nodded.

'I don't know what made me go there. Curiosity, I suppose. I didn't believe the news when I heard. How could anyone?' When his mother remained silent he burst out, 'It's true, I tell you! *True*! Why can't you believe me?'

'I am trying to.'

'You shouldn't have to *try* to believe the truth! I found that ruby by chance . . . saw it half-buried in the carpet . . . obviously, it had been overlooked. What a piece of luck, I thought. It wasn't until later that I had second thoughts and realized that the damned thing could arouse suspicion . . . wrong suspicion. I panicked, and hid it.'

'But took it with you to America? It was concealed in clothes you had made there . . .'

'I'd forgotten I had it! I'd thrust it in a pocket and left it there. When I arrived in Savannah I came across it, didn't know what to do with it, so thrust it out of sight . . . and have continued to.'

'In a very secret pocket . . .'

'Many men have pockets like that, to foil thieves . . .'

Her silence, combined with the brandy, began to lull his fear. Doubt was beginning to touch her, doubt that made her ready to listen.

He said reproachfully, 'Dear Mama, surely you could never think that *I* could be guilty of that hideous thing? I thought you knew me. I thought you trusted me. I – thought you loved me.' His voice broke. 'Dearest Mama, believe me – *please*.'

He sensed that she was trying to, that she wanted to, that she was seizing on his story to allay her own fear. He reached out and grasped both her hands. She didn't withdraw, and he knew then that even if she didn't believe him she would never betray him. That was the only thing that mattered.

She withdrew her hands, crossed to the window and stared out across Tremain's spreading grounds. At length she turned. With her back to the light he could see little of her face, but what he did see was twisted with grief.

When she spoke again, the words came in jerks, choking her.

'Why have you come to me? Don't say "for advice", because you never want it or heed it. You came for help. Tangible help. If it's money to enable you to run away again, you've come to the wrong person. I have none to spare.'

'But you're my *mother*!'

'Yes – your foolish, gullible, doting mother who can be twisted round your little finger. But not this time. All I have to give you

194

now is maternal advice, no doubt unwanted – but here it is. Give the pottery back to Amelia, unreservedly. You can't sell it or raise money on it in any way. It belongs to the Draytons and Amelia has a son.'

'*I* may have sons!'

'And they will be Draytons, too. Time will tell. Time will deal with everything, but you can deal with nothing. You can bring only ruin to Drayton's because you're incapable of running the place. It was foolish of me to believe you could, but I've always been foolish where you are concerned.' Taking a deep and steadying breath she finished, 'If you're really thinking of your unborn sons, you'll heed my advice. If you don't, the men who threatened you – and everyone has heard about that – will carry out their threats. You must be content with the Carrion bequest. As for this ruby . . .'

She picked up the stone and stared down at it for a long moment, then said painfully, 'I'll accept your story because I must . . . because I want to . . . because the alternative would be too unbearable to live with. But belief would be easier if you hadn't hidden this all these years –'

'I've *told* you why I did that! How could I confess to being near the place?'

'In the customary way. By telling the truth. To me, at least.' Her fingers closed over the ruby. 'I'll keep this. It was my mother's. I shall wear it as a pendant. What use would a single stone be to you? You have plenty of rings, plenty of fobs, more than enough jewellery for any man. You could sell it, but you would have done that, had you needed money. The Carrion bequest carried funds for its upkeep so long as you live there, and your pockets have never been to let – thanks to me. Now you must survive with what you have, and be content.'

She sat down, leaned her head back, and closed her eyes.

'I'm tired, my son. Very tired. On your way out, please summon Rose. She will help me to bed.'

He turned his back on her, and left.

When he returned to Carrion House, a phaeton stood at the door. He recognized it as one belonging to Damian Fletcher.

He couldn't avoid the man. He was waiting in the impressive hall; not sitting, but standing beside the hearth, legs astride in a resolute stance which somehow suggested that he had been waiting for some time and nothing was going to dislodge him. But he spoke pleasantly enough.

195

'I came to thank you on behalf of Olivia and myself.'

'Indeed. And why?'

'I think you know. It *was* you, wasn't it, who wrote to Caroline, telling her how prosperous her husband has become? It seems that at long last she's willing to take advantage of it. When I was poor, she refused a divorce. Now I can provide for her more generously, she is eager for it. Her terms are excessive, but I'll meet them gladly. Any price is worth paying to marry Olivia. The result of your interference is ironical, but gratifying, so I'm here to thank you for it.'

'And you came here just to say that?'

'No – something else as well. From the sound of things, it's time you quit the Drayton Pottery. I've made it my business to talk with the men. They want you out of it, and Amelia back. Olivia, too.'

Lionel laughed. It was a mirthless sound.

'You're a bit late. I've already decided on that. My aunt is welcome to whatever is left of it. The place is a mess.'

'Amelia has a talent for sorting out messes, and Olivia has a talent for helping her.'

At the door, Damian Fletcher turned. 'I've just remembered something. It should interest you. Caroline has another reason for agreeing to a divorce at long last – she plans to marry again. A rich landowner from Kentucky, with vast estates and a string of fine hunters . . .'

So *that*'s what she was hinting at in her letter, Lionel thought bitterly. That's what she meant by: *Freedom is very desirable, providing one knows how to use it . . . and I do, dear Lionel . . . I do . . .* And he'd imagined she was hinting at a possible renewal of their once-enjoyable relationship! Freedom, to her, meant the freedom to take lovers as and when she felt inclined – but, this time, more permanently and profitably.

He felt as if a final door had been slammed in his face.

After that, there was nothing to say. Leaving Fletcher to see himself out, Lionel sought escape by opening the nearest door. The choice was unfortunate. It led into Phoebe's tawdry salon. Ornate mirrors glittered. Satin drapes and crystal candelabra gleamed. Artificial flowers festooned the ceiling. Everything was pink and silver and gold; everything was tinsel, bright and gaudy and hideous. Gilded cupids looked down on him, their dimpled faces laughing . . . mocking . . . exactly as they had laughed and mocked when he scrabbled on this floor for scattered rubies, while her contorted face gazed up at them . . . her cherubs . . .

196

her pretty cherubs ... all laughing at her bulging eyes and her swollen tongue and the frantic man harvesting the fruits he had killed her for.

As he flung himself from the room his reflection was flung back from Phoebe's grandiose mirrors – an ashen, frightened man faced with unwelcome imprisonment. He stumbled in his haste and, with shaking fingers, locked the door behind him. Never again would he enter that damned place. Let it gather dust; let it go to wrack and ruin. Let time take it over.

Time! For all time he must remain here because he had no choice. The money bequeathed for its upkeep would cover that, but leave no margin for luxury travel and little for pleasures on the scale he enjoyed. From henceforth those pleasures would consist only of bear-baiting and cock-fighting down in Burslem, but not enough for higher stakes in Stoke and elsewhere, and little for the even more exciting sport of dog-fighting. He might win something here and there, enough to cover his wine bills, but precious little else. His mother had proved to be singularly ungenerous today, and it would be a long time before he inherited anything from her. She was the sort who could live for ever. He was confident that she would rally from shock – the shock, he remembered, which Deborah had observed when seeing Agatha hurrying away from Carrion House. Then she would settle down to good hearty eating again.

For his mother, life would go back to normal. For himself, it would never be the same again.

As for selling Carrion House, how much would it fetch? A fair sum, a tidy sum, but how long would that last? Money had a way of vanishing and when it was gone – what then? Property was at least durable, and its value could even increase ... and of course he was still a Drayton, which was a comforting thought. He might be able to trade on the name; even, with luck, claim some sort of financial benefit from the family business. After all, Drayton descendants had been profiting from it for centuries.

Those who worked for it, you mean ... The words came from nowhere, echoing in his brain, reminding him that this unhappy, doomed house was now his sole legacy.

Fear was an icy chill in his heart. He was trapped for ever in a house of tragic legend and if he ever tried to scoff, his own memories would rise to mock him. Locking the door of that room wouldn't keep them at bay.

CHAPTER 18

If she rode to Merrow's Thicket at about seven o'clock in the morning, she might see him. Deborah had hinted as much when Miguel came to Ashburton, unexpectedly.

'I'm taking up my early morning rides again,' she had said. 'Mama has made me see the folly of my ways. I'm not getting enough exercise, she says. The Ashburton lands are not enough. I must ride further, as before. She also says I shall work all the better for being healthier. Not that I'm *un*healthy. Papa says I'm always "bursting with rude health", which sounds awful . . . and here I go, chattering too much, as usual.'

'I like the sound of it. What route will your early morning rides take?'

'The same as before. Across the valley and then a good gallop across Tremain's fields, down into the dip of Badgers' Brook and across the ford, up the hill at the other side . . . and then the usual way home. Early, of course, because now I'm to have full responsibility at the Ashburton Pottery I must be as conscientious as Olivia and Aunt Amelia have always been.'

It was very exciting, the merger of the Ashburton and Drayton Potteries; Drayton's producing earthenware, china, and porcelain as before, and Ashburton working exclusively in the new white stoneware, which was proving ideal for her own type of work.

'Have you seen the sundial in the Martin Drayton Museum?' Deborah had then asked with some hesitation.

'I have. And the tribute to its donor. Both pleased me – but I wonder how Aunt Amelia persuaded him to be so generous.'

She wondered, too. However it had been achieved, she was glad about it, for already she was working on a better design, a more suitable one for Tremain Hall. She hadn't told Miguel about it yet, but would do so very soon because she had also decided on a course of action inspired by something Olivia had told her – a step Olivia herself had taken many years ago.

Riding now toward Badgers' Brook, Deborah's hope quickened. If he were there, it would be wonderful. If he were not, she would emulate Olivia and ride up to the s'or of Tremain Hall and tell him why she had come. That was what Olivia had done when Damian's wife went back to America, never to return.

'Had she come back,' Olivia had confided, 'she would have found me already installed, and very difficult to dislodge. I knew precisely what I wanted to do, and what *he* wanted me to do but couldn't ask me to. In such circumstances I had to take the initiative, so I did. I packed a bag, told my grandparents the time had come for me to rearrange my life and that even if they didn't give me their blessing, which I wanted very much, nothing would stop me.'

'And did they give it?'

'Of course. They loved me. Then I walked all the way to Damian's cottage and knocked on his door. I knew exactly what I was going to say, and that I had to say it for him. "I've come to live with you because I can't live without you." But it wasn't even necessary. He took one look, seized my grip and drew me inside. And there I've remained ever since.'

'And now you'll be married. Will you feel any different?'

'After all these years? I don't know. An even stronger sense of belonging, perhaps. An even deeper permanence. I shall find out. I shall be glad to share his name, of course; to be Olivia Fletcher instead of Olivia Freeman. He wants that, and so do I. But I've always been glad I took that first, important step.'

So if Miguel didn't appear at the gap leading from Merrow's Thicket, Deborah knew what she would do. She would ride up to Tremain Hall and ask to see him, and when he appeared she would say, 'I'm making another sundial for you. A more apt one. It features our entwined initials. That will be more suitable for the walls of your home, don't you think?'

No – that was wrong – it would have to be 'our' home. And she would stress it.

The ford by Badgers' Brook was behind her. A few more yards, and she would reach Merrow's Thicket. Only the sound of her horse's hooves echoed in the silent air.

Then something else. A footfall. The crunch of dried bracken and fallen twigs.

Her breath caught.

He was there. He was waiting.